Broken Soul

Broken Soul

The Scholar's Legacy - Book I

Joshua Buller

Contents

Chapter 1

The Nameless Man

As I sit to write this, I look back on the long and colorful life I've lived and remember countless strange and fantastic things that I've survived through and how they've all affected me and made me into the woman I am today. None, however, have affected me as deeply as the story of the Scholar and the time that I spent with him after he saved my life.

My name is Micasa, and sadly, I can't tell you the precise circumstances under which I was born. My first real memory was of the labor yards, where I often worked the fields from sun up to sun down. It was tireless, thankless work, and the greatest rewards I got for my efforts were lukewarm soup, half a roll of bread of questionable freshness, and the shackles around my wrists tightened slightly less when I went to sleep every night in that dingy shack they called a boarding house.

My education was all but nonexistent, save for fear of the master's anger and the overseer's lash. I taught myself how to talk from the stories the other slaves told each other at night while the rest of the manor slept. Most of the stories revolved around the demons that supposedly ruled the world, indiscriminately killing people and forcing them to live their lives in constant fear of their wrath.

None of the slaves had ever seen one of these monsters, but the master had more than once threatened to leave disobedient slaves out for whatever bandits or demons came across them. From the somber way the older slaves took the threat, I could only assume there was some merit to the stories.

Despite my ownership, I considered myself fortunate. The labor camp was relatively safe, far from the larger cities and villages where demon attacks and marauder raids were said to be a regular occurrence. There were plenty of guards who lived there too, protecting the estate from anything that might threaten our little corner of the world. They made it clear, though, that if we made any escape attempt, they would hunt us down quickly and punish us gladly.

So we stayed, and we worked, and Hawke Morau – the Master of our household – always made sure we were fed and watered and in relatively good health. Of course, it was he who made all the profit from our toil and lived in the lap of luxury; we were simply assets to be guarded or, if necessary, replaced.

This was the life I knew for the first three years I can remember. It was a nonstop blur of strenuous labor, cracking whips, battering fists and vulgar swearing. The only kindness I was afforded was the rare gesture from the few slaves that took pity on a girl so young as myself. It was sometime around my fourth year of memory that my world was turned upside down by the man whose story I now write.

It was a fairly nondescript day to begin with, as every day tended to be. I was up before the sun had crested the horizon, the sky a blackened bruise fading to blue. It was the best time to tend to the garden, before the heat of the day made the chore even more miserable. We grew a variety of vegetables and fruits, some to help feed the compound and the rest to be taken off to market when the traders came around. I had learned long ago that the slightest damage to any of the stock would immediately lose me twice that amount in rations, so as always I absorbed myself in my work.

I scarcely noticed the figure that was slowly moving in my direction, assuming it to be another slave working his or her way towards where I was picking some apples. It was only after the figure stopped at the foot of the ladder I was using that I turned my attention toward them. When I saw what it was, I immediately dropped the bushel I had been balancing with so much care.

What stared back was human in shape, to be generous; I doubt that any man or woman could ever have such a gaunt and featureless face, regardless of malnutrition or disease. Its skin was so tight and sallow; it was more akin to a walking skeleton covered haphazardly in aged leather than an actual person. It wore no clothing, but likewise lacked any means of determining gender. It gazed hollowly at me with sockets devoid of eyes, toothless maw hanging slightly agape.

Before I even knew it, I had leaped from my perch and was halfway back to the compound before the ladder had a chance to hit the ground. Stories of ghouls were some of the favorites the slaves told at night; they were said to be soulless husks that demons often kept around as pets or servants to torture their unfortunate victims. I had no intention of experiencing whatever foul deeds it had been sent to do to me, even if it meant punishment from the overseer.

And punishment was exactly what I was met with. Even though the overseer saw quite clearly that there was, in fact, a ghoul in the fields and summarily hurried the slaves in to prevent any damage coming to Master Morau's property, I was still beaten and denied my meals for the day for the apples I had spilled in my fright. Still, it was better than having my soul sucked out by some monster, and I considered myself lucky nonetheless.

All the workers were sent about the manor to tidy up as we waited for the ghoul to hopefully wander off so that we could get back to the fields before long. However, the creature seemed to have taken a liking to the area. It shuffled across the garden one direction, neared the boundaries of it, then turned and wandered back toward the other end. As I watched it out a window I was cleaning, I half-mused that it appeared to be looking for something.

The ghoul had still not left by sundown, and that meant an entire day's worth of harvesting had been lost. Master Morau was nearly beside himself with rage, but like the others, he too had heard of what powers these ghouls supposedly possessed. He wasn't about to let his overseers risk themselves trying to drive it off, lest he have to figure out a way to replace them – they were not so expendable as us slaves.

With that likely in mind, he came up with a different idea. The next day, when Master Morau saw that the ghoul had not shambled off yet, he sent one of us to make an attempt at getting rid of the monster.

This particular slave was quite the oddity amongst our stable. He had been here for years, according to the older servants, but never once spoke a word to anyone, even Master Morau. The Master often called him "oaf," but as far as the slaves knew, the man had no name and no past. The oldest slaves said he had been brought in years ago, as quiet and timid then as he was now.

The mute's face was layered with thick stubble that refused to grow to a beard proper. His blonde hair was often dirty and unkempt, and he only made the most minimal effort at keeping himself clean. For whatever reason, Master Morau was slightly more lenient on this matter to him than to the rest of us slaves, who would savor the lash for any deviation from our hygiene.

The worst part was his eyes. Blue as ice, they were, and just as cold. He wasn't blind, but he never seemed to truly see anything. Whenever they landed on me, I could feel a chill creep up my spine.

The nameless man worked almost tirelessly, oftentimes doing jobs well through the night while the other slaves slept, but there was an odd, rather mechanical quality to his actions. Even when reprimanded in the middle of a job, he would continue to work until his task was completed, immediately thereafter setting out for his next job. He was in a way the perfect slave: he slept little, ate less, and worked constantly.

So it was a mystery to all of the slaves why Master Morau would send what was thought to be his most useful asset out to possibly be killed or worse. I heard the overseers say that, according to the Master, it was a "best to take care of a monster with a monster." Why Master Morau considered the nameless man a monster, I couldn't fathom. Still, there were chores to be done, and us slaves had no time to watch and see how the events played out as we got back to our duties.

My curiosity from earlier turned to fear when a great scream came from outside only a short time later. I went to a window with the pretense of cleaning it to take a peek. The nameless man lay out near some of the crops, curled into a ball and clutching his chest. There was no sign of the ghoul to be found.

Overseers had rushed outside to see what had become of him. They stood there, shouting at him to move. Eventually, they resorted to their lashes, but even those failed to move the nameless man from where he had fallen. Finally, they heaved him to his feet and half-carried, half-dragged him off.

The nameless man wasn't seen for the rest of the day, but Master Morau was in a more pleasant mood than usual with the removal of the ghoul. He gave all us slaves an extra ration and let us retire to our bunks early that night, on the condition of making up for the lost time from the last two days. There was a clear undertone that we would regret not meeting those expectations.

The slave's quarters were located outside the main manor, a ramshackle old wooden building lined with dozens of cots. It was left unlocked at all times, and since nothing of much value was kept there, the quarters were usually left unguarded. Instead, we were made to wear manacles around our wrists and ankles through the night. As such, it was no wonder nobody ever seriously considered making an attempt to escape.

The nameless man had been taken back to his own bunk. He lay shivering under his blankets and layered with a film of sweat. Occasionally he would murmur nonsense, and more than once cried out in agony. My fellow slaves whispered amongst themselves that he had been cursed by the ghoul and pulled their rickety cots as far as they could from him to avoid possibly being affected too. In spite of his whimpering, the slaves were too tired to be kept awake and were soon asleep with the aid of smelly moth-eaten blankets pulled over their heads.

The boarding room always grew stifling with so many bodies crammed inside. As poorly insulated as the room was, the air quickly thickened to a soup of sweat and exhaustion. It felt more cramped than usual that night, with everyone's bunks crammed close to get away from the nameless man. I found myself unable to get to sleep so early in the night. I needed to get some fresh air and stretch, if just for a little bit.

Fortunately for me, I had learned a couple years back how to undo my cumbersome shackles. It was a trick I first discovered when I was cleaning an armoire that had been permanently locked since Master Morau broke a key in it. He had to replace all the expensive clothing that was stuck inside, much to his displeasure, but the armoire itself was more expensive than the garments combined, and he refused to have it damaged to recover them.

Still, the slaves always made sure to keep it as spotless as the rest of the house, so it was on one random day when I was maybe five years old that I ended up tending to it. I found myself drawn to the lock, the broken key still visible inside, and for some strange reason I was compelled to poke at it with one of my hairpins. After just a minute or two, I managed to figure out just how the lock worked, the right way to twist the pin, and suddenly the wardrobe popped open, the broken key sliding right out of the lock.

Master Morau came to investigate the loud bang the doors made as they swung open. Rather than praising me as I was hoping he might, I received a round of lashes and scolding, for he was sure I had broken the door in my clumsiness. The only reward I got was an end to the beatings once he discovered that the armoire was actually still intact.

That was the earliest memory I have of my affinity with locks. After that I constantly found myself drawn to anything that had a lock or was particularly stuck, and always found that, with a little effort and my hairpin, I could manage to get the object in question open. It took a bit more effort to learn how to lock those things again, but once I was confident enough in doing both, I naturally tried it on my shackles one night. Sure enough, I was able to slide them right off. By covering up my legs with my shoddy covers, I made sure the overseers never saw I was unchained when they came to wake us in the morning, giving me time to snap them back on before I left to have them taken off properly.

With all the other slaves fuller than usual and taking advantage of the extra rest, I had no trouble discreetly unsnapping my shackles and slinking past the huddled sleeping pallets, stepping outside to enjoy the brisk summer night. I was greeted by a vast tapestry of stars that painted the ink black sky. It was a sight that never failed to take my breath away. I was half tempted to wake the others so they could see this incredible sight with me, but the fear of giving up my secret gift was a bit more than I was willing to part with.

So imagine my surprise when I heard the squeak of the rusty hinges and the muffled jingling of manacles as someone else stepped out of the unlocked boarding house. I had been sitting against the side of the quarters and instinctively huddled as close to the rotted wood paneling as I could, hoping the bright stars I was just admiring wouldn't betray my location. I watched as the lone person stepped out awkwardly, trying to manage their binds, and began peering through the darkness, and I knew that it was me they sought.

"Micasa?"

The man's voice that called out my name was one I couldn't recognize from the stable of fellow slaves. It was a bit hoarse, as if he hadn't had any water in a long while, and creaked not unlike the old hinges on the door he had just stepped through. I ventured creeping a bit closer to identify this man. Of course, I'm sure you could guess by now who it was I saw when he stepped a bit further out of the shadow and into the light of the rising moon.

Yes, it was none other than the nameless man, his pale blonde mop of hair matted against his brow with sweat and his face a mask of pain. His eyes glinted with a liveliness I had never seen in him before, curiosity mingling with the anguish he bore. I was so intrigued by his unexpected appearance that I didn't even think twice as I stepped out from the shadows.

"What are you doing out here, nameless man?" I said, in the foolish way a child always speaks their mind. He started at my approach but let out a haggard sigh of relief when he saw it was me.

"I thought I heard someone come out here, and saw you were gone," he said, clearing his throat a couple times. I suspect he realized when I spoke how much harsher his voice sounded.

"I thought it would be a good night to look at the stars," I said. "I don't get to do so very often."

"Oh...for a moment I thought maybe they had taken you away." The nameless man let out a chuckle that turned into a stifled gasp of pain.

"Are you okay?" I asked.

"No, but I'll manage." He slowly lowered himself to the ground, doing his best to muffle his chains, and leaned his back against the shack.

"Nameless man, why can you talk now?" I asked, confused why he could not only speak but more so why he decided to come out and talk to me. He looked at me for a few moments, his eyes narrowing as he bit his lip, before he finally shrugged.

"I wish I could tell you," he replied in a defeated tone. "I'm more confused than anyone about this. I can vaguely remember the times when I was working in the manor, and out in the gardens, but those memories are all fuzzy. Almost like it wasn't me living them."

"But of course you were. You're you," I said giggling. His words made absolutely no sense to me.

"I don't even know who I am, though. I have no memories beyond a few hazy years here, and that's it. I can't even remember my own name. What I do know is that when I was sent to chase that ghoul off, I walked up to it and felt an irresistible pull to it, something I can't really place. I touched it, and the thing just disintegrated in a bright flash of light. All of a sudden I was gripped by this horrible tearing pain." His breathing was still heavy, and I could see how badly his hands shook. Regardless, he continued.

"At the same time, I suddenly found I could speak again, and the experiences I've had from that moment to now seem so vivid compared to whatever I was feeling before. I have no idea what's going on, and it scares me."

I had seen grown-ups be afraid before. Usually it was under the threat of Master Morau's rebuke and the overseer's lash, but to hear one say they were afraid because of things like memories and feelings was something I couldn't quite understand at the time.

"How'd you get your shackles off, Micasa?" he asked unexpectedly. I told him about my gift of unlocking things, and it was only after I told him that I questioned whether or not I should have. I was always cautious about safeguarding my secret, and here I told him without as much as a second thought.

Perhaps it was because, regardless of how I had felt when he looked at me, he had never actually done anything to show he was untrustworthy. He was unlike some of the other slaves who would steal and lie at any given moment to make life easier, even at the expense of another slave.

"Could you undo my shackles too, then?" he asked, stretching his legs out towards me. Once again, I didn't hesitate for an instant to put my trust in him and reached towards the manacles. His were a bit harder than expected, as they appeared to have never been removed and the mechanisms were slightly rusted from disuse. Still, it took only a few extra moments of playing with it before they snapped open, a bit louder than I had hoped. Thankfully, there was no sound of interrupted slumber from the slave quarters.

The nameless man stood and stretched his legs, bending them back one after the other in a way that moments ago would've been impossible. A sudden pang took him and he doubled over, but he held a hand out to stop me when I approached with concern. When he caught his breath again, he sat back down and looked to the sky. The way he stared, it looked like he was taking it all in for the first time ever.

"Magnificent," was all he muttered, drinking in the sight for a long while without moving. For that moment, his pain had been left forgotten. I looked up too, enjoying it as I always did. Still, I couldn't help notice how far the moon had travelled during our time out here, and I knew I needed to get some sleep before the next day's chores were upon me.

"We should get to bed or we'll be punished tomorrow for being so sleepy," I told him, turning to head back. I was stopped when his hand rested on my shoulder and held me back. It was surprisingly strong, the hand of someone who had been working hard for many years, and it scared me just a bit; it was almost like the hand of the lord of the manor. Still, unlike the harsh blows I suffered at the latter's hand, this was a gentle gesture that the nameless man was showing me. I turned to see his face full of anxiety again.

"Micasa, your gift," he started, looking terribly unsure of what his next words should be. "Could you use it to get into the manor?"

I had more than once, I admit, fiddled with the intricate and expensive locks that closed off the manor, even at the risk of being flayed if I had broken them. They were tricky, but I had managed to undo them and lock them again without anyone being the wiser. I told the nameless man this, once again wondering why it was I could trust him so readily.

"Micasa, I need to get into the manor and see Master Morau," he asked as he clutched at his sides and winced. I knelt beside him.

"Why, are you hurting too much?" I asked. "We can go get an overseer; maybe they have some medicine for it." I knew as well as any slave that the Master never wasted medicines on us, but I figured it was worth a try.

"No, it's not that," he said, his grip tightening ever so little. He must have seen on my face how much his hold scared me because he let go before explaining. "Remember that pull I told you I felt when I was near the ghoul? I still feel it, pulling me towards the manor. I know it has something to do with Master Morau, but I won't be able to get in there myself. Please, it can't wait. I don't want to get you in trouble, but I just need the door unlocked so I can get in. I need to know what this feeling is. Please."

That was the first time I ever knew what it felt like to pity someone. Us slaves had it rough, without a doubt, but I had never seen someone so distraught as the nameless man was at that moment. I knew the overseers would be furious if they saw us sneaking around, but it seemed harmless enough to open a door for him so he could see the Lord.

So with a small nod, I led him by the hand across the field towards the manor. There were no clouds to obscure the moon that night, but it was waning fortunately and cast little light. We kept low to the greenery, slipping from bush to bush. We slowed as we approached the building – the overseers kept their patrol close, in case they needed to beat a hasty retreat from a sudden attack.

The side door was less guarded than the back or front, with only one burly figure standing maybe thirty feet from the door and looking out over the gardens. We snuck around the long way, moving as slow as we could to avoid him catching us from his peripheral, and made our way to the corner of the building. By creeping along the wall, we were able to pass right behind him, though each inch moved felt like a mile, knowing that any sudden sound would instantly draw his attention.

Getting to the door was hardly a victory, for now, the guard was only a stone's throw behind us, and all he had to do to see us was to turn around. Still, we had come this far, and I just needed to get the nameless man through the door. I took my customary hairpin and set to work.

It was a much more harrowing job than usual. Even though I knew just how to undo the lock, doing so without making a single sound was a different matter altogether. The first couple times I messed with it, I made only a little noise, but with the bustle of the day, it was usually easy for me to slip away if I thought I'd be caught after making a blunder. Now, the only other noise I had to work with was the occasional cricket chirp, and I couldn't count on that to cover my tracks if I made a critical mistake. Ever so carefully, I moved a lock pin here, a spring there, and finally I began to feel the handle resist less as I gently tugged it down.

As I slid the final pin into place, the lock popped loudly.

My heart skipped a beat as I looked over my shoulder to confirm my fears, seeing the guard turn sharply and give out a cry of surprise. The nameless man grabbed me around the waist and threw the now unlocked door open with his free hand. It crashed into the wall as he pushed it in, undoubtedly alerting any overseers who hadn't heard the first one's shout, but the damage had already been done.

The nameless man hauled me bodily into the manor, no doubt worried that I would have received the full brunt of the backlash if he had left me alone. Together we flew down the corridors, towards the staircase that led up to Master Morau's chambers. A guard had come through the front door and was standing at the foot of the stairs; but without slowing down, the nameless man put both his arms around me to protect me and charged full bodied into the overseer as he swung down with his supple baton. I heard it crack against my guardian's back, but he didn't slow down in the slightest as he collided with his attacker, knocking the guard backwards several feet. The nameless man hoisted me up in both arms and flew up the stairs before the guard could recover, but our ascent was a short one as we met with the point of a sword staring straight at us.

Master Morau stood on the top step, awakened by the commotion we had made in our endeavors. He was still wearing his night gown and was glaring at us with a mixture of confusion and anger as he realized the two intruders he now brandished his blade at.

I was well acquainted with this sword. It normally hung over the mantle in the Master's room, a brilliant blade made of polished silver (kept in that state by us slaves) with numerous precious gems inlaid in the hilt. The sheath he now held in his free hand was similarly valuable, made of high-quality wood with a gold lacquer and studded with gemstones. I had never seen the Master so much as hold the weapon before, but at that moment I half-wished that I hadn't done quite such a good job keeping it in perfect shape.

"What in blazes is going on here?" said Master Morau, his eyes narrowing in suspicion at the two of us. The nameless man had frozen a few steps from the top of the flight. I heard more footsteps now climbing the stairs and saw that three of the guards blocked our escape. One was the man we had just bowled over, still rubbing his sore back.

"I needed to see you, Hawke," the nameless man said. I cringed at his casual address of the Master, having been taught long ago that doing so was a very dangerous thing to do. Sure enough, our owner bristled with indignation, but also looked rather befuddled; he was likely as confused as I had been at being addressed by a slave who had been considered mute up to this point.

"Why have you decided to barge in here in the middle of the night seeking my audience, boy?" demanded Master Morau in the most command-ing tone he could muster. The nameless man didn't seem to be listening, though. Those piercing eyes of his had glazed over, completely fixated on the Master's face.

"What is this feeling…" the nameless man murmured. "You have…something of mine…"

He took one hand off me and began to stretch it towards Master Morau, whose eyes grew wild with fright.

"You stay back!" he suddenly commanded, backing away. "I am Hawke Morau, the great Scholar! I was a slayer of demons and one of the Old Kings! You keep your filthy hands off of me!"

The Lord continued to shirk away, but the nameless man advanced just as readily. He seemed hypnotized, completely consumed by whatever feeling he had mentioned to me before. Master Morau commanded his overseers to attack, and they stepped forward in unison and lashed out with their discipline rods. The nameless man barely even flinched at their blows.

Master Morau eventually backed himself into a wall, holding his sword out at arm's length. I could see how he shook uncontrollably, unable to hold back his fear. "Stop!" he cried, "I *am* Hawke Morau, I *am*!"

I couldn't understand why he kept insisting on his name, but regardless, his pleas fell on deaf ears. As the nameless man's outstretched hand floated closer and closer to our owner's face, the Master made a wild stab at him.

The sword was heading straight for me; but without batting an eye, the nameless man grabbed the blade and stopped it, the sharp edge cutting deep and drawing blood. Still, he didn't wince, and I started to wonder if the nameless man even understood what was going on. He pulled the sword aside, letting go of it to reach again for Master Morau's face.

Our master was now paralyzed, unable to speak or move, as the nameless man's hand, cut and bloodied, hovered just in front of his face now. There was a tense moment where the nameless man stopped, and I thought that, for the briefest instant, a smile crossed his face. Then he leaned forward and grabbed Master Morau's face.

The Lord screamed, and there came a brilliant flash of light from the breast of his gown. I closed my eyes tight, unsure of what was happening, and could hear the guards shouting behind me. The light subsided quickly, and I felt the nameless man's chest heaving heavily as his breaths came in ragged gasps. I chanced opening my eyes and saw his own were nearly popping out of his head. They looked around crazily, as if he had just woken from a nightmare, but my attention was pulled away from him as I heard a terrible sound come from where Master Morau had been laying.

He was grabbing at his head and rocking back and forth on his back, alternating between quiet sobs and moans of anguish. "Who...where...why?" were the only words I could make out him saying, small blurbs of sentences between his sobs and moans.

"What have you done to the Master, you–you–!" I saw one of the overseers rush forward and swing his rod with all his weight behind it.

Everything that happened next all occurred in the blink of an eye. The nameless man turned with fluid grace and caught the rod, pulled it from the overseer's grasp, and struck the attacker with a single powerful blow on the neck using his own weapon. The overseer keeled over like a rag doll and went tumbling down the stairs. The other two scrambled aside, their mouths agape in shock. One of them lost their footing and went tumbling down after his comrade, adding to the pile the first overseer had started.

The nameless man looked at me, still coddled in one of his arms. "I trust you can stand on your own, Micasa?"

His tone had changed again. Confidence, control, and concern laced his words, things that men broken as slaves rarely spoke with. I nodded, and he set me on my feet gently, but my legs were a little shaky with fear and uncertainty. I had no idea what was going on, but after seeing the nameless man so easily beat down those who had been so terrifying to me my whole life, I felt safest doing what he told me to do at the moment.

He reached down and took the sword and sheath that Master Morau had dropped on the ground, brandishing the former at the last remaining guard who was still standing on the stairway, knees buckling.

"Stand aside, peon," the nameless man commanded. "Tend to your wounded, and know that if you come after us, I'll finish what I started here. Come, Micasa." He sheathed the weapon and started down the steps.

I couldn't imagine just walking out of the manor, but there was a thrill I had never felt welling up in me before. Was I really going to just leave, right past the Master and those fearsome overseers, and never see them again? Never again hear their horrible words or feel the sting of the lash? It was something I had never even dreamed of, yet the nameless man stood at the bottom of the step and looked at me expectantly. The remaining guard didn't lift a single finger to try and impede my progress, shrinking back as I passed by him and followed my savior straight out the front door. The other guards would surely hear of what happened soon, and yet seeing how terribly powerful the nameless man looked as he walked tall and proud, sword in hand, I couldn't help myself; I smiled.

We marched straight through the gardens, the nameless man slowing down only a bit as he looked to the sky again, muttering under his breath as he pondered the stars and moon, before speaking to me again.

"This way, Micasa. Stay close. It's probably going to be a bit of a walk, and it could very well be dangerous."

A part of me wanted to say goodbye to the other slaves, perhaps ask them if they wanted to come along, but I also feared that if I didn't go with the nameless man right now that he wouldn't wait for me. I made a promise to myself right then that one day I'd come back and bring them with me, so we could see the world together. It was a promise I would never get to fulfill.

"Um, thanks for saving me, nameless man," was the only thing I could think to say under the circumstances as we walked off the compound and into the wild, untamed lands I had only seen from a distance before. The sun was starting to peek up, tingeing the sky a pretty aquamarine color, and I felt my heart flutter at the way its rays played off the trees and tall grasses. It was like the world was coming to life before me for the first time.

The nameless man turned to me and looked into my eyes for a second, a slightly confused look on his face. Then his face broke into a small but warm smile. "Sorry, in all this confusion I guess I've yet to properly introduce myself," he said.

"My name is Hawke Morau."

Chapter 2

The Shady Man

The day that followed our escape from the manor was a strange blur to someone like me who had never set foot outside the compound in the short life I had lived up until then. We had brought no provisions with us and had no money to speak of, but the nameless man who claimed to have the same name as our old Master managed to procure some fruits and bread for us to eat. I didn't know how he had acquired it, but we had traveled within range of a small food cart that had set up shop along the road. I half-suspected that he took advantage of the 'five finger discount,' as the other slaves called it when they pilfered food from the pantries back in the estate.

After our meager meal, we napped under a large tree, since both of us had skipped on sleeping the night before. I couldn't shake the feeling that any moment the overseers would be bearing down upon us, reprimanding us for sleeping midday and dragging us back to the compound, but the man who now called himself Hawke had assured me that he was a light sleeper and would make sure no one came to take me away.

It was an incredible feeling, getting to sleep in the shade of that great tree in the middle of the day. Though I only dozed for a few hours, it was some of the most refreshing rest I can ever recall having.

A bit past midday we woke and continued our travels, sticking to the hills and fields just off the main path. Eventually, a horse-drawn cart came rumbling down the road, slowing at the driver's command when he approached us. The man who led the horses was a kind looking farmer with a big straw hat and overalls, clothing that I had only seen on overseers before. I instinctively flinched at even his mildest of movements.

I had never seen the overseers with such sympathetic looks on their faces, though. When he saw me in my ragged work clothes, Hawke said some things about me being an orphan from a demon attack and that my only remaining family was in Changirah. Since it was on the way to where the farmer was making his delivery, he didn't think twice about letting us hop on the back between some crates and milk canisters.

Hawke quietly whispered to me as the cart noisily started down the path again, telling me that a victim of a demon attack was more likely to be helped than an escaped slave. I didn't understand exactly why that would be, but I kept quiet nonetheless. Anything that kept me from going back was a good thing as far as I was concerned.

We made it to the city before the sun began to creep out of sight. I was completely awestruck at the sight of the great walls and the sturdy doors that protected it. I had never been taken on any trips outside of the compound, and seeing the city guards in their shining protective armor and their weapons that made the overseers' rods look like toys was almost more than my racing heart could take. I had no idea what was in store for us on the other side of that giant gateway, but I felt completely safe at the side of this Hawke I was with, a strange thing to think when comparing him to the other Hawke Morau I had grown up with.

We hopped off near a bustling marketplace, waving the old man on as his cart trundled off. Oh, the number of exciting things for sale! I could barely keep myself from running away from Hawke to get a look at everything, but he must have noticed how my face lit up, because he gave a slight chuckle and led us right down the main avenue past the vendors. Most of them scowled at us when we passed by, though looking back I can hardly blame them. We did have all the glamour of two penniless vagabonds who had just crawled out from some filthy gutter.

Hawke's stride quickened as the sound of a particularly loud merchant came within earshot of us. I couldn't quite make out what he was trying to sell, but it wasn't his wares that Hawke was interested in. As he marched up to the stand, the merchant – a small, bald man with large watery eyes and a thin, upturned nose – turned to him and flashed a smile composed mainly of jagged yellow teeth.

"Ah, my good sir, you are looking in need of some new clothings!" The weaselly man spoke hurriedly with the occasional brief pause. He eyeballed the two of us like the other vendors had, but though I could see some disappointment in his swollen gaze, he quickly donned his greasy smile again.

"Yes, yes, why else would you come here but if you had money! Come, we shall get those rags off and suit you until you are suited, yes?" It almost seemed like he would forget what he was saying mid-sentence, remember again, and hurry to say it in case he forgot once more. He clasped his hands together, nodding feverishly as he began to turn towards a rack covered in strange, brightly colored robes.

"Fern, don't treat me like one of your hustle jobs," said Hawke, looking a little annoyed. The man started at the name 'Fern,' turning with a look like he had been caught doing something terrible.

"That name, it does not fit me, no? I am, ah, Banca, yes! No? Kazul? Bill?" he continued to list names as he nervously scratched his cheek, as if hoping to find one that pleased Hawke, but the once nameless man continued to simply stare at him.

"Fern, it's me, Hawke," he said in exasperation. The sniveling man named Fern squinted hard, almost like he was seeing this customer for the first time, then suddenly clapped his hand to his mouth.

"Impossible!" he muttered. "Yet the face, and the tone, and the nose! Yes, the nose, that is where the truth lies!" He leaned in close to take a good look, I suspect, at Hawke's nose.

"Enough of this," Hawke snapped at him. "Let's go to the back and talk business."

Hawke walked around behind the stall, beckoning me to follow as he went. Fern looked around nervously for several moments before he followed a good distance behind me.

The space between the market stalls and the buildings that stood behind them was like a small, secluded alleyway. With all the tents and the shouts of the merchants trying to attract customers, it seemed the ideal place to have a conversation where no one would be privy to eavesdropping.

"I suppose I should apologize for appearing without notice and so, er, disheveled," Hawke apologized, scratching his head.

"No no no!" argued Fern as he scratched his cheek again. "Not disheveled! How can you be disheveled, when I know not the word? You are seemed messed up a bit, though! And where has seen the Chief?"

"I'm still trying to piece that together myself." Hawke gave a small sigh. "But all things in due time, Fern. First, I need some things, as you can plainly see." He made a motion towards the sad towels he called clothing.

"Oh, I'd love to just give, Chief," said Fern, his voice dripping with what I assume he thought was pity, "but the family has fallen on hard times. With you gone, our best items also went! Best items gone means best fences gone! Hard times arrived, and now–"

"–Now you're selling cheap knockoffs in a bazaar full of people much smarter than you," Hawke finished for him.

"Yes," Fern agreed without a hint of indignation. "The family might be familiar with Chief, but we have little to spare, even for who as you still might be."

"Calm down, Fern, I didn't come for a handout. Here," he handed a long bundle of dirty rags to the sniveling man, "This should fetch a fair price for your trouble."

Fern unwrapped the parcel and nearly dropped it on his unwashed bare feet. It was the sword that Hawke had taken with him from the manor, which he had concealed in a strip from his own threadbare robe before we started our ride to Changirah. He had made sure to clean it when we had rested prior, so the silver blade shone with a beautiful luster, even in the dingy light that broke through the tent canopies. The gems in the hilt and on the sheath were dazzling as ever, and I had thought they must have been heavier than I remembered, for Fern's hands shook as he held it.

"This – this is real?" he could hardly get the words out of his mouth, which concerned me. He already seemed to suffer from that problem just speaking normally.

"Every inch of it. Got it from a lord who lives just down the way. I was an unwilling guest of his for several years, and I considered this, shall we say, fair payment for the duties I performed." Hawke leaned in and placed an arm around Fern.

"So, here's the deal: You give me what I need from whatever stores you guys have left – and I'm sure you still have enough left to meet my simple demands – and in return, I give you this sword, and I'll do what I can to send more like it your way in the future. It'll be just like old times. Sound fair?"

"Oh, this is the best, Chief, the best!" Fern jumped up and down as he hugged the ornate blade and sheath tightly. "With news of Hawke Morau's return to the family, we will be back in business before I know it! Oh, and the girl," he turned a cheery eye towards me, "is she for sale too? We were talking before about expanding to the servants' market, no?"

Hawke struck a fierce backhanded blow across Fern's ugly mug, leaving a terrible welt where he made contact. It did little to improve his twisted features. He almost dropped his prize, but even the odd little merchant was smart enough to know that it was more valuable than his discomfort at that moment. The glare Hawke gave Fern made him wince more than the strike did.

"She was just freed from her bonds, and you dare to speak of putting her back in them? Watch your tongue, Fern, or you'll be looking for a new one." Fern tried to stammer something akin to an apology, but Hawke waved it away. "Next time, think before you speak for a change. Now, about what I need..."

I couldn't help but feel a little bad for the spindly man. He had no idea where I came from, so I didn't see how it was fair to hit him for something he didn't know. Still, seeing someone stand up for me so boldly was something I was still rather unaccustomed to. Hawke couldn't see how I beamed at him as he spoke to Fern, reeling off a list of odds and ends that he wanted.

He spoke so quickly I couldn't make out half of what he was asking for, and for a moment I wondered how Fern would possibly remember the demands made to him. He had already proven to be more than a little dimwitted. However, after only being told once, Fern nodded furiously, his eyes darting around as I suspected he was using every ounce of his brainpower to recall what he had just been told, and without another word, he bundled up his new treasure and scurried off at incredible pace.

"We'll stick around here and pretend to run to the stall while he's off procuring what I want," Hawke said as he turned back to me. "Stay put for a moment."

Hawke walked around to the front of the tent, leaving me alone. I badly wanted to explore the marketplace and see all the knick-knacks and such that I had only gotten a glimpse of, but a life of servitude had also taught me well the dangers of wandering in strange places. He returned after only a moment, holding a bundle of robes.

"It'd be better for us to not look like we just crawled out of a privy," he said, handing me the smaller of the two robes. "Sorry, it probably won't fit terribly well, but it was the smallest size I could find."

The robe was indeed a couple sizes bigger than what I normally wore, but it cinched up well enough that it made little difference. It was a vibrant orange color, and while Hawke commented on how gaudy the clothing was (as he put on a robe of bright blue with a slight grimace), I was ecstatic to put on something that shimmered the way that cloth did. It was almost like getting to wear something straight from Master Morau's old cabinet.

Thinking of the manor we had just come from the other day reminded me of a question I had meant to ask Hawke. He led me around to the inside of the tent, where he flung himself into a folding chair Fern had been using and kicked his feet up on the baubles that sat on the counter. Several of them were sent clattering to the ground, yet not a single market-goer spared any of them more than the briefest glances.

I sat down beside the chair cross-legged and watched the crowd meander by as I worked up the nerve to ask him.

"Hawke, why do you use the same name as Master Morau?"

I turned to look up at him, and he gave a great sigh, his eyes sliding out of focus as he fell into deep thought.

"Mmm, I wish there was a quick and easy way to explain that," he said as his gaze wandered aimlessly around the market. "I'm still trying to piece together everything that's happened that led me to where we are now. I guess the easiest way to put it for the time is that the Master Morau you knew was an impostor pretending to be me."

"But he's been Hawke Morau for as long as I can remember," I said. "You just started calling yourself that today." Hawke raised an eyebrow at me, but he let out a low chuckle and gave me one of his soft smiles.

"I suppose that it would be confusing to you, then," he agreed. "Come to think of it, I *was* just the nameless man to everyone there up until yesterday. It would seem strange that anyone would want to pretend to be me, wouldn't it?" He leaned his cheek against a calloused hand.

"Still, I was Hawke Morau long before that fake was even born. Like I said, it's all a little complicated to explain right now." He tousled my hair a bit with his free hand. "Once Fern comes back and we have a little time to rest and recover a bit more,

I'll try to explain it better. Hopefully, by then I'll have a better idea of how to put it."

We didn't speak again until Fern's return. He was carrying a small knapsack that he held onto tightly, but that didn't stop it from clinking musically the few times it bounced. I also noticed he had a bundle similar to the one holding the sword he had left with, though the tough hide that hid its contents and the belts that secured it made it clear it wasn't the same one. He was out of breath and sweating quite a bit, but he seemed pleased to see us tending to his booth.

"Ahaha, feel free to rest your toesies on what you wish, Chief," said Fern as he glanced sideways at Hawke's makeshift footrest. "Rubbish, they are, now that you're back! I see you picked out the two finest robes I had on stock. Fine choice, fine choice! You have good taste, and without your tongue even–"

"Just give me the loot please, Fern," Hawke interrupted as he held out his hand. Fern winced at the gesture, hastily shoving the bag and bundle he had brought with him at my companion. Hawke snatched both up in one arm and flicked the knapsack open with his free hand. He spent a few moments rummaging through the contents, nodding every so often before finally closing it again and giving the now jittering Fern a tiny smirk.

"See, Fern? I knew it wouldn't be too hard for you to fulfill such a paltry request. The family has my thanks. I'll let you get back to your business. Micasa and I have our own to attend to."

The squirrely man had a confused look on his face, as though Hawke had just spouted gibberish at him. Nonetheless, he got enough of it that he knew his patron was satisfied and nodded enthusiastically as he scratched nervously at his cheek once more. It was only then that I happened to see the spot that Fern constantly scratched had a strange mark: a single black line drawn straight down just below his left eye. I wanted to ask about it, but before I could, Hawke led me to the back of the tent again.

"Here, Micasa, it isn't much better than what you have right now, but then again anything is a step up from the dregs Fern is pawning here."

From the knapsack Fern had given him, Hawke unearthed a robe of a deep plum color, with a sash to tie it off at the waist. I had been quite enjoying the orange robe he had already given me, but this was also the first time I had ever had more than one change of clothes in my life, and the idea of getting choices on what to wear was too tempting. I changed quickly while Hawke was standing watch at the entrance to the alley, making sure to fold my orange robe as neatly as I had the old Master Morau's clothes and set it gingerly on the bag where it wouldn't get dirty.

My new robe wasn't quite my size either, but fit better than the other one did and was made from a much softer material that felt blissful against my skin. I imagined that this was what lords and the wealthy must feel like all the time. It was exhilarating to think I got to experience the same.

"Heh, that's a big step up from those rags we came here in," said Hawke when I showed him my new robe. While I had been changing, Hawke had slipped on a pair of plain glasses with silver rims.

"I didn't know you had trouble seeing," I said. He pressed the glasses up the bridge of his nose with a finger and looked away.

"Yes, well, it's just a slight astigmatism. It's no big deal... oh, don't cinch up your new robe too tightly just yet. We're both still rather scruffy from the trip here, and it'd be a shame to dirty your new clothes right after getting them. Come on, I need a hot meal and a hotter bath."

Considering how much Hawke had been complaining about the bright blue clothing he was wearing, I had expected him to change first as well, but instead, he took me by the hand and started leading me gently through the bazaar. I had instinctively flinched when he took hold, but it was nothing like when the overseers had apprehended me so they could drag me off to be punished. His touch was strong, undoubtedly, but also kind, and he didn't force me along so much as he did coax me to follow him. I felt bad for flinching, but if he had noticed he made no sign of it.

Our second trip through the marketplace saw a dramatic drop in the number of dirty looks we got, though there were plenty of people who snickered as they passed by Hawke, pointing to his bright robe. I thought it looked fine on him; he stood out more than anyone else on that street, and the bright shade of red he was turning complimented it well. Still, he picked up the pace as he looked up and down the buildings. His expression relaxed as he caught sight of a particular sign and led me to the door of a large wooden building that was emitting some delicious aromas.

Hawke didn't knock as we entered the door, but rather than being reprimanded, a large woman looked up from behind a counter and waved us into the room. It was much like one of my former lord's old sitting rooms: large and comfortable, with several candles illuminating a number of large comfy chairs surrounding a fireplace that would likely be roaring if the weather had been colder outside.

A couple men sat in two adjacent chairs, a board laden with several stone pieces sitting on a table between them; at the moment, they seemed to be having an argument over the arrangement of the pieces. I had seen such parlor games played by the old Master Morau at the estate when he had guests over and was sorely tempted to ask the gentlemen how it was played, but I quickly noticed that Hawke had already walked up to the counter to speak with the woman, leaving me to hurriedly return to his side lest I be scolded.

The woman spoke with a thick accent I hadn't heard before, but this didn't seem to bother Hawke, who was asking something about 'room rates.'

"Tventy roopulls per night, mai deer," said the woman in her strange drawl.

"Acceptable, as long as the room has a private bathroom so we can wash up," replied Hawke.

"We've come quite a ways and need to scrub off the weariness of the day." He reached into his bag, where I heard the clinking of coins.

"Prayveet bafroom is fife extra, deery," the woman replied, sounding a bit harsher than she had before. Hawke flashed her a smile, though, and jingled the coins in his bag a bit more.

"I'll tell you what, I'll give you thirty-five for one night, but I want a hot bath drawn immediately and a hotter meal ready for us when we've tidied up. How's that for a deal?"

The woman's eyes glittered as she put on a smile that showed off teeth whiter than any I had seen before, even the old lord's. Hawke looked satisfied with her silent response, pulling a large handful of coinage from the bag and setting it on the countertop without so much as checking how much he had just put down.

The innkeeper double-counted very quickly, something she looked well practiced in, before snapping her fingers. A tall, lanky boy in a plain linen robe appeared from a door underneath the staircase that led to the second floor.

"Bostwick, geet ze bafwater drawn for rewm tvelve und tell Roscoe to vhip up sumtink for our new guests!" she barked at the wiry lad as she swept the payment off the counter and into a purse she produced from thin air. Without so much as a glance at us, the boy named Bostwick nodded fervently and, strangely, ducked back into the closet he had just stepped out of.

"Room twelve it was?" asked Hawke, to which the innkeeper replied by flicking a key at him as she walked towards a door towards the back of the building. The purse she had shoved our payment into still jingled merrily in her hands.

"Hawke," I spoke up, "outside you said you wanted the bath hotter than the food, but just now with the lady, you said you wanted the food hotter. Which is it?"

Hawke looked at me for a second with a puzzled look before giving another chuckle, something he seemed to be in a habit of doing when I asked him questions. "I did say both, didn't I? Well, I like surprises, so let's see how it turns out. Now come on, if I don't scrub up and change out of this silly robe soon, I might go crazy."

The room was on the second floor, yet another wonder in my young eyes; I thought only lords and the like got the privilege of having rooms upstairs. The furniture was modest in comparison to my old master's bedroom, but still far more extravagant than anything I was accustomed to. A curtain hung on the far side of the wall that could be drawn to effectively cut the room in two for privacy.

I was more interested in the beds, which looked much softer and more comfortable than my dirty cot I used to spend my nights in. I was all ready to go test that theory when Hawke grabbed my shoulder and gave a soft shake of his head.

"I think the lady downstairs would be rather cross with us if we jumped into the bed *before* we washed up," he explained. "Why don't we see how that scraggly boy is doing with our bathwater."

As it turned out, the small private bathroom in the side chamber already held a sizable tub nearly full to brimming with steaming hot water. It seemed that Bostwick was far more competent than he looked. Apparently, Hawke thought so too because he looked around with his brow furrowed for several seconds, scratching his chin as he looked back at the tub over and over. Finally, he shook his head and shrugged.

"Well, whatever," he muttered, "you clean yourself up first and I'll take my bath afterward. I'll be back shortly. Don't leave the room until I return, okay?" I nodded, though I had no clue why he thought I would go wandering off myself. He seemed content with my answer and closed the door to leave me to my bath.

When I finished and left the bathroom, Hawke was gone, but the lady from downstairs was waiting with a hairbrush. "A preety yung think like you needs to be vell kempt," she said with a big smile, and she proceeded to help me try and tame the unruly mess that sat on my head.

"Such a bewteeful deep black, you vill be so lovely vhen you grow up," the landlady cooed softly as she ran the brush through my hair what felt like the hundredth time. I had never paid much attention to my looks; it had always seemed pointless. My deep tan was simply part of working outside for so many hours, though I was the only slave on the compound that had black hair and did hold some small sort of pride in that. To hear someone else compliment me on it, I couldn't help but grin.

Hawke returned sometime later with a couple new bulging sacks, which he quickly deposited on the bed. The innkeep woman had left a short time before, leaving my hair silk smooth and shining in the room's candlelight thanks to a dose of oil she had combed in. I had already donned my plum robe again, now feeling comfortable closing it tightly without fear of getting it dirty. Hawke nodded approvingly at me.

"One always takes little things like bathing for granted until they go without them for awhile," he mused. Taking one of his new satchels in hand, he made his way to the washroom. "Dinner should be ready by the time I'm done," he called over his shoulder. "Make sure you're ready!"

It was maybe a half-hour later that we were finally both cleaned up and seated downstairs in the inn's quaint dining area. Hawke looked like a new man, his hair neatly combed and parted so it fell down either side of his head. He'd taken a razor to the stubble I had been so accustomed to seeing on him, making him look much younger than I thought he was; he couldn't have been much older than twenty.

He'd also switched into a strange gown after his bath comprising of a large white shirt that opened in the middle but had been cinched closed with a sash, as well as a pleated kilt that extended down until it almost dragged on the floor. The deep crimson dye of the kilt reminded me of blood and made me fidget. I had switched back to the orange robe for our dinner, even after Hawke suggested the plum-colored one instead multiple times.

In front of us lay several large dishes of food I had never gotten to try before. Some I could identify from my former master's table, but I had almost never so much as gotten to smell those; tasting his food was punished with severe tongue scalding, so few slaves had been daring enough to ever try it.

Here, though, Hawke encouraged me to have as much of each plate as I liked. Between the mashed potatoes, the crisp roasted duck, the piles of peas and the sweet milk, I couldn't decide which I liked better. Compared to hard bread and thin broth, each and every one was a delicacy I felt almost guilty tasting.

"Now, Micasa, we have to talk about what's going to happen to you," Hawke started saying when we were nearing the end of the meal. I had a face full of mashed potatoes and ended up spraying quite a bit on him when I tried to respond, but he seemed more amused at that than upset.

"Just keep eating and hear me out," he said while he dabbed his face clean. "Now, the question is what you want to do from here. There aren't a lot of options for someone as young as you, but if you wanted to, I could find you someone to apprentice under learning a trade like sewing or–"

51

"Can't I stay with you?" I cut him off before he could finish his thought. "I don't want to be with someone strange." He looked at me with a raised eyebrow.

"I…don't know if that would be the best idea, Micasa," he responded slowly. His eyes drifted towards the wall, and he weighed each word as he spoke on. "I have a lot of business I need to tend to, and I couldn't guarantee your safety." He paused for a moment, then added quietly, almost to himself, "I don't even know if I can guarantee my own safety, for that matter."

"But you beat up the overseers!" I pointed out, "I don't think even demons could beat you! Please, you're the nicest adult I've ever met!" I pounded my small fists on the table, like that would somehow embellish my reasoning in any way.

Hawke leaned back in his chair and rubbed his face briskly, looking hard into my eyes. After what must have been minutes of silence, he closed his eyes and shook his head. "No, Micasa, I think the best thing would be to send you to an orphanage. Changirah is a nice town, better protected than most out here. There are plenty of opportunities to be had. With a few more years, you could make something of yourself."

I could feel the heat rising in my face but stubbornly looked at the ground and forced myself not to show my disappointment. After all the kindness he had shown me, I wasn't ready to give up the one person who had given me so much. Hawke let out a hefty sigh from the other side of the table and leaned across it, tilting my chin up softly.

"Hey, it won't be so bad. Here, I'll tell you what – take this little trinket to remember me by." He reached into the pocket of his robe and pulled out something wrapped in a plain handkerchief, which he slid across the table and set in front of me. I curiously pulled back the cloth to find a crystal a bit smaller than my fist, milky white in color. Even in my sadness, I couldn't hold back a cry of delight.

"Is that a shinestone!?" I exclaimed in hushed awe. I had seen such crystals before in my old master's possession. Supposedly they were very rare stones that gave off light when touched with bare skin. According to some of the handmaids, the stronger the glow was, the luckier you would be in life. I almost couldn't contain my excitement as I stretched my finger towards the crystal, and a squeal of happiness escaped on its own as the rock radiated a soft blue glow when I touched it – it was the real deal.

"I'll love this forever! Thank you Hawke!" I snatched the shinestone in my hand and ran around the table to engulf him in a massive hug, my sadness replaced with pure and simple joy for a bit. Hawke, on the other hand, was looking at the glowing crystal as if he had never seen it act like that.

"Glad you like it so much," he finally said. "Just take care not to show it off too often. I wouldn't want someone trying to steal it from you."

I nodded, knowing that others would be jealous of my new treasure and that I had a responsibility to protect it. I quickly whisked it back into the handkerchief Hawke had put it in and slipped the bundle deep into the pockets of my robe. A couple reassuring pats and I was certain it was as safe as houses.

Even with the gift lifting my spirits, there was a somber silence between us as we retired to our upstairs room. Hawke drew the curtain hanging in the middle of the room, hiding us from one another. I couldn't even properly enjoy my first night's sleep in my own feather bed, tossing and turning while the worries of where I would end up come the morrow filled my thoughts. As a result, I spent most of the night dozing in and out of night-mares.

I was startled out of one of these fits in the early morning to the sound of a pounding at the door. I looked over to see Hawke pulling at the doorknob as he twisted it to no avail.

"A-apologies, suh!" came the meek and muffled sound of some poor boy on the other side, accompanied by a constant thudding. It sounded like the boy was throwing himself bodily into the door. "The lock seems t'be stuck!"

"No worries," called back Hawke. "I just hope we don't have to bust our way out. Seems like such a waste of a good door."

I finally shook off enough of my sleepiness to remember forcing the lock shut in the middle of the night after one of my nightmares, terrified that someone would burst in and take me back to the plantation.

"Sorry, I did that Hawke! I'll get it!" I cried out as I hopped out of the bed, snagging one of my hair-pins from the nightstand as I darted to the lock.

Hawke watched carefully as I picked the lock free again with a few deft wiggles of my pin. The door flew immediately, and Hawke and I were just able to jump out of the way as the boy on the other side collapsed onto the floor.

Hawke stared at me with an unreadable expression. "Micasa, you locked the door by yourself? Where did you get a key to the room? I had the only one in my pocket all night."

"Oh, I just used my hairpin like always."

"You... you can lock and unlock *anything* with just your hairpin?"

"Yep!"

His face scrunched up in thought for a second, then he took a breath. "Right, change of plans. Get your things together. We're leaving after breakfast."

Chapter 3

The Sandwich Man

I had seen caravans before on the rare occasion they passed by the plantation to do business, but getting to ride in one was a treat completely new to me. Hawke had bought us passage to a town he called Sapir but told me it would take us days to get there. Clutching my meager possessions consisting of one spare robe wrapped around my shinestone that I had moved from my pocket, I watched as the countryside passed at a leisurely pace from the inside of our horse-drawn carriage. I had been sorely tempted to try and pet the horse, but one dirty look from the driver was all it took to make sure I reined in that curiosity.

"Micasa," Hawke said late our first afternoon, as we clacked across a bridge spanning a narrow stream shortly after lunch, "you were wondering why I call myself by your former master's name before. You really want to know the reason?"

I was already sitting in rapt attention before he finished his sentence and nodded vigorously.

"Here, then," he said, "pull out your shinestone and I'll try and explain as best as I can."

I fished out the stone from the depths of my bunched up robe, holding it out triumphantly as it exuded its soft blue light.

"That glow you see is from an energy your body gives off," Hawke stated. "Most people who know about this energy call it essence."

"I heard the brighter it glows, the luckier you are," I told him. Hawke laughed a little at this.

"Not quite, though how bright it glows does depend on who's holding it. For the average person, it's very dim, barely any different from the stone just sitting out on its own. Yours, you see, is actually fairly noticeable. It means you have a stronger essence than most people."

It was my turn to laugh. Even as young as I was, I knew I wasn't very strong at all. Plenty of the other slaves could lift more than twice what I could. Being told I was strong in any sense was just silly to me, and I told him this.

"It's true!" he insisted, "There's much more to your essence than how much you can lift. Here, hand me the shinestone and I'll show you why I handled it with a handkerchief before."

I offered up the crystal to him, and no sooner did he snatch it from my fingers that it began to radiate a brilliant orange light. It could have easily passed for a lantern in the dark, and I let out an involuntary gasp of surprise.

"Your essence is the measure of your potential as a person," he explained. "Er, that is, it's what some people call their soul. It holds your memories, your skills, your likes and dislikes – all of these things are stored in your essence. It's not just your body, but also your essence that makes you unique from everyone else."

He tossed something onto the seat next to me. I picked it up, puzzled to find it was a simple padlock.

"I grabbed this before we got on the caravan," he said. "You said you can lock and unlock anything with your hairpin, right?"

"I can do it with lots of things," I admitted. "I just always have a hairpin on me."

"That's fine, just use whatever and undo that lock."

It took me a couple seconds of fiddling, but the lock popped open nonetheless. Hawke nodded, then stepped towards me and used some loose string from his bag to tie the shinestone to my wrist, where it sat idly shining.

"Now, force the lock shut the same way you did to our door at the inn, and pay attention to the stone."

Forcing a lock open was fairly easy for me, but to lock something in a way that couldn't be undone with its key was much trickier. As I worked the lock, I was caught by surprise as the soft blue of the shinestone intensified until it was almost purple.

Hawke clapped his hands together and let out a guffaw. "I knew it! You have a talent!"

"A talent?" I was thoroughly confused.

"Here, I've got a book that will explain things to you," he said, reaching into his seemingly endless bag of supplies and pulling out a thin hardback with a hand-drawn picture of a man making food. "It's a classic children's book. I made sure to have Fern grab a copy just for you."

He handed the book to me, but I simply stared at it puzzled.

"Something wrong?" he asked.

"I can't read," I replied plainly, looking up at him.

"...Right, I knew that," he said too-casually. "I'll teach you in time, but for now, let me read it to you. It's called *The Sandwich Man*." I giggled at the name as he seated himself next to me and flipped it open. He began:

There was a boy, all full of joy
Who made a sandwich grand.
And as he grew, the village knew
He'd be a Sandwich Man!

Honeyed ham or leg of lamb,
Wet dirt or branch of pine,
It mattered not what things he got,
He made a sandwich fine!

And as word spread, like fresh baked bread,
His reputation grew.
The Lord Ordained himself proclaimed
To taste one with his stew!

His loyal slave to 'wich Man gave
The best ingredients.
When it was made, farewell he bade
And stole it off at once!

Late that night by candlelight
The Lord began to dine,
But then he gasped, his throat he clasped
and perished in his wine!

"Poison!" they cried, Sandwich Man tried
To fight the law of land,
But still he failed, and so was gaoled,
poor foolish Sandwich Man!

The final picture was of the Sandwich Man behind bars, frowning while somehow still looking disturbingly cute. As Hawke closed the book, I looked up at him.

"Are you saying I'm gonna kill someone?" I asked in a squeak.

"What!? Nonononononononono," he waved his hands as if trying to shoo the notion away. "Just...no. That's not what I was going for. The story is usually told by parents as a warning about doing things without thinking. The Sandwich Man didn't check the ingredients he was given and ended up poisoning the Lord Ordained without meaning to. Mothers and fathers always warn to 'remember the Sandwich Man,' like saying 'think before you do something.'

"That's not the most important part, though. What's important is *why* the Sandwich Man could make a sandwich out of dirt, or pine branches, or even poison, and people would still enjoy it."

"Is that the 'talent' you were talking about before?" I asked.

"Yes and no. A talent is something you can do better than most other people. Usually, it's dependent on how you grew up, what you think and feel. Someone who has never seen a horse will likely not have a talent for horseshoeing. Your lock handling talent was likely born from being in manacles for so long and playing with them constantly. The next step after that is what the Sandwich Man has in the story: a power."

Hawke returned to his knapsack, this time pulling out a simple lantern and some matches. After lighting the lantern, he sat holding it between us.

"Now watch this," he instructed, and before I could ask what I was looking for, the flame began to flicker. At first, I thought there was simply a draft inside the cabin, but then I saw the way the flame stretched out, how it swayed back and forth, almost like it were dancing. I was so entranced, I didn't realize that Hawke had opened the lantern and shoved his hand in.

I cried out, afraid he was going to burn himself, but instead he pulled his hand out with the flame still burning in his palm. I watched, hypnotized with wonder, as the little fire slowly crawled up his arm, around his back, and down his other arm. Once in his opposite palm, he gingerly set it back into the lantern and closed the shutter. For a final show, Hawke snapped his fingers, and the flame went out in a puff of smoke.

"A talent is something concrete," he started as if nothing strange had just happened. "Make a candle, bake a cake, grow really good cabbage, these types of things are talents. When you start using your essence to expand the range of that talent, it becomes a power."

"You can make fire dance...!" I whispered breathlessly.

"Well, sort of," he said, scratching his head. "Working fire like this is a power, but it's not *my* power."

"You can use other people's powers? Could you use mine!?" I got excited at the prospect of watching Hawke work with the locks too. He laughed, shaking his head.

"You can't lend another person your power, if that's what you're asking. It's part of your essence; it'd be like trying to give someone your arm to use. My real power does, however, let me learn how to use other people's powers."

"So you can learn how to lock things like me then! I want to see!" I grabbed the lock to give him another demonstration, but he put his hand on mine and stopped me.

"Er, that's where things get complicated," Hawke said. "Even more than they already are. You see, Micasa, someone has stolen my essence."

"But you just showed me the shinestone. It was so bright!" I argued.

"I got some back, true, but that's only a little bit of it. Remember what I said about your essence 're-membering' what makes you unique? Well, there are people out there that can rip those memories out of you."

"Like your name!" I exclaimed, realization dawning on me.

"Like my name," he agreed. "The Master Morau you knew was holding onto my real memories and name. That's why I couldn't recall who I was or where I came from. The person who stole those from me gave them to the plantation owner, so he thought he was me. And that wasn't all she stole. I remember who I am, but there are talents and powers of mine that were ripped from me and still out there, and other people might be using them. That's what I'm going out to find."

"Why are you letting me come with you now, though, when you were going to make me stay before?" I asked. Hawke hesitated, squirming a bit before answering.

"In truth, I'm bringing you for selfish reasons," he admitted, looking away from me. "Your undeveloped talent is fascinating, and I would hate for you to waste your life doing something so mundane when you could train your power and do something great with it."

I had no idea what a "mundane" life was, but any excuse to stay with Hawke longer was fine by me.

"Just stick close to me while we travel, and I'll protect you," he promised, "but remember: when you feel like using your talent, always remember the Sandwich Man."

I swallowed and nodded solemnly. The last thing I wanted to do was get in trouble for something I did so often without thinking. I vowed at that moment to always think before I picked, or something along those lines.

By the time our conversation about powers and essence had ended, the sun had already dipped away and given the sky to the stars. The driver assured us that the carriages would ride through the night, and one of the stewards for the caravan showed us how to convert the seats into a bed that filled the whole cabin. Hawke hopped out and let me have the bed to myself, even when I offered to share.

"I don't need to sleep much," he assured me. "I'll just walk alongside the carriage until you wake up."

He gingerly pulled the covers over me and tucked them in, but as he turned to leave I grabbed his robe.

"Hawke, can I ask you something?" I said.

"Sure."

"When you talked about the person who stole your essence, you said 'she' did. Do you know who took it from you?"

Hawke paused for a long time, looking at nothing in particular. When the silence between us threatened to become deafening, he finally broke it.

"Goodnight, Micasa."

And without another word he closed the carriage door.

Chapter 4

The Musical Man

The next few days we spent on the road, Hawke dedicated it to trying to teach me the basics of using my power. He had me lock and unlock the padlock he'd given me what must have been a thousand times, each time with a different twist: make the key work, don't make it work, try to lock it so a *different* key worked.

It wasn't long before I was so frustrated I would've ripped the lock to pieces if I had the strength. When at last I had had enough, I simply forced the lock so badly that I doubted I could ever undo it and chucked it across the cabin. Even that seemed to please Hawke, though.

"Pushing your limits like that will make you grow more in the long run!" he tried to praise me, but he clearly could tell I was at wit's end.

"I'm tired of that lock!" I whined. "Can we do something else please?"

When I wasn't working with that stupid lock, he tried his hand at more basic things. True to his word, he started working on teaching me to read, which was much easier than I had expected it to be. Near the end of our trip, I was almost able to read The Sandwich Man by myself. To be fair, I had heard it so many times by then I probably could have recited it by memory.

What interested me more than reading was the music that constantly played in our cabin. Hawke had told me he paid extra coin to get a carriage with a phonograph inside it. For me, phonographs were practically sacred. Our old master had one, him being a collector of pricey and often gaudy trinkets, and though he did occasionally play it, I was usually forced to clean something far away from him as he enjoyed the music. Getting to experience the beautiful noise firsthand was yet another perk of the freedom I never knew until recently.

"I'm glad you like it," said Hawke, "because where we're going, there's one of the only theatres left in the world. We're going to go hear a live performance there!"

I was both excited and confused at the prospect of hearing live music. Hawke did his best to explain how instruments worked, but it was practically as confusing as essence to me. He finally just shook his head a little and promised it would make more sense when I saw it.

He spent the last leg of the journey leaning back in his seat, one leg crossed over the other and eyes closed. His suspended leg jittered in time with the music, and I was left to my own devices: namely, trying to sneakily pet the horse without raising the ire of the coach driver.

As we approached Sapir, I got to see for the first time just how different two towns could be from each other. Where Changirah had been surrounded with high sturdy walls and the gates guarded by fearsome armor-clad warriors, Sapir had little more than an archway that declared entrance to the city. What an arch it was, though: I was able to read the name by myself, but the fancy and overindulgent font they'd chosen to use for the welcome sign was almost impossible to decipher. The archway itself was a masterpiece carving, apparently made from a single piece of wood hewn with the utmost precision.

"Sapir is a city of artisans," Hawke explained as he leaned close to look out the window with me. "People come from all over the land to see some of the greatest art, eat the finest food, and listen to the best music mankind has to offer."

A soft tune was playing through the air, and as the caravan continued down the street, it swelled until we found the source as a man cranking a handle on a large box. As the cheery ditty played, two monkeys on leashes danced a jig around the man. I cackled in delight, and Hawke even gave me a handful of change to toss to the performers before we passed them by completely. From that moment, I was on the edge of my seat to see just what other wonders this strange town had to offer.

"Aren't they afraid of demons attacking with no walls or guards, though?" I asked as our coach began to slow down near a central square.

"Those types of attacks are fairly rare this far inland," he said. "Most of them occur near the coast, when they wash up on the shore. Bandits would be a bigger threat, but Sapir is plenty safe, don't worry. They have their own form of protection."

I wanted to ask him what he was referring to, but we got caught up in the caravan unloading its haul and shooing us on our way. I quickly forgot my question as we moved through the town to find a place to stay.

The bazaar in the central square wasn't quite as large as Changirah's, but the streets were lined with cobblestone rather than packed earth so the overall appearance was much less of a dirt storm, and the curiosities were even more curious. Trinkets chimed and shook and spat and gave off pleasant aromas as we marched through the throng of people wearing robes of every color imaginable. The buildings came in many shapes and sizes, their unique architecture noisily clashing with one another as if they were all fighting to be the most eye-catching on the streets.

"Yeah, the Sapirians have a taste all their own to be sure," Hawke agreed when I asked him about the buildings. "Like I said, this is the place to be if you consider yourself any sort of artist. It's a rather cutthroat world, to be honest. A lot of dashed dreams and sad endings line these cobbled roads."

He caught sight of a particular merchant and led us to the stall, where he began to speak to the man in fast, hushed tones. I caught sight of the same black line under this merchant's eye that Fern had, and figured they were probably friends, so I took the time they were talking to rummage around the table for anything interesting. The man gave me a rough look, but Hawke vouched for me and no more was made of the matter as I continued to sniff around for anything interesting.

The best I could find was a ball that spun wildly in the holder's hand while giving off a wonderful whirring noise, and several beautifully crafted music boxes that I entertained myself with, laughing at the noise made when several were opened and playing simultaneously.

Hawke finished talking with the man as I was toying with locking and unlocking a particularly sparkly sapphire colored one. He pulled me away from the stand so quickly I had no time to unlock it as it tumbled from my hands back onto the table.

"We have a couple things we need to pick up before we hit the inn," he told me as he led me to the other side of the bazaar. "Namely, some nice dress robes for the concert. I thought we'd have a day to prepare, but we're behind schedule it seems."

We spent the next few hours bumbling between clothing stalls, trying on various robes with different fancy sashes and chains on them. Owning several sets of robes was exciting enough for me, but I had never even dreamt of getting to wear the extravagant types of dress robes my former master's guests would wear during visits to the old estate.

When Hawke finally helped me pick out one with a rich forest green color and a shimmering lighter green sash that crossed my shoulder, I felt my eyes start to water.

"Micasa, is something wrong!?" Hawke said with concern. "Is the sash too tight?"

"Hawke," I whimpered, "is this fair?"

He startled a bit. "What do you mean?"

"Is it alright for me to be this happy? With all the other slaves still stuck at the manor, is it fair for me to get new clothes and a shinestone and get to travel and see so many things with you?"

I didn't cry. Crying was one of the easiest ways to earn a brutal punishment at the estate, and I had learned that lesson early. But the emotions welling up in me were threatening to overwhelm that conditioning. I didn't dare get anything on the beautiful clothing I had on, so I instead planted my face in my bundled up plum robe and hastily rubbed my eyes dry.

Hawke's expression softened as he knelt down next to me. "I'm sorry we couldn't bring them with us. It would've taken too long and put all of their lives and ours in a lot of danger. It's not your fault, though, Micasa. Don't blame yourself one bit. You have every right to be happy."

I nodded and sniffed a few times, even though I wasn't completely convinced. Hawke smiled and ran his fingers through my hair, which helped me feel a little better as he went to pay for our robes. He had chosen a dark maroon one with a chain belt.

Again with the bloody color, I thought, seeing how it matched his kilt, but I shook the thought from my head.

The rest of the afternoon, Hawke tried to divert my attention with various street shows around the town, yet even with all the musicians and puppet shows we passed, I couldn't help but notice the uneasy way Hawke started carrying himself. He was getting extremely fidgety and never stayed at one performance for more than a few minutes before ushering me towards some new distraction.

It didn't take long for him to dismiss every show on the street and whisk us away to the inn down the road. The common room through the entrance was similarly quaint and well-furnished, like the one in Changirah, but boasted the added benefit of music being piped through the ceiling as well as several gaudy paintings lining the walls. No matter how hard I stared, I couldn't make heads or tails of a single one, and when I asked Hawke what they meant he simply shrugged and gave a noncommittal grunt.

We had just reached the rooms when a distant bell sounded seven times, striking the hour. "Damn, I completely lost track of time, we need to get moving," Hawke muttered as he tossed most of his belongings on the bed and shot to a side room with his new robe. "You change here, just let me know when you're done so we can be on our way."

I had more trouble getting into the robe than I thought I would. The robe itself was simple enough, but I never worn the type of flourishing sash it came with before, and it required a level of finesse I wasn't accustomed to. Fortunately, Hawke was well-versed enough to get it straightened in almost no time, but I didn't even have time to appreciate how I looked in the mirror before he was whisking me out the door.

"C'mon, we don't want to be late!" he said breathlessly, barely able to hide the excitement on his face. "Oh, could you give the lock your special touch on the way out? I feel our stuff would be safer that way."

With a simple twist of the lock, our room was as secure as it ever could be, and Hawke practically carried me down the main street towards the most impressive building I had ever seen in my life at that point.

A great gilded dome covered the top of the enormous structure, with flags poking out every so often on the rooftop, creating a sort of crown around it. Already hundreds of people were milling towards the massive gold doors that stood at least twice as tall as even the considerably lanky Hawke, and we wasted no time in queuing up behind them to enter.

A surly looking man and a bored looking woman waited at the entrance, in resplendent robes of lavender and emerald respectively. As we approached, I saw that they were checking tickets for everyone else, and wondered when Hawke had taken the time to buy ours during our busy day. When we reached the doors, though, Hawke scratched his left cheek and murmured something to the two. They returned the gesture, bidding us to enter afterward, and I couldn't help but notice the same line under their eye that the merchant from earlier and Fern had. As we entered a massive foyer, I finally asked Hawke about it.

"Oh, you caught on to that?" he gave a slightly forced smile. "Yeah, let's just say that they're part of the same family, and I'm well acquainted with them."

"So they're like your brothers and sisters?"

"Not quite, it's more that we help each other out, and... oh!" The lights started dimming at that moment. "The concert's starting, let's get to our seats!"

I was struck speechless at the sight of the auditorium, packed full of patrons waiting for the show to begin. There must have been hundreds of people seated, wearing robes of satin and velvet so rich it made my old master's wardrobe look shabby in comparison. Even more people were seated in balconies high above ground floor, some using small binoculars to get a better view of the stage far below. Hawke marched me down the center aisle straight towards the front row, and more than a few heads turned and appraised us with sneers and snorts of disapproval. Even with our dress robes, it appeared we were woefully underdressed for the occasion.

Right in the front row, two more rough looking bouncers with the line tattoo had taken a couple of the best seats. They rose as we approached, nodding and scratching their cheeks, and as they left, Hawke bade me to sit.

Afraid of seeing the looks of disgust likely aimed at the backs of our heads, I tried to make sense of what was about to happen. The stage was so large it made up a third of the massive room and rose so high I almost couldn't see what was set on it. Dozens of chairs were placed in a semi-circle pointed towards the audience, and in front of those was a single wooden podium, standing ominously alone.

Before I had a chance to ask what was going on, two concentrated lights brightened to illuminate the entire stage. Thunderous clapping filled the auditorium as men and women began to file onto the stage from behind the drawn curtains, each one dressed in black satin pants and vests and carrying an instrument. Hawke whispered the names of them as they walked in: violin, clarinet, flute, cello, tuba, trumpet, and oboe. Three men wheeled in three massive drums Hawke pointed out as tympani.

When all were in their place, a lone woman Hawke identified as the conductor paraded onto stage, the only one on the stage wearing a white vest. She bowed to the audience, and instantly an expectant hush fell over everyone watching. The conductor turned, raised her baton into the air, and brought it down.

The first note the orchestra played made me jump. Listening to music on the phonograph did nothing to prepare me for what live music offered. I was spellbound by the magic they wove with their instruments, their play flawless as they complimented each other's sound to create something more than the sum of their whole.

As the song swelled louder and louder until I almost wanted to cover my ears to keep from going deaf, the entire orchestra stopped suddenly. I thought it over, but after the slight ringing in my ears subsided, I heard a single violin cut through the silence, its note high and sad. I looked around to see who was playing, but the sound seemed to be coming from offstage. As the note continued to linger, a figure stepped forward slowly, his violin bow pulling so slow across the strings you might have thought it wasn't moving at all.

The player was more boy than man, young and smooth-faced. His auburn hair was artfully tousled, and though he wore black like the rest of the orchestra, there was fine gold filigree that lined the seams of his clothing. He stepped forward, past the rest of the players and even striding by the conductor, until he stood in front of the podium looking over the room. All the while, his lonely note wafted without faltering.

Then he began to play.

I want to stress that the rest of the performers were quite good, and by themselves, they put on a decent show, but the entire song changed when that boy tore into that violin. The orchestra didn't miss a beat as they picked up the song right where they left off, but now they seemed to only exist to support the young violinist. The conductor worked valiantly to keep them in time, but the boy needed no guide – standing at the forefront, there was no doubt that he was setting the pace that everyone else had to keep up with.

When he struck that final tumultuous note at the end, it shivered in the air for a lifetime. As it faded, it was as if I had lost a dear friend and ached for more.

The applause that followed shamed the applause from the beginning of the concert. A few people whistled, and I swear someone in the balconies screeched, "Give me your children!" The boy paid no attention to any of it as he strode to one of the trumpet players and handed them his violin. The trumpeter exchanged instruments and rushed off the stage as the boy took the podium again.

The song began at the conductor's mark, but it wasn't long until the boy was blowing away at his new instrument. Unlike the soft melancholy of his violin, his trumpet was fast and electric, playing notes so fast he might have been mistaken for playing two instruments if you weren't watching.

The concert continued on for over an hour in this way. After every song, the boy would swap his current instrument with one of the orchestra's that he had yet to play, and each time he seemed to get even better. By the end of the third song, the audience was too entranced to even applaud, instead waiting feverishly for the next song to begin.

I glanced over to see how much Hawke was enjoying it, but his reaction was even more than I expected. He sat at the edge of his seat, eyes wide and unblinking, and he gripped the armrests so tightly they creaked like they were about to break. It was disconcerting to see him so intensely focused on the performance, but when I nudged him his expression lightened and he assured me he was fine.

For the final song, a man stepped onto the stage with a most peculiar instrument: a twin-necked violin, ebony traced with jade. My confusion gave way to astonishment when he proceeded to play a harmony with himself for the entirety of the song, as the rest of the orchestra simply watched on in reverence. Even the conductor, who had been stern of demeanor for the rest of the performance, had a look of wonder on her face as his fingers danced along the strings and his bow carved an entire story out of sound alone.

When at last he rested, the entire room seemed to explode with applause, cheers, and whistling. Even I couldn't avoid clapping until my hands were raw, yet Hawke only continued to stare with mouth slightly agape.

"Who was that boy? He was amazing!" I asked Hawke as the lights came back on and the patrons chatting animatedly to one another. He startled out of his concentration and looked to me.

"His name is Claudio Johann. He's often referred to as the Young Genius – apparently he's been able to play like that since he was only nine years old. That was seven years ago..." he trailed off as his eyes lost focus, but he snapped back to attention quickly.

"Would you like to meet him?" he asked out of the blue.

"Wow, could we really?" I wanted nothing more at that moment than to thank the boy named Claudio for the wonderful show he put on. Hawke nodded and took me by the hand, leading me around to the side stage.

Two more guards with the face line stood close by the entrance to the backstage, but with a single scratch of Hawke's cheek they stepped aside and ushered him into the cramped hallway. Hawke walked so quickly I had to jog to keep up as he moved past several identical doors until stopping with purpose in front of one no more remarkable than the rest. Without so much as a knock, he twisted the knob and pulled me inside.

Claudio stood in the back of the lavish dressing room, staring into a wide mirror that covered most of the wall. I hardly noticed the expensive looking furniture that practically littered the floor, nor the gaudy paintings that papered just about every inch of the wall the mirror didn't take up. Both Hawke and I had our sights glued on the boy as he gasped in surprise and turned when we appeared in the mirror before him.

"Who the blazes let you in?" he said with a wild look in his eyes. "Where are the guards? Lousy oafs!" He spoke loudly and angrily, but it was easy to see how frightened he was as he looked around, perhaps for something to defend himself with.

"Come now, Claudio," Hawke said in his softest tone, "is that any way to talk to your teacher after so many years?"

The Young Genius' eyes narrowed, taking in Hawke for a long time.

"No, that's silly," he muttered as he tilted his head in thought. "He vanished after only a few lessons, and that was so long ago I almost forgot about him."

"Yes, seven years to be a bit more exact," Hawke agreed as he stepped closer. Though he was smiling at the musician, there was something terribly unsettling about it that made my flesh crawl. The boy shook his head.

"I think you're mistaken, my dear fan. Nobody has seen that lout in—"

"Seven years. Yes, we just discussed that." Hawke's smile was gone now, replaced with the face I saw him wear when his patience grew too thin. "The name Morau should strike a chord with you, I should think?" Hawke gave a short mirth-

86

less laugh, taking another couple steps towards the boy. Claudio tried to back away but could only press himself ineffectively against the vanity on the wall. Glancing around in a panic, he gave a pained smile that could have been mistaken a grimace.

"W-why, Lord Hawke, is that really you!? Goodness, I'm so glad you could make it to my performance! I've come quite a ways, wouldn't you say? Even with those scant lessons you gave me, they most certainly shaped me as I climbed to the top of the music world!"

"Show me it."

The growl that escaped Hawke's lips was unlike any tone I'd heard him give before. Hunger was drawn across his face, and now I recognized the other time I had seen him look like this: the night he accosted our old master, his impostor. Claudio wilted at his gaze.

"I r-really have no idea what you're talking about..."

Hawke had closed the distance and was now standing inches in front of the trembling boy. He reached a hand up towards Claudio, eliciting a cry of fright and a flinch, but he only set his hand gently on the mirror. Instantly cracks splintered from where he touched it, and Claudio tumbled to the side clutching his head.

"I could take it whenever I wanted to, child, but I need answers first. Who gave you the shinestone?" As if on instinct, Claudio put a hand on his chest where I saw a peculiar bulge protruding.

"It… was one of those wretched gypsies," he said weakly. "Black hair, skin like strong ale. She came to our hut sometime after your last visit and gave it to me. 'Keep it safe. You'll know what to do with it,' she said and was gone. I would say she was beautiful if she hadn't been one of *those*—"

The rambling boy was dragged to his feet by his shirt, and Hawke's face scowled inches from his own tear and snot streaked pout.

"You are not allowed to speak like that about the gypsies ever again. As your teacher, this is my last lesson. Not one more foul slander will escape those lips ever again. Are we clear?" Claudio nodded once, his eyes locked onto Hawke's.

"Good," said Hawke, "then all is forgiven." He reached up again and tenderly touched Claudio on his cheek.

Almost instantly, a blinding light dazzled from the bump under Claudio's shirt, filling the room and forcing me to turn my head away. It only lasted for a moment, but after it subsided, I still had to blink furiously to clear the spots swimming before my eyes. Hawke was kneeling on the floor, gasping for air as sweat trickled down his brow. Behind him, Claudio stood stock still, save for a slight quiver in his lip.

"No, no, I can't remember. I can't remember!" The Young Genius screeched. "You took it from me! I can't remember how to play!"

Hawke had seemed to compose himself a bit, leaning against a large stuffed chair as he hauled himself up. His eyes floated around, looking at nothing, and his fingers flexed open and closed. He gazed at his hands, wiggled them a bit, and gave off a small chuckle.

"I really am sorry," he said as he turned to look back at the panicking musician. "It's not your fault at all, but that talent you've been celebrated for was never yours to begin with. I merely took back what was mine."

"How will I perform now!?" Claudio raved on, oblivious to Hawke's apology. He began staggering around the room, smashing anything he could get his hands on and flipping over anything too sturdy to be outright destroyed. "They're expecting an encore any minute! I can't show my face out there!"

I could only watch on confused. Hawke took my hand and led me out the door while the screams of Claudio Johann and the din of his tantrum slowly died behind us, ending with a horrible wail of despair.

"Will he be okay?" I asked as we marched down the tight corridor back towards the auditorium. Hawke sighed heavily.

"He's not hurt, but his performing days will be over. Possibly for good."

"Oh no! His music was so wonderful, I would be so sad if no one to get to hear it anymore!"

Hawke slowed his pace, looking at the floor. We were right at the backstage entrance, the sounds of happy patrons still bubbling from just down the stairs.

"You know, you're right, Micasa," he said as he gave me a little smirk. "The least I could do is give the encore they've been waiting so patiently for."

He tightened his grip on my hand and led me away from the stairs leading back to the seats, instead leading me behind the curtains and towards the stage. He stopped at the edge of the wing, pulling the curtain back and taking a peek at the full house.

"How lucky for you, Micasa, you're getting the best seat in the house!" He gave me a thumbs up, and stepped out onto the stage.

The idle chatter quickly became a buzz of confusion as Hawke strode towards the podium where Claudio had performed. The twin-necked violin had been leaning there, waiting for its owner's return, but it was my guardian who took it back into hand. One of the stagehands began to step out from the opposite side, but with a scratch of Hawke's cheek the bouncer stopped, nodded, and backed away. The confused murmur in the audience rose and made way to angry shouting as some people started to stand and leave.

Then Hawke raised his bow, gave a little bow to the mob, and attacked the strings.

Chapter 5

The Savage Man

We remained in Sapir for a couple days after the concert, and I spent most of that time reading through a few books Hawke had purchased for me while he was off running various errands. Most of them were schooling books, helping to reinforce my understanding of basic reading. I grew bored with them quickly and ended up spending more time letting myself out of the poorly secured room and walking around the inn instead.

You'd be surprised how many different types of locks you can find in the average building: doors, windows, pantries, the errant diary a careless guest had left lying around. The last one I enjoyed the most. I could honestly tell Hawke I had been practicing reading when he returned, though all it had were the names of various men and women and lists of activities that, had I been more world-wise at the time, would've made me blush.

It was midafternoon on our third day in town, as I was toying with the idea of seeing how difficult it would be to crack the lock on the safe behind the downstairs reception counter, that Hawke returned much earlier than usual and handed me a knapsack.

"Alright, Micasa, load up your things. It's time we get going," he said as he piled his own belongings into his travel bag.

"Are we going on the coach again?" I asked expectantly. Another long ride in a caravan sounded great after so many dull days cooped up inside the inn.

"No, sadly, the caravan won't be going the way we are," he said. Likely seeing the disappointment in my eyes, he gave me a reassuring grin. "I think you'll enjoy the next leg more than enough. There's a surprise waiting downstairs for us."

With the promise of something special, I hurriedly lumped my few precious items into my new knapsack, save for my dress robe; that, I folded and placed carefully on top. With both of us packed, I scurried down the stairwell and out the door, bouncing on my heels as I waited for Hawke to catch up.

"There's our ride," he said as he pointed toward the side of the road. I gasped as I caught sight of the beautiful chestnut stallion that stood tied to a post nearby. Its tail swished back and forth lazily while it looked around with mild disinterest at the goings of the passersby.

Hawke took my travel bag and tied it securely alongside his own behind the saddle strapped to the horse's back, our belongings joining a small pile of sacks and boxes already waiting on the horse. Apparently, all his time away had been spent on getting provisions for the journey to come. Once everything was secure, Hawke reached down and hoisted me up by the waist into the saddle.

"Can I pet it!?" I gushed while he pulled himself up.

"Of course!" said Hawke. "We'll be riding him for quite some ways likely, it's best for you two to get off on the right foot and make friends."

The fur of the horse's mane was amazingly soft, and I laughed as I ran my fingers through it over and over. The horse merely snorted.

"I'm gonna call you Sir Brown Horse!" I declared. Hawke grabbed the reins and started our new steed off at a slow trot.

"That's, er, not bad," Hawke said as he led us down the road towards the gate. "We can play around with names while we're on the road, though."

I found myself continuously reaching out to pet Sir Brown Horse as we trotted leisurely through the countryside that flourished beyond the walls of the city. Between the abundant groves of trees and fields of uncountable flowers, I found it hard to believe I had spent most of my life believing the stories told about constant demon and raider attacks.

"Enjoy the scenery while you can," Hawke advised. "The path we're taking will be a lot more barren before long."

"I love the horse, but I wish we were still in that caravan. That was so much fun!" I said.

"It's because of where this road leads that we couldn't take it," he explained. "We're going to be leaving these farmlands and heading into some dangerous territory. You have that map I gave you?"

I nodded and pulled it out of my sack with a bit of difficulty from the bouncing of the horse ride. Hawke held me steady with one hand while I clumsily unfolded the large piece of parchment, revealing a large jagged shape that covered most of the paper.

"All the land we live on is this one massive island, the land of Astra," he said as he traced his finger over the shape. "The land itself is divided into two main segments. Where we are right now is known as the Fertile Lands." He swept his fingers over the right side of the map. "Most food and other goods are made here, to be shipped all over the country. The other side is known as the Old Kingdom. It holds a massive amount of natural resources that they use to trade for those goods. Because of that, most people in the Fertile Lands are farmers or artisans, while people in the Old Kingdom tend to be nobility or simply wealthy."

"What about this weird line between the two?" I asked, touching a large jagged red fissure that divided the two areas.

"That, sadly, is the only way to get between the two territories. It's a short expanse that runs from coast to coast, a desert area with no towns to speak of and where bandits and... other unsavory sorts like to hide out. No law touches that desolate little strip of land. The people call it the Madness for that reason: anything can happen there, and nobody will be there for you when it does. Don't fret, though," he said reassuringly. "It only takes about a day to cross over it, and we'll make sure to be well prepared for the trip."

I nodded, but couldn't really visualize what a lawless land could be like. Every place had to have some sort of rules, that much I knew from my experiences, so how a little line on that map could be any different was beyond me.

What I did know was that the bouncing motion of the horse had begun to hurt my backside, and I was hoping desperately for a rest. Hawke conceded and let us down near an overgrown oak to break for lunch.

"Hawke, will you tell me what a gypsy is yet?" I asked as I worked over an apple from our stores. I had broached the subject a few times after the night of the concert. The mean words Claudio Johann had used to describe the gypsies made them sound like terrible people, yet Hawke had been staunch in his defense of them. He always shook his head when I asked, or changed the subject abruptly, and it looked like he was about to do the same. He paused with his mouth open, then let out a sigh of resignation.

"Well, I suppose there's not much to say about them anyways. The gypsies are a group of people who travel in a caravan of their own, dozens of people with no one place they call home. They're sort of jacks of all trade, but they're particularly good at entertaining: music, acrobatics, parlor magic, they're the best of the best when it comes to those things. They rove around, only stopping to make some money or get supplies in exchange for their services."

"They sound a lot like us. We travel a lot too."

"True, but this kind of life is all they know. There is no one place the gypsies call home." Hawke carved himself a piece of particularly hard cheese, sniffed it appraisingly, and took a bite.

"Why would Claudio have talked so badly about them, though? They sound nice."

"People fear things they don't understand, Micasa. Their life is very different from most people's, so when they appear, others tend to get very paranoid about their intentions. It doesn't help that there are lots of horror stories – mostly untrue –" he added pointedly as he took a dignified bite of the cheese, "that float around about the gypsies and only stoke the fear more. Speaking of wandering, though…"

I noticed that his gaze drifted past me and down the road some distance. I turned to see what appeared to be a man hobbling slowly down the way, clutching at his shoulder where a dark red stain covered most of his tunic. Hawke stood and stepped between me and the approaching traveler, watching.

The man took almost a quarter of an hour to make it near our campsite, and as he came into view, it was clear something was very wrong. Where he clutched at his shoulder, only a bloodied stump remained, and his torn and battered clothing revealed innumerable cuts and bruises that peppered his body. One of his eyes was swollen completely shut, and the other was cast at the ground as he dragged himself one step at a time forward.

"Oy, you want to rest for a while stranger?" Hawke called out, "We've got food and some bandages for those wounds!"

The injured man startled, apparently just aware that there were people not a stone's throw from him. He stood transfixed like a deer, his one good eye lingering with suspicion. At last, he gave a furtive nod. Hawke jogged over and helped the man towards our picnic area, gingerly sitting him against the tree.

He ate almost nothing, but when Hawke offered him a water skin, he drank most of it in a few gulps and used the rest to clean the dried blood from his face.

"Aye, thanks, mate," the man managed to croak when he was done. He leaned against the trunk of the oak, the last drops of water still dripping from his tangled bronze hair. "Dunno if'n I woulda made it to town alive without that." His eye rested on me, then Sir Brown Horse with all our goods laden on him.

"You two headin' where I was comin' from?" he asked as his head lolled to the side. When Hawke gave him a small nod, he spat, "Then best you turn back. Find another way around, or a caravan strong enough to cross the Madness."

"Is it that bad?" Hawke asked. He had procured some linen from our supplies and started to dress the man's wounds.

"No more than usual, but it's startin' to creep into the area around it too. Town I just came from is practically in Madness itself. Place by the name o' Grits...some big lummox with a great honkin'

sword took the town for his own, demandin' payment from anyone passin' through. If'n you can't
pay with coin, you pay with blood. He says you
can go without coughin' up anythin' if'n you can
make him give up, but guy's strong as an ox. You
keep down this road, it's the only place you can
reach."

Hawke listened closely while he worked, occasionally stealing a glance down the road. The injured man gave a shrug.

" 'Pose you could try the hillside around it, but
th' ground's not so good for horses, and bandits
like to prowl th' forests. Like I said, best turn and
find some protection."

"Thanks for the heads up," said Hawke. He
walked to Sir Brown Horse and busied himself for
a few minutes, returning with a bulging satchel.
He tossed it at the traveler's feet.

"That should last you until you reach Sapir.
Sorry I can't take you back myself, but I doubt the
horse could handle all three of us. Rest well and
take your time, and you should make it to Sapir
within a day or two."

"I really don' wanna see nice folks like yourselves meanderin' off to danger, 'specially not the

little one," he said with a pointed look in my direction.

"We'll be fine. Micasa, let's get going."

Hawke helped me back onto the horse, though even with the break it still hurt to sit the saddle. As we took to the road again, I chanced one more look at the stranger. He was already fast asleep under the willow.

Our trip was relatively uneventful after that strange encounter, save for my growing discomfort with horse riding. Hawke assured me that I'd get used to it each time we took one of our frequent stops to let me rest, but the initial magic I felt for our adventure was already wearing thin. Thankfully, by our fourth day of travel Hawke's promise had more or less come true and I found Sir Brown Horse's rhythmic plodding growing bearable.

It was on that day that we finally caught sight of the first signs of human habitation we had since leaving Sapir. This town was far different from what I had been used to after seeing the likes of Changirah and Sapir. Most of the buildings were small houses of mud and brick with thatched roofs, tiny picket fences quartering off their territory. Chickens and pigs clucked and snuffled around the loosely packed dirt roads, and a couple farms could be seen quietly growing a ways off some side roads, but not a single person could be found nearby.

"I was hoping we could get some supplies here, but it might as well be a ghost town," Hawke murmured to himself as we clopped down the road. He vaulted off Sir Brown Horse and took him by the reins, guiding us both at a slower pace towards the edge of town where the only wooden structure stood. Above its awning stood a sign that, with trouble, I made out:

SHERIFF

"What's a shuriff?" I asked him, struggling to figure out how to pronounce the word.

"I'm the one who's haulin' in this scruffy vagrant."

I started, almost falling off the horse, while Hawke whipped around to see who was speaking right behind us. With some trouble, I was able to crane around to get a look at the biggest man I had ever seen. While Hawke was about twice as tall as me, the giant was almost three times my size. His greasy black hair was pulled back into a hasty topknot, and his beard was short but almost completely unkempt, a mass of wiry oil locks suffocating his face. His dirty burlap robe was pulled tight around his massive frame, tied loosely with a piece of rope. By far, though, the most alarming accessory was the massive broadsword he leaned against lazily like a cane. Its blade was as long as I was tall, and despite his grimy appearance, the blade was meticulously cared for, gleaming in the late afternoon sun.

"Ah, you're the sheriff then? Wonderful, I was looking for the nearest inn so we could rest up before setting out tomorrow. We're heading towards the Madness and might need—"

"Shut it," snapped the giant even as he put on a swinish smile. "We don't tolerate vagabonds in Grits. You got a choice – give your coin to the town, or give your flesh a taste of m'steel here." He patted the flat of the blade almost affectionately.

"Is that really necessary?" Hawke held up his hands in a surrendering gesture. "We're just weary travelers from Sapir here to settle down for a night before we're on our way. We'd be glad to spend some money for what little we need, and we'll be gone before we're a nuisance."

The brusque sheriff pulled the tip of his blade from the ground with a soft 'shink' and pointed it at Hawke's throat. "There's no negotiations. Pay now or find yourself a weapon and get ready. I'm not unfair, though," his slimy grin widened. "If you can make me cry uncle, I'll let ya go with all your limbs and your purse a little heavier than otherwise. Pretty good deal, eh?" He took a step forward, but a cry from a nearby house gave him pause.

"Oy, Boss Man Apollo! Why not give 'em a spell to sleep it off?"

All our heads turned in unison to see a small balding man with a very large mustache waving from the window of the house nearest the sheriff's office. "Won't get a good fight out of some straggler fresh off a day's ride! We'll hole him up here for the night, so he can't run off and will be ready and rarin' for you tomorrow!"

The man called Apollo narrowed his eyes but didn't lash out at the interruption like I thought he would. After a quick glance back, he nodded slowly.

"Yeah, okay, why not? Looks like you got some time to get your things in order, scum." He lowered his sword and started dragging it back towards his office. "Go ahead and take the night to make your decision. I'll be within hollerin' distance, so don't think you can bail out in the darkness. I'm looking forward to sunrise..." He snickered coldly as he pulled open the dilapidated door to his office and slammed it shut, wherein it promptly fell off.

The mustachioed man had meanwhile jumped through the window and ran to us, though even such a short distance had seemed too much for him as he doubled over gasping for breath. Unlike most people I had seen on the journey, this man wore the type of white shirt and blue coveralls that I mostly saw farmers wear. It was a dress style that always reminded me of the overseers. I shuddered, almost able to hear the snap of the lash.

"Sorry 'bout that," he huffed as he tried to look up at Hawke. "You picked a bad, bad town to wander into, fella. Here, tie up yer horse and bring the little one in, and I'll explain things over the missus' stew."

It turned out that the man's house was similarly furnished to the few inns we had stayed at so far, making me wonder if maybe it was one at some point. The man's wife had already laid out four bowls of stew on a table, her face sporting the smallest of frowns. As I sat to eat, I had a strange hankering for a sandwich to go with it.

"Name's Earl, stranger. This is m'wife Giselle," mustached man said, his wife bowing ever so slightly at her introduction. "The 'sheriff' you just had the misfortune of meetin' is Apollo: meanest S.O.B. this side o' the Madness."

"Any reason you elected such a crazy fellow as sheriff?" Hawke asked as he leaned back, brow furrowed and arms crossed. His stew remained untouched.

"Elected? That's funny. Yer a funny one," Earl said through a spoonful. "Tha' beast just wandered in one day some years back an' said the place was under his protection. The old sheriff tried to drive 'im off, but he's a dang vicious one. Cut down him and half a dozen good men before we wised up and gave in. Even built him tha' eyesore of an office t' keep him satisfied."

"Earl, why are we wastin' time and good food on this lout?" Giselle spoke up. Her hands rested on her hips, and she glowered at her husband. "Should've just left 'im to pay or limp off half a man. Didn't hold him back when tha' last poor bloke came amblin' through, did ya?"

"THA' ONE—" he started to shout, but almost immediately quieted down and stole a furtive look out the window towards Apollo's office. When he was sure there was no movement, he spoke again, much softer. "Tha' one didn't have a little one with 'im, did he?" He looked to me with sad eyes. "Why would you bring such a lass to such a terrible place?" The question wasn't for me.

"There was no other way for us to go. We're destined for the Old Kingdom. This was the best way." Hawke played with the spoon sitting in his rapidly congealing gruel but still didn't touch a bite. "My question is, what does Apollo get out of this? If he just wants the money, why doesn't he just attack travelers and take the money afterward? Why the ultimatum?"

"Ulti-whata?" Earl said, digging his finger into his ear. "Tha' question's easy, though. Apollo's a bloodthirsty beast, bu' he wants to prove he can beat anyone in a fight." Earl stopped talking to whip out a pipe and stuff it. He lit, took a puff, and let the smoke dribble from his nose. Hawke frowned and stole a glance at me, but remained silent.

"Yer right," Earl kept on, "this is the best road through the Madness. Tha's why he holds up here waitin' for lone stragglers to pass by. He doesn't need the coin, he weasels plenty outta us for his 'services', but he figgers the people with coin to pay aren't worth the trouble anywho. He *wants* people to try an' fight their way out, so he can show off how good he is with tha' sword. And if there's one thing he is, it's dang good with a sword."

"And if we try to sneak away right now, you're the ones who'll have to pay my price, won't you," Hawke added. Giselle turned from the dishes she was doing in surprise, and Earl swallowed hard.

"Aye, so you could tell? Usually, the townsfolk hole up in their houses when they catch wind of someone wanderin' through. Don't wanna chance being taken for an accomplice if they get away from Apollo. Sorry, boy, but we're not much better than them. I'll call for the Boss Man if I see ya runnin' too. I hope ya understand."

Hawke lowered his gaze, and for a moment I thought I saw a flash of emotion come over him. Anger? Guilt? I couldn't quite tell, but he raised his head and nodded.

"That's all I need to know," he said. "Thanks for telling us. We'll be off to bed then. The sheriff said he'd be by at sunrise for me, yes?" Earl nodded, looking away.

"Thanks for the stew, Ma'am!" I said as I hopped from the chair. She looked at me with a pained expression.

"Weren't nothin', dear," she replied hesitantly. I smiled at her and followed Hawke to the room Earl had pointed out for us to use.

The bedroom was more of a closet, almost completely overtaken by the straw stuffed-mattress covered in sheets that counted as a bed. A small oil lantern hung from the ceiling, which Hawke lit before planting himself in an empty corner. He had the long, belted bundle that Fern had given him across his lap, and was undoing the clasps on a small bulky case I had seen tied behind our other things on Sir Brown Horse.

"Best you get to sleep early, Micasa, we're heading out early tomorrow," he said. He reached into the case and pulled out an instrument. It was similar to the violin I saw at the concert, only much larger.

"Did you get that in Sapir?" I asked as I climbed under the massive sky blue quilt. He nodded, plucking a couple of the strings while fiddling with some pegs at the top of the neck.

"It's called a guitar. I considered taking that double-necked violin with me, but that kind of instrument is far too fancy for my taste." He toyed with the strings a bit more, then started to strum out a quiet tune. Even with how softly he played, it filled the room with a warmth that made me want to drift off, but worry kept me from being able to.

"Will you be okay?" I asked as I pulled the covers over my chin. The bed was lumpy and a little itchy from the odd straw poking out, but with Hawke's song wafting in the air, it somehow felt more comfortable than any bed I'd been in before.

"Against Apollo? I think it'll work out," he mused as he strummed absentmindedly. "He has some of my essence. I figure that's why he's so dangerous, and why I wanted to come this way."

"You can tell that?"

"It's like I said to you before, I can feel my essence like it's pulling me. It was the same with Claudio in Sapir, though I didn't know who had it exactly until I saw him in the concert. Now that I've started gaining some of it back, the pull's getting stronger, and Apollo definitely has it. I just need to touch him, and like the others, I'll take it back."

I recalled back to the fake Master Morau's manor and to Claudio's dressing room, to the bright flash of light when he touched them and how he became something more with each one.

"What did he take?" I asked, growing sleepier with each passing moment. Hawke's song wasn't helping – the gentle noise only made it harder to keep my eyes open.

"He has my ability to fight, I'd wager," he said, his song never faltering. "It would explain his propensity for starting fights. If that's the case, it shouldn't be too bad. It's a lucky thing we met Johann first..."

His words were already fading as I tumbled into the irresistible pull of sleep.

* * *

It was a pounding at the door that snapped me awake some hours later. For a second I looked around panicked, thinking I was late for my chores on the plantation, but the call from the other side of the door was that of mustachioed Earl.

"Rise up, Mr. Stranger! Boss Man's here for your answer, and he won't wait too long!"

Hawke stood from the corner almost immediately, making me wonder if he had slept at all last night. The guitar was back in its case, but he shouldered the other bundle and pushed his glasses up his nose before looking to me.

"Stay where I can see you, but don't get too close to us. Things might get a bit hairy."

I nodded and jumped out of bed, stretching the kinks from my back as Hawke marched out the door with purpose. I was right behind him, past Earl (who all but threw himself backwards out of our way) and straight out the door.

Apollo stood in the street, leaning against his sword once more. It seemed to be shining even brighter than yesterday. It wouldn't have surprised me if he had been up all night polishing it.

Hawke, in turn, took the buckles off the wrap and pulled off the cloth, revealing a plain black scabbard with a long straight handle at the end. In one swift motion, he grabbed the hilt and tossed the sheath aside, revealing a plain but sharp looking longsword, its steel unscratched and gleaming in the early morning sun. It looked as if it had never been touched until now.

"Damn it, Fern, I wanted a curved sword," Hawke murmured as he looked over the blade. "At least it's good steel."

"Well, this one's got more gumption than the others!" drawled Apollo. He snorted in what must have passed for appreciation from him. Hawke locked eyes and walked into the street, holding his sword at an angle towards the sheriff. Both stood perfectly still save for the gentlest of breezes that ruffled their clothing.

It was Apollo who swung first, bringing his hefty sword up in a great carving arc. Hawke stepped aside, but Apollo wasted no time bringing the blade around in another huge swing. This time Hawke ducked, narrowly avoiding losing his head, but still the giant continued with one great blow after another.

"Boy's not bad," commented Earl. I looked around and saw several other faces peering cautiously from behind curtains or doors cracked open. One by one, the folks of Grits joined the audience as Hawke patiently stepped away from every blow their "Boss Man" threw at him.

"Step-in-and-bleed-already!" Apollo grunted each word as he attacked, sweat starting to dot his brow. It was clear that any strike landed would take a limb off, yet the way Hawke moved, it was almost like he could see what was coming well ahead of time.

"If you insist."

Even as he said this, Hawke's blade rose for the first time. Instead of striking at Apollo, his blow landed on the flat of his enemy's blade, knocking it aside mid-swing. In a single step, Hawke drove himself chest to chest with Apollo. The sheriff's eyes went wide, but Hawke only smirked and placed his hand over Apollo's face.

There was a cry of surprise, but I knew what was coming and I turned away just before the cascade of light poured forth. The next shout came from Earl, doubtless blinded, and I felt a little guilty for not warning him before.

When I looked back, Hawke was already stepping back, his sword held out again and his eyes still completely fixed on his opponent. Apollo, on the other, hand, was quivering, his eyes darting back and forth in confusion.

"I knew it," Hawke said with a fierce triumph. "What a way to use my art, holding farmers hostage to get some cheap kicks swinging a sword. What a beast you are."

Apollo ground his teeth together and bellowed, lunging forward with his blade pointed straight at him. Hawke pushed it aside with his bare hand and spun in a single move, closing the gap instantly again. Somewhere in that movement, he had brought his blade directly under Apollo's chin, but I hadn't noticed until Hawke started talking again.

"Now, normally I'd do this myself, but I think it'd be better to leave this to the people of Grits to mete out your punishment. I'll just give you your payment–" in a few deft flicks of his sword, Hawke scored a number of cuts along Apollo's arms, legs and back in the span of a couple seconds, "–and take my leave, as you promised."

The sheriff replied with a howl pain, as if only just realizing he'd been hurt. He crumpled to the ground shaking, dropping his sword as he clutched his face for protection. Hawke walked back to the house, expression blank, and put the sword back in its sheath.

"Mind if we grab a few things before we hit the road? I'll just need some food and maybe a book or two if you have them," he said nonchalantly to Earl. The farmer was still staring at their brutal sheriff curled in a fetal position in the street.

"Wh-what in tarnation did you do to the big lug?" he said in hushed amazement.

"Took something of mine back that he had, nothing more." Hawke glanced sideways at the pitiful thing now whimpering on the ground and spat. "He's still a big guy, but that sword might as well be a steel stick in his hands now. With enough men, you should be able to do whatever you need to and be rid of him."

"If…if that's true, damn, *take* whatever ya want from the town, stranger," Earl said before taking off down the road we had come in from screaming. "HEY, JEFF, GITCHER ASS OUT HERE! ROUND UP THE BOYS, THE BRUTE'S DOWN!"

Hawke knelt next to me and rested his hand on my shoulder. "Hope I didn't give you too much of a scare."

"I was gonna worry until I saw you dance around him like that. It was amazing!" I felt my adoration for him grow as he smiled at me. "What did you do? You were so fast!"

"He had my style of sword fighting, but it's based off of fast, rhythmic sword strokes. I call it Sword Tempo; it doubles as a sort of dance performed with a blade as well. Apollo's too big and ungainly, no coordination at all. On top of that, his huge sword moves too slow to get the most out of the style. I might have had a bit more trouble if I didn't get my music sense back from Johann. It helped me find his ungainly beat."

I stared at him, trying to suss out what he said. When he saw my clear confusion, he laughed. "I'll teach you about music a bit later, then maybe it'll make a bit more sense. Now, go get our things from the room and I'll meet you near the horse."

I started back towards the inn, but stopped at the threshold and looked back. Hawke had returned to where Apollo still lay quivering. Hawke said something in a low voice that I couldn't make out, but Apollo replied in a loud stammer.

"Th-the gypsy! She said go west, through the Madness! Tha's all she told me, swear it on m-muh worthless life! Please don' kill me!"

Hawke growled something else I couldn't hear, and Apollo cried out and curled into a tighter ball. I hurried back to get our things like he asked, but now I had heard about the gypsies for a second time. Whoever they were, Hawke knew something about them he still didn't want to tell me for some reason. I wanted to know but was scared that asking Hawke would make him mad, maybe even make him leave me behind. Above all else, I would go to any lengths to avoid that.

It took two trips to grab my things and Hawke's guitar. When I got back with the unwieldy case in tow, Earl was standing next to Sir Brown Horse along with several more men in coveralls, who I guessed were some more farmers from town. They were busy loading our horse with bushels of food and various dry goods.

"Now now, not too much guys!" Hawke said with his hands up. "The horse still needs to carry us too!"

"We ain't lettin' the two o' ya off without as much as yew can carry!" a farmer with a wide-brimmed hat said as he tried to stuff an entire ham into a pouch that was clearly not designed for the task. "We can finally get rid o' that skidmark thanks t' ya!"

When at last Hawke managed to persuade them that yes, we had enough food, and no, we didn't need five pints of ale, he helped me on Sir Brown Horse's back and climbed on. The villagers gave us lots of cheers and friendly waves, but as I waved back I saw each one clutching a pitchfork, or a scythe, or a meat cleaver. Hawke gave them a single wave of his hand and kicked the horse's sides to set her off at a steady canter down the road leading west. I chanced one last look back, before the houses blocked my view, to see those friendly villagers slowly circling in on the still cowering Apollo.

"What'll they do to him?' I asked Hawke, who kept his eyes fixed straight forward.

"They'll give him what he should know plenty about," he said. "His payment to leave."

Chapter 6

No Man's Land

Up until now, our travels had been remark-
ably relaxing. Between cart rides, accommodating
coaches, trotting along casually on horseback, and
the most luxurious sleeping arrangements I'd ever
been privy to, my new life was as close to perfect
as I could imagine a life could be.

That all changed when we encountered the
Madness.

Hawke had warned me before that the journey
through this stretch of land would be difficult, but
having been raised on farmland, I'd yet to experience what a desert precisely entailed. My first
glimpse of it sent a chill through my bones, in
spite of the brutal heat already washing in from
the sands.

"Where is everything?" was the only thing I
could think to ask. It seemed a fair one, too:

bleached sand and the occasional small boulder was all there was as far as the eye could see. Hawke tightened the cowl he had secured around his face, double checking to make sure mine was equally snug.

"It's not a comforting sight, is it?" he said. "Most of the Madness is like this. Very few things can survive out here, and most of those live off the left-overs of those who try to make the journey and fail. It'll be better once night falls, but we'll have to weather this heat until then."

We climbed off Sir Brown Horse and tied him to the tree we were taking shelter under. Even with the shade, I found myself baking inside my thick robe.

"These clothes make me sweat too much," I complained, tugging at the head wrapping that barely had space to see out of.

"I know, but if you don't cover up you'll get sun-burned something terrible," Hawke said apologet-ically as he handed me a water flask. I did what he told me to, only sipping a bit to make sure we had enough to last, but it didn't even slake my thirst.

"You can take a short nap if you want. It'll make the time pass faster," he suggested. He had pulled out his sword and was wiping it down with a cloth, the little bit of sunlight that snuck through the leaves jumping off its gleaming edge and right into my eyes.

"You should too then. You never sleep," I said, perhaps more sharply than I meant. I was afraid he'd be cross, but he just chuckled.

"I only need very little rest each night. Besides, this isn't like the Fertile Lands; we need to be on our toes constantly from now on. They don't call this the Madness for nothing."

"Is it really bad?"

Hawke considered my question for a moment. "The Madness certainly can be, but that's why only strong towns tend to settle anywhere near it. The Old Kingdom we're heading to isn't quite as dangerous as here, but it's definitely not what you're used to. War is a normal part of life over there – it's partly why nobody tries their hand at farming on that side. It would just be ransacked before long."

"But we really have to cross this?" I watched the heat shimmer off the dunes, getting so dizzy from the way it warped and twisted I had to close my eyes.

"Yeah, I can feel the pull of my essence. It's definitely coming from this way."

"How do other people get across?"

"Same way we do," he answered with a shrug. "Though most people hire lots of guards when they do so. There are whole businesses around protecting people across the Madness, but you'd need to be a very well off merchant to afford that kind of insurance. We'll just have to make best with our horse friend here, and hope nobody notices two little travelers creeping around."

An arid breeze whipped into my eyes and I blinked furiously. All *I* hoped was that the journey would be as cool as he promised it would be when night fell.

Hawke spent his time caught between strumming idly on his guitar and sharpening or polishing his sword. He made frequent checks on Sir Brown Horse, who seemed to be only slightly less annoyed by the heat than me.

I tried to occupy myself with the small library Hawke had been accumulating for me, but the texts were even more tiring with the sweat slowly drifting down my face. I toyed with some of my practice locks too. He had purchased a few more in Sapir after the one he had originally acquired held no more challenge. One after the other I mastered a black iron monster of a lock, a burnished steel one with three separate keyholes, and a queer one that used a series of tumblers in the place of keys.

Eventually, I could lock and release any one them with one hand. I glanced skyward hoping daylight would soon creep away, but for all I could tell, the sun hadn't moved at all. There was little point in continuing practice on my trinkets anymore. Hawke promised me with an apologetic smile that he'd find some new ones in the next town.

All that was left for me was to drift in and out of uncomfortable, muggy sleep. The sun continued taking its sweet time that day in crossing the sky, but after a dozen mini-naps, I breathed a sigh of relief as I saw the familiar purple glow of evening pass to the soft blue haze of twilight.

"It's time. Let's get going."

I had never been so happy to hear Hawke say those words, and before he had a chance to stand, I was already on my feet, pack neatly filled. The weather had been cooling off steadily, and it filled me with a renewed energy to continue our journey.

Right away there were troubles as we set out. Sir Brown Horse's hooves proved a poor match for the desert sands, and Hawke began idly muttering a lot of words I didn't understand then and couldn't write down now in good conscience. In addition to our slow pacing, I began to notice that the drop in heat that I had been so glad for earlier hadn't let up, and as the night grew darker, the cool breeze I had been enjoying so much now began to carry a biting frigidity. The sweat that still clung to me only made the cold that much worse. I found myself desperately wrapping my clothing as tightly as possible.

"It'll be okay, Micasa," Hawke assured me as our steed fought its way up a fairly unremarkable sand dune. "In a couple hours we'll stop and warm ourselves. I can make fire dance, remember?" He placed a reassuring hand on my shoulder, but at that moment a little dancing flame would've been much more appreciated.

Even with the frigid temperatures and our mount difficulties, we still continued forward steadily. I was astonished to find that the sand was, in fact, not infinite, even in the desert. There were entire stretches of land that gave way to hard packed earth crossed with so many cracks that it looked like someone had shattered the ground itself. Every now and then, something would crawl or slither from those fissures, quickly scurrying off at the unwavering "clop clop" of Sir Brown Horse carrying his two passengers. I even forgot my discomfort momentarily when I caught sight of my first cactus. Hawke had to explain several times why I couldn't go and touch the fuzzy looking tree.

The ever increasing cold put me on edge, but what made me feel the most unease was the utter desolation I felt as we crossed an infinite stretch of the same flat land. I had never been so long without seeing evidence of another person, whether a fellow traveler or some quiet house nestled in its own little nook in the world. I kept glancing around uncomfortably, waiting to catch glimpse of anyone else, but aside from Hawke and myself, we were beyond alone.

At least, that held true until some hours later.

I had resigned to watching the moon creep across the sky, feeling like I could relate to its pace, when Hawke pulled the reins on Sir Brown Horse. The horse snorted and pawed at the ground, likely just as eager as us to get out of this freezing badland, but Hawke held him steady. His eyes were fixated far ahead.

"What's wrong?" I asked, pulled from my moon watching.

"Light," was all he said. I couldn't make it out at first, but it did seem that beyond the small dune a few minutes off was the faintest of glows.

"Is someone camping over there?"

"Probably. That's why we're gonna give them a bit of a wide berth." He nudged the horse forward again, veering off to the south of where the blush of light radiated. Unfortunately, our detour was shorter than anticipated as we crossed the dune and found ourselves facing a full-blown canyon.

"Damn," swore Hawke. He swept his head back and forth as if hoping beyond hope a bridge would be waiting to lead weary wanderers out of this barren landscape. I took the time to peer as far over the edge as I could from the saddle. The bottom of the canyon was visible, even with my small stature, but it was obviously too deep to just jump down. It wasn't terribly wide either, but much too far to even think about jumping.

"This is bad," said Hawke. "Who knows how far we'll have to go to get around this? We might be stuck out here another day." He garnished the end of the sentence with a few more choice swears.

"Look, Hawke, a walkway!" I pointed towards a wooden ramp that had been crudely assembled at the cliff's edge, sloping down into the canyon. Far below where it disappeared, the light we had seen earlier diffused a warm orange.

"They probably built it to get quickly up and down…" he mused, pulling out a pair of binoculars from his satchel and training them on the side directly opposite the ramp, "…and there's one over there as well. The problem is sneaking around whoever's down there."

"You don't think they'll help us?"

"Micasa, I'm sorry, but only one type of people lives out here: outlaws. They're not likely to spare us anything, even mercy. If we're lucky, though, they might be asleep."

Hawke hopped off Sir Brown Horse and led him by the harness towards the ramp, stopping just at the edge. He tied the reins to one of the guard rails and slowly crept onto the central platform to the walkway. It creaked a little, but he seemed satisfied with its durability and continued until he was able to look down upon the supposed camp. He pulled his binoculars up again and scanned for a long quiet moment before pocketing them and coming back.

"I think we're in luck. There are a few people down there near the fire but they look like they've passed out. There are bottles littered everywhere

– they probably were drinking heavily. As long as we're not too loud, we might be able to slink right on by."

He untied Sir Brown Horse and started leading him as slowly as possible down the wooden ramp. There was a tense moment where it gave out a painful groan, but the planks didn't show any signs of giving under the animal. Hawke took a deep breath, then began leading us into the canyon.

Even with our glacial pace, every hoof beat and every crack or groan of the rickety structure caused Hawke to flinch. I looked at the canyon floor, which seemed so close before, but now it seemed to stand a mile below us, and I felt a flutter of nausea. From our new vantage point, I caught sight of the campfire that sat in the middle of four plain cloth tents, casting long shadows all over the small valley. Even at a distance, I could make out the tiny figures of people lying around the fire, amongst a mess of objects strewn about near them. With Hawke's slow pace and constant wincing, I kept my eyes glued on the supposed bad people, watching for any sign of them stirring from their slumber. Thankfully, they remained right where they were as the ground drew ever closer.

When we finally made that last step off the shoddy structure, Hawke and I both let out soft sighs of relief. It wasn't far to the other side of the valley, and the ramp leading to the other side was directly in front of us. As we started our creeping pace forwards, though, the flames of the campfire flickered. A light breeze whipped through a moment later, blowing past the camp and us. With the wind came something else: a horrendous, cloying sweet smell. Hawke stopped in his tracks, looking towards the camp.

"What is that?" I whispered as quietly as I could.

"There's something wrong with this camp…" he said, staring for several seconds. He looked back and forth between our exit and the camp multiple times before turning Sir Brown Horse and myself towards the camp, creeping as slow as we could.

It was only as we drew closer that we caught whiff of that stench again, threatening to be so overbearing that I had to put my hands to my nose or risk vomiting. Hawke's nose wrinkled too, but that only made him pick up his pace. The horse was snorting and trying to shy away from the camp, but Hawke kept his grip firm on the reins.

When we rounded the first tent and came upon the fire, I wished that we had just gone up the ramp.

Now, I had seen dead bodies before. While not common, slaves did on occasion pass out from overwork and never stand back up. The overseers usually hauled them off shortly thereafter, though what became of them, nobody knew. Those people who collapsed always just looked like they had fallen asleep on the job.

The situation that was sitting right in front of us was an entirely different matter. The four people that were around the fire were lying on the ground, as well as strewn on the tents, resting in the flames, and coating the rocky outcroppings. One man's entrails showed the path he took as he crawled from the tent he had been eviscerated in, before depositing himself several feet away in a heap. Another man sat glass-eyed against one of the tent poles, his severed arm lying a few paces away with a sword still loosely gripped in its cold blue fingers. For all the mess made, there might very well have been more than four of them.

"Micasa, don't look," Hawke warned a little too late. He turned his back to the carnage, and even in the dim moonlight I could see that he had paled a few shades at the campsite. I was still a little too confused and shocked to understand exactly what I was looking at.

"This is all wrong," said Hawke as his eyes darted around. "These bodies have been here for at least a couple days, but scavengers haven't gotten to them yet. This fire was just started recently too..."

That's when someone lunged from the empty tent.

There was no time to see who had emerged, as the horse immediately reared and screeched in terror. Hawke was kicked in the chest in its panic, sending him hurtling backwards, and I had no time to try and keep myself from being thrown backwards and off the mount. I landed hard enough on my back to blow the wind out of me. I laid there desperately gasping for breath, trying to twist see where Hawke had landed. He had been sent sprawling into one of the tents, pulling it down all around him where he lay, motionless. Sir Brown Horse took off, leaping over the campfire and out of view.

After tense seconds that dragged on to tenser minutes, I finally found enough strength to stand on my own. Hawke had also begun to stir, thrashing about in an attempt to free himself from his entanglement.

"Are you okay?" I cried as I tried my best to pull the mess of a tent off of him. It took some work, but eventually he stood shakily, clutching at his chest.

"I should ask you that," he managed to wheeze. "You were lucky you didn't break your neck." He turned back and forth, sucking in a painful breath. "We're in trouble here. The horse has our supplies, and we'll never make it through the Madness without him. Stay close." He drew the sword at his hip, pointing it forward while keeping a protective hand on my shoulder.

"Did you see where the horse ran off to?" he asked. I nodded and pointed where I saw Sir Brown horse take off. With a nod of his own, he started slowly leading me down the canyon.

We were barely past the campfire when the sound of falling hooves reached our ears. "Sir Brown Horse is coming back!" I cried hopefully.

"Maybe, but those footsteps are too fast," was all Hawke had time to say. Sir Brown Horse erupted from the darkness at full gallop, and he wasn't alone. All I saw was a bright flash of red before Hawke pushed me out of the horse's path, throwing himself backwards and just narrowly avoiding the trampling hooves. I heard a clash of steel and tried to push myself up to see what had happened.

Instead, I found myself being hauled up bodily by the waist. At first, I thought Hawke was trying to carry me somewhere, until I heard him call out for me from the other side of the camp. Whoever had grabbed me was the person who had tried to ride us down, and he was rushing towards the scaffold leading out, fast.

I tried to call back to Hawke, but no sooner did my voice start to rise that my captor struck me sharply, all but knocking me out. As I laid limply in their grasp, my abductor started climbing directly up the walkway at astonishing speed without so much as bothering to follow the ramps in the slightest. In seconds we were at the top, and my captor was already sprinting away at full speed.

When I tried once more to call out, he struck me even harder, and everything went black.

* * *

How much time passed until I woke up, I couldn't tell you. The first thing I noticed was the musty smell, not unlike a certain nauseating scent

I had just been introduced to recently. Despite the pulsing pain in my head, I forced my eyes open. They had swollen near to shut, leaving me with only faint slits to peek through.

A dim bonfire was the lone source of illumination, and for a brief moment, I thought I was back at the campsite from before. With some effort and a lot of throbbing, I was able to look around a bit. Immediately I realized that I couldn't have been farther off.

Course, mildewed stone surrounded me on all sides and comprised the floor, leading me to figure that I was in some sort of cave. The cave itself was about the size of a large den, but the only furnishing was a stray boulder and the largest pile of bones I had ever seen. It teetered precariously towards the ceiling, and though it was made of a mass jumble of various animals, there was no mistaking the small pile of round, clearly human skulls stacked neatly around the base.

I tried to push myself to sit, but my hands and feet had been bound together behind me. Even rolling side to side was almost too much for me to do, and my whole body throbbed so much it wasn't worth the effort.

"Eyes open. Good."

The voice startled me, a voice unlike anything I had heard before. I looked around, but no one seemed to be there with me. However, there was one spot that the light didn't reach: the sole entrance to the cave. Something was moving there, but I couldn't make it out in the shadows.

"Glasses will come for Little. Glasses protected. Glasses will watch Little die."

I shivered at the sharp, stilted way it spoke. It felt like a cheap imitation of how a person would speak. When the speaker stepped out into the reach of the light, I saw I was far more correct in my assumption than I had hoped to be.

Its skin shimmered bright as a drop of blood in the glow of the flame, crossed all over with faded pink scars. Its eyes were like bleached bones, reflecting nothing, yet I could almost feel its perverse gaze settle on me. Two gaping holes filled the space where a nose would be on a normal person, sitting just above a massive mouth that I could have fit my whole head inside. Its teeth were tiny saws, perfectly locked together in a monstrous grin. It lumbered towards me, back hunched while lanky and muscular arms dragged along the floor. In place of hair, long horns grew down and curled around the smooth, earless sides of its head.

The beast stopped in front of me, bending even lower until I could smell the decay and iron on its breath. It ran a finger along my cheek, almost carefully, before smacking me across the face again.

"Don't die yet. Glasses must see. Glasses will regret."

It lumbered back towards the exit, and all my pains were forgotten as fear roiled in my gut like an illness. I had lived most of my life in the grip of a demonic man, but my former master paled in comparison to the genuine article.

Chapter 7

The Inhuman

I couldn't tell you how many hours I spent in that festering, oppressive cave with that monster. There were hundreds of questions buzzing through my mind, but I learned quickly that whenever I even looked like I was going to speak, the only answer I'd get was a punch to the stomach or a slap in the face. I was lucky to even be able to see out of my swollen eyes, looking back on the experience.

Instead, I spent the untold hours watching the thing pace in and out of the cave. Sometimes it would go to the pile of bones and rearrange them ever so slightly. When the fire started to die, it would go down the passage and return with wood from who knows where. At one point, the creature left for at least an hour. When it returned, it was chewing slowly while holding a large piece of something lumpy and dripping a dark liquid. What it was eating was one question I pushed far out of my mind.

The worst part was when it started talking to me.

"Who Little. Where see Glasses first. Ever see *grinel.* Ready to die."

It spoke everything in a very short, terse manner, and never changed its tone, yet I wondered if its bizarre voice could even inflect like a person's as it did its best to ask questions to me. Of course, it struck me whenever I tried to answer, so I quickly figured it was just thinking out loud, and kept my mouth shut.

Most of my time, I thought back to all the stories I had heard about demons when I was growing up on the plantation. It was one of the favorite subjects for the slaves to talk about when we had a little bit of free time to converse over our meals; there had been dozens of tales of demons laying entire towns to waste, leaving them as nothing more than burning fields and razed buildings. Some stories told of their ability to slip in amongst humans in disguise, where they'd spread their progeny who would one day grow up to destroy their homes and everything within their reach. Others spoke of them unleashing ghouls and thralls that did the dirty work for them, that they would claim domain over wherever they sowed destruction.

The main consensus, no matter the story, was that they existed only to destroy. Sitting in the safety of our ramshackle hut, it was easy for the slaves to talk about what they had never seen or experienced. Oh, of course they *knew* it's how demons were, but aside from the strange ghoul that had wandered onto the estate that fateful day, one had never been seen on old "Master Morau's" compound. Seeing what one was like in the flesh was far more sobering than any scary story.

After what felt like days, the monster returned again, fixing those dead white eyes on me. It stepped right over the fire and put a hand on my shoulder.

"Cry now."

It began to press down, hard. My bones popped and I gasped in pain, but tears refused to come to my eyes.

"Need cry. Scab Kahlot need Little cry." It pressed harder until my shoulders felt like they'd snap. My face scrunched in pain, yet still my eyes remained dry.

"Littles always cry. Little don't. Scab Kahlot dislike."

There was no point in trying to explain that crying from pain was something I hadn't done in years. Overseers and masters hated nothing more than a worker prone to bawling, and those who couldn't learn to shelve their pain or anger or sadness were not long for this world. It was something I just couldn't bring myself to do on command.

It smacked me around a bit more, practically bouncing me off the walls. While its expression never changed, I could tell it was getting aggravated. Apparently, it didn't often encounter someone who was used to being beaten and lashed on a regular basis.

"Need cry or Glasses won't find until dead. Cut arm maybe." It started towards the pile of bones, but froze when a soft noise echoed through the exit. It looked at me, the grotesque grin plastered on its face growing wider, before loping down the corridor. More tense moments passed as I watched the dark opening, with only the faint crackle of the burning wood to keep me company.

A sudden piercing cry rang through the cavern, like a saw trying to cut through another saw. It twisted and warped more as it bounced around the walls until the whole room was filled with such a horrific din that I would've gladly cut off my own ears if it would've ended the noise. Before the sound had time to subside, the demon tumbled into the room, clutching at a stump where it once had an arm.

"Where is she?" I heard in an all too familiar voice.

"Hawke!" I tried to scream, but it came out as barely a hoarse whisper. The demon had done much more harm than I thought. Even through my bruised and inflamed eyes, though, there was no mistaking the tall figure that stepped into the firelight, sword raised before him. The reflection from his glasses hid his eyes, and his face was an expressionless mask, but cold fury snapped his words.

"If you don't bring her here right now, you'll wish you could–" He froze as he caught sight of me on the floor. I must have looked even worse than expected, as his only response was a breathless, "Oh lord, what has he done."

The demon was huddled against his bone collection, rasping breaths between its gnashing teeth. I found grim satisfaction in seeing it distressed, but that little joy curdled quickly as it removed its hand from the stump Hawke had left it with.

The wound bubbled and stretched, contorting as it grew at a rapid pace. Within seconds, the demon was flexing the fingers on its newly grown arm, just as dangerous looking as the one it had lost.

"Little is alive. Glasses watch die."

Hawke's glasses flashed for a moment, and though I couldn't tell exactly, I thought I saw a terrible fire burning in those eyes.

"Touch her again, Scab, and you'll lose a hundred arms," he swung the sword to point straight at the demon. It winced away, but let out a stuttered screech that almost could be mistaken for laughter.

"Respect *Grinel*, Glasses. Scab Kahlot. Name right."

Hawke stood without saying a word for the briefest pause. "*Scab Kahlot jhogaka teppet,*" he suddenly uttered in the same stilted way the demon had been speaking.

Scab the demon stood frozen, mouth agape. When it finally found its voice, it began to screech in a tirade of words just like what Hawke had said. The two began what sounded like an argument, back and forth in the jagged language, losing me completely.

While my captor was distracted, I began to struggle a bit more freely against my bonds. The knots were incredibly tight, and my fingers were far smaller than I would have liked to try and undo them, but I didn't want to just lay there doing nothing.

"*Mikhasa sago teppet!*"

I startled as the demon spat something that sounded like my name. I froze, afraid it had caught me trying to escape, but its blind gaze still locked onto Hawke. My guardian opened his mouth to retort but remained silent as his eyes flicked towards me, narrowing just a bit. His shock only lasted that one moment. He turned his attention back to the demon and spoke again.

"Look, Scab Kahlot, this is pointless. You can't kill me, and I can do things to you that'll make you yearn for death. Release the girl and we'll leave you be."

The creature cocked its head sideways, as if thinking, but only responded with its shredded imitation of laughter. "No deal. Little dies until Glasses surrenders."

Scab walked to its array of dismantled skeletons, the filthy excuse for a loincloth that clothed it dragging like its ungainly limbs. It shuffled through the bones for a few seconds, eventually pulling out one that was longer, thinner, and darker than the rest. After a couple seconds, I realized it was actually a very worn looking sword sheath with an even older looking hilt. Hawke sucked in a breath.

"Tell me who gave you that," he hissed. It wasn't a question; it was a command.

"Found," was all Scab answered, his demonic smile stretching into a painful grimace. "Crazy Glasses sword. No edge but left scars." It traced a finger along the faint lines that crossed all over its skin. "No sword do that but crazy sword."

Scab grabbed the hilt and freed the weapon from the aged sheath, and even with my bad eyesight, I could see what it meant by no edge. The blade looked more like a rusted piece of thin iron curved into the vague shape a sword. Still, the demon visibly shivered at the sight of it exposed.

"Now deal. Glasses let Scab Kahlot cut until death with crazy sword. Or Little gets instead," At this, Scab stepped to me and placed a hand on my face, pressing until I was certain my head would cave in.

"Fine." Hawke stepped forward until he was dangerously close to the fire. "Get off her now or no deal."

Scab released the pressure immediately, and I gasped at the sudden relief. I was fortunate the demon wasn't paying more attention – I had worked most of the way through my knots and it might have gone berserk if it saw how close I was to freeing myself. I could only hope that Hawke was capable on taking such a beast head on.

Scab walked until he was standing directly on the fire. It sputtered and licked up its leg, but the demon seemed completely unaffected as a thin tongue flickered over its teeth.

"Arm for arm," it hissed. Without missing a beat, Hawke stuck his left arm out, the sleeve falling aside to expose flesh. Scab shook his head, looking with scorn at the sword Hawke still held in his other hand. Hawke glared but obliged and offered his other arm, dropping the sword with a clatter to the stone floor.

Licking its thin lips, the demon took hold of the proffered arm with its free hand and set the rusty sword to Hawke's bicep. The beast let out a throaty chuckle as its fingers tightened around the hilt and it gave a hearty tug of the blade. Hawke's face tightened, but he didn't let out a sound as his blood began to run to the floor. After several agonizing seconds of sawing at the appendage, Scab gave a final wrenching pull and ripped the sword all the way across his arm, leaving a deep gash. It looked at the wound, then spat in anger.

"Sword no sharp. Barely cut arm. Cut Scab Kahlot and left scars but not take arm off Glasses. Why." Its tone got less and less coherent as it ranted until it dropped common language altogether and started spewing its strange demon tongue in rage. It raised the sword high overhead to bring the blade down on Hawke's head.

Hawke dove out of the way of Scab's strike, grabbing the sword he had dropped and rolling to a kneel. As he rose, the blade bit upward into the demon's extended arms, taking both off and sending its rusted weapon spinning across the ground. Scab snarled and dove for it, but Hawke was already lunging across the cave towards the liberated weapon. Both reached for it, and the demon would've won with its longer arms if they had still been attached. Instead, Hawke took firm hold of the fraying hilt and brought the blade around.

As he did, a bright flash filled the cave and blinded me even worse than I already was. When

I finally blinked the glare out of my eyes, Hawke had already closed most of the distance between him and myself. He stood only a few feet away, but Scab Kahlot was some distance behind him, one of its clawed hands freshly regrown and digging into Hawke's back.

"No need sword to kill. Scab Kahlot rip out Glasses heart easy," the demon growled. Hawke took a heavy breath and pushed his glasses up the bridge of his nose.

"You should know better than that, Scab," he scolded. "I don't turn my back on an enemy that can fight." He looked at me and frowned. "You probably shouldn't watch what's about to happen, Micasa."

I had no time to ask why, as just then the demon let out another unearthly roar before gurgling and collapsing into an indiscriminate pile of its former parts. Hawke didn't bother looking back as he knelt beside me, reaching forward but looking hesitant to touch my numerous injuries.

"I'm sorry. I should have been paying more attention, but this still happened. I'm so sorry. I'll get those ropes off you soon, just take it easy."

I responded by pulling my arms free of the weak bonds and sitting up, a feat that was far more difficult than even I had expected it to be. Hawke took a step back in surprise.

"It's okay, I got free while you were fighting the demon," I explained, still barely able to talk above a quiet croak. "It was easier to undo the knots when I thought of them like locks." As if to demonstrate, I reached for the bindings at my legs and undid them in moments, despite them being nearly tight enough to cut off my circulation. Once again free, I took the opportunity to stand and stretch, though that was enough to double me back over in pain.

"Don't overdo it," insisted Hawke as he set a ginger hand on my shoulder. "I'll carry you back to the horse. You need to rest."

"It's okay, Hawke, really," I said. "I was beat a lot at the plantation and still had to work afterward. Scab wasn't even as bad as the overseers. I just want to go."

He looked at me, a fresh frown creeping onto his expression, but he nodded. "Alright, let me just take care of one more thing."

I started hobbling towards the exit while Hawke sheathed the rusted sword and tucked it into his robe sash. I tried not to look too closely at the mess of viscera that once was Scab Kahlot as I dragged myself past it, but I couldn't help but jump when it began to pulsate wildly.

"Step back, Micasa," Hawke ordered. He had just picked up the straight sword he had brought in with him and proceeded to drive it directly into the pile of gyrating parts. The mess let out a scream of pain as it continued to pull itself together around the sword. It only took a minute or so before Scab Kahlot was once again whole, pinned to the floor of the cave by the sword. The demon let loose a terrible string of indecipherable words but was unable to extract itself from the ground. With a hand on my back, Hawke ushered me towards the exit as the creature continued to curse us.

"How did you find me?" I asked. Every step I took throbbed through my whole body, and I didn't look forward to how badly it was likely going to hurt on horseback, but the more distance we put between ourselves and the cave the better.

"I almost didn't. Scab escaped with you so fast I couldn't follow on foot. By the time I got the horse calmed and up the cliffside, you two were long gone." Hawke paused. "But I felt the pull. I thought it was coming from the other side of the Madness, but I realized soon after that it was *in* the Madness. It was my best bet for finding you, and apparently, luck was on my side."

"Like the pull from Claudio and the big sword guy? What part of your soul did the demon have?"

"This." I couldn't see Hawke in the inky blackness of the tunnels, but I heard a soft clack as he shook something.

"The sword? It looks so old."

"It is," he agreed. "A friend made it for me a very long time ago. It's my most treasured possession, so much that it's almost like a part of me."

"The demon couldn't cut you well with it, but you…" I shuddered at the thought of what Hawke had done to my captor, "…did all *that* with the same sword."

"Essence can do more than just the powers I've shown you. Things like giving a deadly sharp edge to an old blade, for example. This sword is worthless to anyone but me." He sighed. "I just wish I could know why Scab Kahlot had it."

A white circle of light came into view as we turned a corner, and before long we were standing out in the waning light of the moon as it prepared to slink away for the night. Had it only been a few hours since I was abducted?

Sir Brown Horse was hobbled nearby with a rock pinning the reins into the dirt. Hawke quickly trotted to him and removed the rock, stroking its mane gently as the horse stood.

"Sorry, buddy, I didn't have time to tie you up properly," he cooed apologetically as he kept petting it. After a few treats, the horse seemed to have forgiven him for its discomfort and allowed us to mount. We were off as fast as we could manage, every bounce sending me a fresh jolt of pain.

"We're gonna have a rough ride ahead of us. I hope we can get out of here before it gets too hot," Hawke said. The light of dawn was already beginning to paint the sky. From behind us, something howled, and I couldn't be sure whether or not it was the wind.

Chapter 8

The Medicine Man

The sun pounced on us much faster than we had hoped, and the searing heat returned with full force. Sir Brown Horse's pace slowed to a crawl as we forced ourselves through the blistering sands. Even when both Hawke and I dismounted and walked alongside him, our poor steed was suffering much more than either of us and both of us were suffering plenty in our own right.

A night of incredibly poor sleep sprinkled with constant beatings had left me with barely the energy to stand. The stifling heat bore through my heavy clothing, leaving me coated in a film of sweat that stung my cuts without remorse. Hawke was trying his best to keep a strong face, but he regularly clutched at the deep gash the demon had left on his arm, and bloodstains continued to grow slowly on the back of his clothes.

Between us and the horse, we drained our water supply in only a couple hours. The food stores held up, but only because we were too thirsty to eat more than a bite at a time. Sir Brown Horse shunned any food we offered him and, on several occasions, tried to lay to rest. Hawke stubbornly dragged him back to his feet for us to continue, but finally, the horse's sheer weight won out, and it collapsed to the ground exhausted. No matter how much we both tried to get him up, he refused to budge.

"Alright, Micasa, grab your things and as much food as you can carry," Hawke said with a sigh as he started unloading packs onto his back.

"What about Sir Brown Horse?" I did as he asked but was more than a little reluctant to leave our equine friend just sitting there.

"He's just tired, he'll follow us when he's had a bit of a snooze. Here, I'll leave this with him too." Hawke set one of our water bottles next to the horse's face. I already knew the bottle was empty, but I could tell that Hawke was getting frantic and didn't want me to worry too much. Without another word, I loaded up the last of my things into my travel sack with a few rations of cheese, bread, and nuts. Hawke tossed me an apple from the supplies he had scavenged, and I bit into it eagerly. The juices ran down my chin, but I couldn't care less as I savored the first moisture I'd had in hours.

"If only we hadn't eaten so much of the fruit beforehand," Hawke said sourly as he shifted the weight of his pack. "Thank the Almighty we're not too far from getting out of here." He pointed towards where the sun had been slowly creeping upwards, and I could just make out some craggy shapes lining the horizon.

"Is that the end of the Madness?" I asked.

"Yes, and there's a beautiful forest not too far inland of the Old Kingdom. It should be nice and cool there, and we can take our time resting back up." He gave me a weak but reassuring smile and started tromping through the sand once more. I hoisted my belongings a little higher on my back and started behind him.

"Have a good rest, Sir Brown Horse," I whispered as I passed him by, trying to swallow back the lump in my throat. I knew enough to know that we wouldn't see him again.

Salvation looked to be within reach, but the sun appeared to have stopped moving as we trudged on for another eternity. *Surely days didn't always last this long,* I thought to myself. We had marched for so long that the sweat had completely dried from my body. That small comfort made way to a much larger concern as I felt a terrible flush begin to overcome me.

Hawke was having just as hard a time, his light skin turning a brilliant red as his tongue lolled from his open mouth, his breaths coming in ragged gasps. I tried to ask and see if he was okay, but my tongue was so swollen and sticky I couldn't make the words and quickly gave up trying.

Finally, the blinding light of day began to fade, and the heat started backing off ever so little. The ground was quickly changing from sand to packed dirt, and the odd shrub could be found poking its branches out here and there. The indistinct shapes on the horizon took the more definitive shapes of trees, and when the ground began to slope and the first splotches of greenery and life came within view I wanted to cry out in joy.

What I got instead was a strange floating sensation, like falling in a dream. My legs seemed to have stopped listening to me, and before I could wonder what was going on I felt a massive jolt blast through me. Suddenly I was rolling sideways down the decline, my arms flailing limply at my sides. Even still, I felt completely detached from the situation. From a great distance I heard Hawke call my name, but all I saw through my blurred vision was his own limp body sliding face down in the same direction I was heading. I blacked out long before I stopped rolling.

* * *

The first thing I remember distinctly after that was the ground bumping and heaving under me. I thought for a bizarre moment that it was an earthquake, but when I opened my eyes, I caught sight of the night sky slowly crawling past me, hidden beneath a canopy of needled branches. A quick glance around told me I had somehow found my way into a cart, and I was far from alone.

At least half a dozen men and women sat at the edge of the cart, amid a pile of sacks and bushels full to bursting. All had kerchiefs, either tied around their necks or covering their faces, and their eyes were set in a perpetual squint. One was looking directly at me, eyes similarly narrowed, but when I returned the gaze they widened.

"Aye, the wee lass is awake!"

The others turned and jostled around me, all talking over each other in a cacophony of inquiries, but the woman who spoke first raised her hand for silence.

"How ya feelin, wee one?" she cooed softly as she bent over to inspect me. As she pulled her mask down, I could clearly see how her face was etched with lines of weariness and tension. Her skin was bronzed from the sun and her short stubbly hair bleached almost white, but despite her hardened appearance, there was no mistaking the concern she wore openly.

"Haughey..." I tried to call out for my companion, but my tongue was still sticky and dry, and I could barely make a sound. The woman peered at me confused for a moment, then snapped her fingers.

"Oy, the lass needs a drink! Hop to it, ya manges!"

There was a lot of confused bustling, and suddenly I found a water skin being forced between my lips. Never had I tasted anything as delicious as those first precious swallows of water I nursed from the skin, deliriously cold and wonderful. I smacked my cracked lips a couple times and felt a bit of my strength return.

"Where's Hawke?" I managed to mutter as my eyes still rolled around, looking for any sign of him.

"Hawkeys? Don't get many a'those around here, lass, but the falcons are a sight t'see," a man with a bushy beard and half an ear missing answered. I shook my head as much as I could manage.

"No, Hawke. He's my…" What *did* I consider Hawke, come to think of it? Friend? Guardian? Dad? I went with the easier choice, "…my friend."

"Oh, the blonde lad with glasses." The woman's eyebrows raised in realization. "He's in the cart behind us. Both o' ya had a real bad scrape wit' somethin' mean, I'd wager. Found ya at the foot o' the forest, ready to call it in. Don' ya worry, though, lass, we got a friend our own tha' can patch ya up in a jiff."

The helpful lady propped me up sitting on the side of the cart and offered me a hunk of bread. I bit in and found it sweet and moist to my delight. It didn't survive long.

"I'm Jo, leader o' this band o' ruffians," she introduced herself as I ate. I could see the way the other men and women puffed up a bit with pride as she pointed around at each of them, rattling off names. "The bearded one is March. The lass with the long brown hair and steely eyes is Cassie – ya, ya, we see yer hair, ya wench! Stop rubbin' it

160

in mah face! The two o'er there with th' matchin' blue kerchiefs are the Bello brothers – no relation – an' the scrappy one in the corner tryin' to hide is Mx. Blake." The smallest of the group poked out a head topped with a stringy mess of short black dreadlocks and glowered at Jo but nodded nonetheless.

"Mixter Blake?" I asked, unfamiliar with the title.

"Neither 'he' nor 'she,' more of a 'ze.' Don't let that bother ya, lass. Blake there is the nicest o' this gaggle o' marauders an' bandits!" The group cheered in unison, followed shortly by a return call from what I assumed to be the group in the cart following us. Blake waved at me cheerfully before returning to what ze was doing before: sharpening the head of a particularly brutal looking axe.

I started feeling better and tried sitting up a bit more, but a bolt of pain rocked me and I collapsed back onto the cart bed. Jo rolled me onto my back and stroked my face with a calloused, tender hand.

"Easy there, lass, yer a lot worse than ya might think. Don' worry a mite, though, we have the best doc this side o' the Madness at our camp. He'll get ya both back ta tiptop afore ya can say 'Ya want HOW much money?'"

I was curious what she meant, but my head was swimming so badly I could only force out a nod and lie there, feeling every minor bump in the road and wondering how Hawke was doing behind us. The black of night and the light from a swaying lantern mingled in the trees, throwing veins of shadow to dance over the wagon and its occupants. The thin strips of darkness brought back memories of cracking whips. A lump formed in my throat as I tried to shove away the thought.

The only experience I had with doctors was the one overseer on the plantation who patched up the slaves after particularly gruesome punishments. Thinking of his excuses for treatment was enough to make me blanch, but I tried my best to remind myself that the situations were completely different from my old life. Besides, if Hawke was truly worse off than me, even that sort of paltry help would be better than nothing.

I fell asleep again at some point, awakening as the wagon shuddered to a halt, but it couldn't have been long as the sky was still black as ink. The group jumped out and started unloading their cargo with an efficiency that showed they had done this hundreds of times before.

Jo, on the other hand, cradled me in her arms and hopped over the side with little effort. We had stopped in a large camp with a number of modest tents placed sparsely around. The only light came from the wagon's lanterns and a lone bonfire in front of one of the tents that made me recall the Madness with a shiver.

"Oy, wake up ol' Medicine Man! We got a couple o' new patients t' bilk!" she called into the gloom. A high, lilting voice keened out in response.

"Keep it down, ya moron! The old man needs rest too! They can wait 'til the morrow, they can!"

"Not this it can't! Found 'em half thirsted ta death in the Madness, covered in beatin's, and one's jus' a wee lass! Get 'im up!" Jo barked everything without the slightest hesitation; there was no doubt that she was someone important around here. The voice in the darkness grumbled a bit, but I heard the sound of footsteps plodding away, no doubt to get this Medicine Man.

There was a grunt and thump behind me. I looked over to find Hawke standing next to the wagon that had pulled up behind ours, clutching his chest and panting for air. His arm gash had been crudely bandaged, the wrapping already crusted with black and yellow.

"Whoa, buddy, take it easy an' lemme help ya!" cried a scrawny man who was climbing out behind him. Hawke shook his head and glowered at Jo, his eyes resting on me.

"I'm fine. I've had worse," he insisted. "Micasa needs the help far more than me."

"Yer crazy, buddy!" retorted the scrawny man. "That slice ya got is already rotten an' yer half-addled with fever! Yewd be lucky ta make it through the night!"

Hawke turned a sharp eye to the man, who cowered back and said no more, before addressing Jo. "I mean it. There *will* be hell to pay if you try to help me before Micasa is well."

"Shoulda thought o' that afore ya dragged the poor lass across the Madness, ya moron," she replied venomously. "We'll be back for ya when the li'l lady is up an' at 'em, if I'm feelin' generous." She stormed away with me in tow, a pained look on Hawke's face. It was clear that her words had cut deep.

Jo had taken the cart's lantern with her, but even its radiance made little difference in the shadowy camp. More than once a tent or tree seemed to appear from nowhere just a few feet in front of us, but every time the bandit leader stepped around it without slowing in the least.

Finally, one structure loomed out of the darkness, large as a circus tent and surrounded with burning braziers. Their glow was dim, but they all wafted a thick incensed smoke that filled the air with perfumed scents. The moment she crossed the threshold of the tent's opening I understood why.

The stench assaulted me almost immediately. It was the smell of excrement, urine, and death, hanging in the air more strongly than the flowery aromas outside. Playing as a perfect accompaniment were the constant moans and wails that rose from several of the thirty plus cots that filled the tent space. Most of them were occupied, though the symptoms of their ailments varied: some sported bloodied bandages, a few had terrible lesions and welts dotting their bodies, and a thankfully scarce few were missing entire limbs. One poor man lay with both arms and legs missing, rocking his head back and forth in what looked to be a nightmare-riddled sleep. In the far corner I could see a massive tarp laid out, covering multiple large and lumpy shapes. It didn't take much imagination to guess what was underneath it.

A few people walked between the cots, checking on the bedridden and speaking softly to them. One was toweling the sweat off a red-faced man who was shivering violently. Another slowly changed the bandages on a woman's leg, tears streaming silently down both their cheeks. Jo walked me past numerous victims and caretakers and set me in a vacant cot well apart from most of the others. Kneeling beside me, she stroked my brow and watched for signs of worsening, every so often stealing a glance at the entrance expectantly.

Eventually, another person did step through the tent flaps, stifling a yawn with a massive hand. He was one of the shortest, stoutest men I had ever seen; he was only about a head taller than my own modest height but carried a gut that made me suspect every meal he had was a banquet. His robes strained over his stomach, but his shoulders and arms were corded like a man who had worked hard his whole life. His face, in contrary to his strong looking body, looked like it belonged to a young boy just on the cusp of manhood, though his expression was clouded with sleepiness. He rubbed his bald head with one of his giant mitts as he glanced around with bleary eyes, slowly waddling to Jo when he spotted her.

"What's the condition?" he asked without so much as a hello, blinking rapidly as he tried to clear his grogginess. Jo stood and started talking very quickly and very quietly, the large man nodding every so often. The way she had been waiting for him, I guessed he had to be the Medicine Man, yet I didn't see any sign of medicines or first aid tools on him. After just a few seconds of conversation, he held up a hand to quiet her and knelt by my bedside.

"Does it hurt, dear?" he asked as he grabbed my wrist gently and looked over my face, assessing my injuries.

"Just a little," I admitted. Truth be told, it wasn't anything I hadn't felt before, but I was more worried about how difficult it was for me to move than the pain associated with it.

"I understand. Just relax and you'll be fine soon. I'm quite good at my job." He chuckled and ran his hand over my forehead.

"Are you sure you'll be okay, Old Man?" Jo asked.

"Does it matter? You're the one who woke me," he chided. "Let me do my job. You know it won't kill me." His hand pressed a little harder on my forehead but not enough to hurt me. I could almost feel the pain starting to ebb away as he hummed soft, tuneless notes.

It wasn't long before I realized that the pain *was* receding. My face felt less swollen, the itchy cuts that covered my arms and legs no longer bothered me, and my sore chest and stomach relaxed into blissful normality. At the same time, I watched as the Medicine Man's face started to contort and bloat. Angry red lines opened on his arms, and his eyes narrowed as he stifled a groan of pain. Almost as fast as the injuries mysteriously blossomed on him, though, they faded away and left him looking the same as when he walked in.

When he finally removed his hand from my brow, I felt better than I had before Hawke and I had entered the Madness. I sat up, looking over myself, but couldn't find the smallest hint of the punishment the demon had inflicted on me.

"What did you do?" was all I could manage to say, still amazed over my recovery. The Medicine Man, however, collapsed onto his backside, sighing as he massaged his temple.

"That never gets easier, no matter how many times I do it," he complained. "But it's always worth it to see what a difference it makes."

At that moment, Hawke staggered into the tent. He looked far worse off than I had originally thought now that I could see him clearly. Blood-shot eyes darted around inside a face pale and slack, his hair matted with sweat. He gasped in pain, clutching at his bandaged arm. Even from a distance, I could see the blood and pus oozing through the wrappings and down his arm. When his eyes landed on the Medicine Man, he took a deep breath.

"It's you, isn't it? I knew I felt the pull coming from here. You have a piece of my essence."

I looked to the healer, surprised. Was he really like Claudio and Apollo and the demon Scab Kahlot? Was he going to fight against Hawke like those others?

The Medicine Man dragged himself to the feet with Jo's help, his gaze fixed on Hawke. "That blonde hair, those glasses... it really is you. Lord Hawke has really returned."

Hawke took a step back at the name as if attacked. "I'm surprised you could recognize me so easily."

"How could I not?" The healer stepped forward slowly as he spoke. "You helped me with your own two hands when I was at my lowest. You don't forget the face of someone who saves your life, and yours hasn't changed even after three decades. There's no one else you could be."

Hawke reconsidered the man, who had stopped several feet away, then clasped his uninjured hand to his head dumbfounded.

"Lord Ordained? Is that really you?" he managed to wheeze out. The Medicine Man chuckled weakly.

"Now *that* takes me back. I haven't held that station in ages. People around here just call me the Medicine Man. Or Old Man, for those lacking tact," he added with the slightest glance at Jo.

"You're looking well," Hawke said, almost accusingly.

"Much better than I should be. You, on the other hand, look like you've seen better days. I'm glad I dragged these old bones out of bed tonight."

His words were very confusing. There was no way the man who had healed me was any older than Hawke; not a single gray hair or wrinkle marred his plump, boisterous body.

"What is all this?" Hawke asked as he glanced around at the surplus of cots filled with injured and sick. "You running a hospital out at the edge of the Madness?"

"Close enough," the Medicine Man said. "There's no end to people who need help in such a dangerous place, and you'd be surprised how much good you can get done with a pack of bandits at your side."

"So you're a common thug now?"

"I heal the common thugs, as well as anyone else who needs my treatment. A man who serves a higher purpose doesn't refuse a call for help because of a person's mistakes."

Hawke looked like he was going to retort, but instead, his eyes rolled back in his head and he fell forward. I cried out and bolted off the cot, pushing past the Medicine Man and Jo to kneel at his side.

"Please, heal him! He'll die!" I begged the Medicine Man as I cradled Hawke's head in my arms.

"That'll be no trouble, little one," he assured me as he started towards Hawke. "He's very lucky to have found me. It's true, I do have a piece of his soul, left to me quite some time ago. I assume you know of his condition?" I nodded.

"Well, it so happens that this piece of him I have contains a miraculous power: the ability to regenerate from any injury and return the body to when it was its healthiest. Just look at me – 83 years old, yet as strapping as I was in my twenties!" He patted his rotund belly and chortled. "All I have to do is give him this power back and he'll be better than new."

"Wait."

I startled as Hawke spoke. His eyes fluttered as if it took all his strength to keep awake, but they were firmly frozen on the Medicine Man.

"You have my power to regenerate, but that power doesn't explain why Micasa is perfectly healed. I saw how bad her wounds were; she should be worse off than me. My regeneration can't be used to heal others. What did you do?"

The Medicine Man looked over the injured man before him, brow knit in thought. He took a deep breath through his nose. "You're right, it's not such a convenient power. At least, by itself. I have a power of my own."

Hawke's eyes widened ever so little. "Since when?"

"A few years after last I saw you." The Medicine Man's face darkened. "I was tired of watching my patients dying in front of me, one after the other. Most I couldn't do any more than ease their pain as they passed, but every death was another needle in my soul. I prayed to the Almighty that I could take on their pain, that I could pull the suffering from their flesh and bones and bear it myself. One day, as a young woman lay dying from a stab wound, those prayers thundered in my head as I desperately tried to keep her alive... and they were answered."

Hawke tilted his head in confusion, but after a moment he let out the smallest of gasps. "Empathetic healing," he said quietly. The Medicine Man nodded.

"It almost ended up killing *me*, but the young lady had not a blemish to show for it. The forces that be had given me my wish, but it was much harder to bear than I had expected. Now I could heal broken bones or bleeding wounds in moments, but in exchange, I had to spend weeks at a time recovering from the same debilitation. Even then, fatal diseases were still out of the question. If I died to heal one person, many more still would perish without me to tend to them."

"...unless you could heal immediately from any wound or illness." Hawke shook in my arms, but

I couldn't tell if it was the pain or his deduction that caused it.

"Can you imagine how I felt when this was handed to me?" He pulled out a necklace he had been wearing underneath his robe. At the end of it was a shinestone giving off a gentle green light. "My youth restored, the ability to shrug off any ailment I suffered? With my own power and this, I became like something out of legend. A healer who can work miracles! An immortal Medicine Man! What servant of humankind wouldn't want such a gift?"

Hawke stared at him, his eyes occasionally darting to the many who still lay moaning or whimpering nearby in their beds.

"Looks like you've been slacking," he shot. Jo grimaced and reached to her sword hilt, but the Medicine Man waved his hand in dismissal towards her.

"You're right. My power is far more exhausting than I ever expected. I heal a person in moments and I recover in about as little time, but it drains me heavily. More than once, I've passed out in the middle of my treatment. The worse the condition I'm healing, the faster I tire. Even the vigor of youth can't help me when it comes to this."

"Stop!" I cried out, taking everyone aback. "Even if you get tired, please, just heal Hawke! Then you can sleep all you want!"

"Micasa," Hawke said, "if he touches me, he won't heal me like the others. It's like with the others: my power would return first."

"But then you'd heal like he did when he made me better, right!?"

"Yes, and he would lose that power."

I went silent as I understood what he was saying. I looked back and forth between the Medicine Man and the man who saved me from a life of slavery as he died in my arms. What was the right choice?

The answer came from a large, calloused hand that alighted on Hawke's forehead.

"You idiot!" Hawke cried out as a flash of light filled the tent.

When all had settled, I looked to Hawke and watched as the color seemed to bleed rapidly back into his pallid skin. His bruising faded to a healthy skin tone, and through the holes in the back of his robe, I watched as the punctures Scab Kahlot had left bubbled and sealed until not a trace was left. His right arm convulsed, and Hawke wheezed as he tore the bandages from it, watching as the last remnants of his infected injury faded to nothing. Aside from a thick sheen of sweat still embracing him, Hawke looked as good as new.

"Damn you!" he panted at the Medicine Man. "How could you put that on me!?" I didn't get what he meant, but the Medicine Man must have because he puffed up in anger.

"*I* put that on *you*!? It was your lady friend who put this on me! I didn't ask to hold onto this trinket for so long, but she made me swear to keep it safe! She was the one who said to let no one else use it until you came back for it! If you have a problem with this, take it up with her!" Hawke's mouth opened in shock, but he remained silent.

"Now, you two might be healed, but you still need rest," the Medicine Man said with a tone that brokered no argument. "I, for one, could use a good nap too. Find them some place to sleep if you would please, Jo."

The healer waddled towards the exit, muttering just under his breath, "We'll need all the energy we can spare. Things are going to be a lot harder around here from now on."

Chapter 9

The Conflicted Man

I didn't see Hawke for several days after the encounter with the Medicine Man. The bandit camp was much larger than I had thought, and the more I looked for him the more I got the feeling that he was actively avoiding me. The only assurance I got that he hadn't moved on without me was from Jo, who insisted he was still around.

"Sometimes people need a little time ta think things out, hon," she told me after she spotted me one day checking inside another random tent on my hunt for him. "Give him some breathin' space, and I'm sure he'll show eventually."

With nothing else to do, I took to tailing the Medicine Man, who spent almost all his time in the sick tent. When he caught me loitering about while watching him tend the patients, he decided to teach me the basics of treating various injuries.

I learned to set a broken bone, how to disinfect a wound and dress it, and what symptoms pointed to what illnesses. Through all his treatments he never once used his power, but his skills with medicine were more than adequate in its absence.

On his rare breaks, he was willing to entertain my questions. "Do you always have so many people to look after?" I asked one afternoon while we ate under a gazebo not too far from the hospital tent.

"Sadly so, child," he sighed as he took a small bite out of some buttered bread. "You've seen how dangerous the Madness is. A man can find himself broken quickly around these parts. It's why I decided to stay here."

"Aren't these people scary, though? I thought they were thieves."

"They are," he said with a slow nod, "but a simple label is never enough to define a person. They do steal, true, but they tend to prey only on the other bandits that attack those traveling through the Madness. They also help those who would otherwise die in that horrible desert. You and Hawke would know that firsthand."

I looked into my rapidly cooling porridge, thinking hard. "So there are such things as good bandits?"

The Medicine Man sighed and tilted his head in thought. "I suppose if there was such a thing possible, these ruffians would be as close as they come. There's no denying their experience with the Madness, and they know how to survive and travel it better than anyone. They even call themselves the Mad Riders. Like a bunch of children, they are." He shook his head, but he couldn't hide the smile that crept onto his face. I decided it was the best time I would find to ask about what was bothering me most.

"Medicine Man, do you know what's wrong with Hawke?"

His smile faded immediately. "The man has more than a little wrong with him, child. He's a good man at heart, and powerful in many ways, but even I wouldn't know where to start to ease the suffering he's been through."

"So you can't heal him?" I hung my head in disappointment. If he wasn't capable with all his expertise of helping Hawke, who was?

"I'm sorry, child, but his ailment is far beyond my capabilities. Even my power couldn't fix him.

Everything I could do for him was done the other night."

His mention of that night reminded me of something else that had been bothering me. "Who gave you Hawke's power?"

He paused for a second, looking at me. His brow furrowed, and I could tell he knew, but something kept him from answering straight out.

"I'm afraid that's not a question I should answer," he finally said. "If he hasn't told you yet, then it means he probably isn't ready to face the truth himself. You'll probably meet her eventually if you continue with Hawke, so just let it be for now."

He finished the last of his bread and dusted the crumbs from his hands. "Now, if there are no more questions, I should be getting back to my rounds."

"Oh! There is one more I have!" I suddenly remembered. "What is a Lord Ordained?"

"Oh ho!" he exclaimed, raising an eyebrow. "I didn't realize one as young as you would have any interest in the workings of the Holy Tenet! It's been dwindling for years, so seeing children still interested in the Almighty's teachings does my heart good!" He beamed down at me.

"Oh, I was wanted to know because I remember it from *The Sandwich Man.*"

His smile instantly soured. "Oh. Well, I suppose I can explain it later if you'd like. If you'll excuse me." The Medicine Man stood abruptly and took his leave, muttering about "damn insipid children's rubbish." I decided not to broach the topic with him again.

As for the subject of Hawke, the healer said nothing more after that talk. He would only make light conversation about the camp or different uses for medicine, and though I still helped him with his work, I found myself wandering away from his company more and more.

The only other person I spent any considerable time with at the camp was the bandit named Blake, whom I remembered from the wagon ride to the encampment. Ze found me one day as I was sitting idly on a fallen log and watching the various people bustle about as they tended fires and unloaded things from the carts constantly coming to camp, among other things.

"Hey, it's Micasa, right? You want to come help me tend the camels?" ze asked. Up until now, I hadn't heard them say a word, so as soft as their voice was it startled me.

"What's a camel?" I asked.

"You've never seen one before?" Blake chuckled. "Well, in that case you *have* to help me. Come on." Ze took me by the hand and dragged me all the way across the camp, towards where Hawke and I had originally been brought in. Near some unused carts was a gazebo that had been erected as a sort of makeshift stables, and under those stood some of the most bizarre animals I had ever seen.

"What are these lumpy horses!?" I exclaimed as I started towards them excitedly. Blake held me back.

"Careful now! They bite if you surprise them." Blake led me carefully towards the camels, who watched our approach with heavily lashed eyelids drooping languidly. Once we had refilled their troughs with bales of hay, Blake let me brush their fur and pet them while they were distracted chewing on cud. I could have spent all day with them, but Blake insisted that there were other fun things to do in the camp. I grudgingly allowed them to pull me away but silently vowed to weasel a ride out of one of the animals before I left.

After our brush with the camels, I was feeling a lot more comfortable around Blake, and ze took the opportunity to suggest a slightly more robust activity.

"Hey, ever throw an axe?" ze asked as we weaved between the tents and cooking fires. I shook my head, which made them grin wickedly. "You'll get a kick out of this then."

Blake took me by the hand again and forced me towards a small grove of trees that had been scored full of holes and large gashes. Some distance from them stood several weapons caches full of bows and arrows, swords, axes, and many other weapons I had never seen before.

"Go on, give it a try," Blake encouraged. I walked to one of the caches and grabbed a small hatchet. I was familiar with using axes to chop firewood but had never had any reason to throw one. I gripped it in both hands and swung it sideways, sending it flying wildly a short distance before it bounced against the trunk of a tree off to our left and landed with a dull thud. Blake broke into a fit of giggles.

"No, that's so wrong," ze said. "It does no good if you don't hit with the head. Here." Ze strode to a different stash of weapons and hefted out a beast of an axe, with a haft half the length of Blake's body and a double-headed blade large as a melon.

"This one's my favorite. I call it the Twins." There was a touch of pride in Blake's voice. "Now check that tree there." Ze pointed to one particular tree covered mostly in massive gouges.

With a grunt, Blake hauled the axe over their right shoulder, gripped it with a single hand, and pivoted their whole body as ze whipped their arm forward. The monstrous weapon pinwheeled through the air, filling it with a deadly sounding hum, before embedding itself deep into the meat of the trunk with a resounding thunk. I gasped and clapped with enthusiasm.

"I've never seen someone do that before! Amazing!" I exclaimed to Blake, who wore a wide grin and crossed their arms. My compliment made them turn away, cheeks flushing a bit.

"It's not that big a deal, just takes practice," Blake tried to downplay it, still looking very pleased.

We practiced at the range for a while, Blake continuing to throw axes with scary accuracy while I struggled to get mine to hit the tree I was aiming at. After a while, Blake gave up trying to teach me the delicate art of axe hurling. Instead, they started going over all the various weapons stored there, showing me the basics of using swords, daggers, and maces. Ze even made an attempt to show me the short bow, but I couldn't even begin to draw it far enough to make a passable shot.

I was enjoying our time for the most part, but something was bothering me as Blake continued to lecture me on the finer points of each weapon. When it finally dawned on me, I blurted out my thoughts in the middle of one of their explanations.

"Blake, have you killed a lot of people?"

Ze stopped talking immediately, staring me right in the eyes. I averted my gaze, afraid that I had said something terrible, but Blake dipped their head and fidgeted. "Yeah, I guess I have. Do you hate me for it?"

"Why do you kill people?"

Blake bit at their lip. "I guess only because sometimes I have to. Whenever I kill it's out in the Madness. Nothing but marauders and demons out there, and they're usually attacking us first. If I didn't kill them first, I'd die."

I thought about that for a moment. "I don't want you to die," I said at last. Ze laughed at my decision.

"I don't want to either. That's why I'm still here. Y'know, I wouldn't want anything to happen to you either, Micasa," Blake admitted. "If someone tried to hurt you, I'd kill them too."

"I don't want people to die because of me," I protested, shaking my head furiously.

"Fine, I'll just whup them so bad they can't hurt you then," Blake amended with a shrug.

I smiled. "You'd really protect me?"

"Of course! No one hurts a friend of mine!" Ze struck an awkward pose I assume was supposed to be heroic, and I laughed. I had felt safe with Hawke around to protect me, but knowing that there were other people in the world willing to stand up for me made me feel better than I had in days. Soon we were both laughing for no good reason, and without another word between us, we went back to throwing axes around with abandon.

After one particularly impressive throw Blake made with the Twins that looked like it almost felled the tree it hit, I was tempted to try my own throw with the axe. I ran over to where it sat embedded and tried to pry it out, but the head had sunk so deep into the tree that I couldn't so much as budge it.

"Oy, look, the weirdo managed to find itself a fan!" guffawed a gruff voice from nearby. I turned to see a man and a couple women in rough leather armor standing nearby, laughing amongst each other. There was no telling how long they had been watching us practice.

"Bout time li'l Blakey found someone who'd actually want to hang aroun' wit' such a freak," drawled one of the women, sneering with a mouth full of crooked yellowed teeth.

"Oy, lass, maybe later ya can go solve the mystery of how it's plumbin' is arranged!" the other woman cried towards me, grabbing at her crotch obscenely. "It's one o' the great myst'ries o' the world, y'know!"

"Shut up."

Blake had stepped forward in front of me, face frozen like a glacier. Ze was breathing heavily through their nose and pinching their lips so tightly together they become a thin line.

"Well, it won't be no myst'ry if ya jus' pull tha' robe o'er yer head an' give us a peek!" the man said, with snickers of agreement from his companions. "Or jess whip it out if'n ya got it to show! 'Ere, I'll show ya how!" The man began to work at his belt buckle with a lewd grin on his face.

Before I could tell what ze was doing, Blake wrenched the axe free from the trunk and launched it in one motion. It drove headfirst into the ground right at the man's feet, missing the front of his pants by a hair's breadth. Silence fell on the trio as they looked wide-eyed at the weapon.

"Pull that thing out here and you'll lose it, you pig," Blake warned, unsheathing a small hand axe from the folds of their robe. "You know as well as any I only miss on purpose. Now, get going."

"Y-yessir," the bandit replied meekly, his eyes still locked on the axe that stood between him and us. All three backed away until they were far enough that they felt safe turning their backs on Blake and setting off to the camp at a very brisk pace. I only realized once they were out of sight that I had been holding my breath the whole time and exhaled heavily.

"That was scary," I said. "Do they do that a lot?"

"Every so often," Blake replied with disgust. "They forget I'm not some kid they can toy around with. Gotta give them a reminder when it happens. You okay?" Ze turned to me, looking worried.

"Mmhmm," I gave a small nod. "I don't get what they were talking about, though. What's 'plumb-ing'?"

Blake's eyes darted around nervously and ze scratched the back of their head. "Er, they were talking about whether I'm a boy or girl."

"Can you be something else?" I had never heard of being anything other than one or the other.

"Well, I've never really considered myself either. I'm just me," Blake tried to explain with a shrug. "Never have seen a point in labeling myself just because I was born with some body parts other people don't have."

I understood the difference between boys and girls well enough: the slaves of the manor had to bathe together, so I saw that there were obvious differences from the two. I had never realized that it made such a difference in the way people treated others, though.

"Do they hurt you because of that?" I asked.

"Oh, they try, but I made up my mind a long time ago not to let them just do what they want. If you stand up for yourself, you'll find most people like that are just all talk."

"Have you ever... killed someone for that?"

"What?" Blake seemed taken aback but shook their head a chuckled after a moment. "Nah, I told you, I only kill those who try to kill me or my partners. They act like jerks every once in a while, but when things get bad, even those three would have my back in a fight. I wouldn't kill someone just because they make an ass of themselves on occasion."

"Why would they try to hurt you anyways? You're so nice."

"I guess people are just afraid of something they don't understand."

Their words reminded me of what Hawke had said about the gypsies when we left Sapir. Hearing Blake mentioning it too made me realize just how often people jumped to conclusions with little understanding. The more I thought about it, the more I realized that if I wanted to keep traveling with Hawke, I had a responsibility to learn as much as I could so I wouldn't make the same mistake.

"Blake, do you know where Hawke is? I need to talk to him." Ze looked at me, lips pursed in thought.

"I think I've seen him wandering around the woods just outside our camp a few times," Blake answered, looking slightly unsure. "He never seems to be doing anything in particular, but he scurries away quick if someone tries to approach him. I'll show you where I'm talking about."

The place Blake was mentioning ended up being on the other side of the camp, out of sight from any of the tents. Near a cluster of trees sat a large rock overgrown with moss, and on that rock sat Hawke, his back towards us and his head in his hands. Without a word, Blake gave me a reassuring pat on the back and headed back to the encampment.

I was unsure whether Hawke would be upset by my appearance, but I didn't want to stay in the dark any longer. I wanted to know more about the person who had done so much for me and asked so little in return. If I could give him nothing else, perhaps I could give him someone he could confide in. With that in mind, I took a deep breath and approached.

"What are you doing, Hawke?" I asked as I drew around the front. His head jerked up, but he let out a breath of relief when he saw me.

"Careful sneaking up on people, you caught me off guard there," he said with the smallest of smiles. He shifted around nervously, and for a moment I was afraid he would simply leave. He eventually settled down and looked to me, expectant.

"Hawke–" I started, but he suddenly cut me off.

"Micasa, I'm so sorry." He bent his head into his lap, hands clasped on his knees. "I almost got you killed because of my poor planning and selfishness."

I didn't know quite what to say. Was this why he had been avoiding me for so long?

"It's okay, Hawke, I just—"

"It's *not* okay," he interrupted again. "I knew how dangerous this journey would be, and I brought you along just because of your power. I should have left you in Changirah; it was stupid of me to—"

"NO!" It was my turn to cut him off. I didn't know why I was screaming, but I didn't let up. "I don't care why you brought me! I've gotten to do so many great things because of you! I like being here with you! Why do you want me to go away!?"

Hawke recoiled away from my anger. When I stopped my rant, my chest was heaving and my face felt hot, but I was determined to get the answers I came for.

"I don't want you to go away, Micasa," he said after some silence passed, his voice oddly small, "but what I've done up until now hasn't been fair to you. I brought you all this way, yet I'm practically a stranger to you. What right do I have to make you trust me?"

"Then tell me!" I demanded. "Let me know about you!"

Hawke slipped off the boulder and landed on his backside on the leaf-strewn ground. He leaned against the rock, rubbing his temple with one hand. When our eyes met again, I mustered up the best angry look I could manage. All it did was make Hawke laugh.

"I suppose if I had done that from the beginning, things would have been a lot clearer," he said through his laughter. "I guess I'm just not very good at talking about myself. It's gonna take some time, though. You sure you want to sit through it?"

I nodded, quickly sitting next to a tree facing him. He sighed, took his glasses off and wiped them absentmindedly.

"Well then," he said, still polishing his glasses, "I guess my story begins over 400 years ago."

Chapter 10

The 400-Year-Old Man

"The world was a very different place then. There were millions and millions of people, and the idea of demons was just fantasy. Imagine a world filled with people like in Sapir: scientists, artists, bakers, businessmen and businesswomen, farmers, all spread across half a dozen continents. They traded their crafts across the vast distances through ships and airborne vehicles and could communicate with each other using devices that sent messages through the very air, making those distances feel that much smaller. It was a golden age for humanity."

I was already struggling to keep up with what he was telling me, but I did my best to hold my tongue. He paused for a moment, as if expecting questions, but when none came he put his glasses back on and continued.

"I was a teacher myself, back in those days. There were schools all over the world, where young people went to learn the knowledge and skills necessary to pursue whatever goals they had. The school I was in a quiet port town called..." he trailed off, thinking hard. "...I can't seem to remember what it was named." He pursed his lips in frustration but shook his head after a moment. "Either way, it was a small town, but well known for the boats that were built there, and the college that I taught at."

"What's a college?" I asked, finally failing at keeping silent.

"They were schools for young adults. College was usually the last schooling a person would take before looking for the job they were trying to do. I was a literature teacher. Er, that is, I taught people about books."

"Oh, so that's why you like them so much," I mused. Hawke chuckled and nodded.

"It's more the other way around: I became a literature teacher because of my love of books. To be honest, though, I was a terrible teacher. I was a sharp student in my own right when I was in school and figured my love of books would translate well into teaching. I couldn't have been more wrong, though; I was always more interested in reading and studying books for my own sake than helping the students in my care learn the things they needed. Because of that, my classes tended to dwindle in number quickly, the students either transferring to better teachers or just quitting altogether. To this day, I have no idea why the heads of the college kept me around for as long as they did.

"Since my classes often ended up empty, I ended up with a lot of free time on my hands. Being a small town, there was very little to do in way of entertainment. Most of the kids who lived there would travel to the larger cities nearby to kill time. Nothing out there interested me, though, so when I wasn't reading something I took to wandering the docks.

"I would watch the dock workers for hours, primarily the ones who were tasked with building the ships the town was so famous for. One particular worker caught my eye, a metallurgist who made propeller blades, capstans, and cleats among other things for the vessels being built there."

"What's a Me-tah…metalerg…" I couldn't even get the word out of my mouth.

"Sorry, he was a metal worker," Hawke said, abashed. "Almost any metal parts needed for the ships they constructed there were made by him. He was sort of a genius when it came to smithing. He even did all his work with an old fashioned stone forge, while the few other metal workers who did business there used more conventional means. Watching him work was so fascinating that one day I struck up a conversation with him. Before I knew what happened, we became fast friends."

It was strange to hear about Hawke having any sort of friend he could relate to. Aside from the kindness he showed me, I found him usually very standoffish towards most other people. Without thinking, I asked, "What was your friend's name?"

He paused for a long while, his eyes looking right through me as his thoughts trailed. When he spoke again, it was with the same distance his gaze held.

"Uraj... Uraj Kuznetsov."

His expression grew darker as he muttered the name, and for a moment I thought I had angered him. It only lasted for a second, though, before his face softened.

"Uraj thought I was odd for being so entranced with his work, but the way he handled the blistering heat of the forge for his craft was a work of art. Heating, shaping, cooling: he had a gift for taking that blistering, backbreaking work and making it beautiful. It inspired me so much I started absorbing every work I could about sea life: captain's journals, sea charts, boat manuals, you name it. It was the first time I was so interested in anything other than just reading, and Uraj was always there to help me understand the things that confused me. We would talk about all sorts of topics when he wasn't working, whether just sitting on the piers or sharing drinks in the tiny pubs around town.

"In turn, he would ask me innumerable questions about the world of higher education. He had grown up in a large and barren country, dirt poor and unable to attend school, so learning more about what he never experienced was somehow gratifying to him. Of course, he often laughed at how I spent more time lounging around with him than actually doing any schoolwork." Hawke smiled and leaned his head back. "Those were some damn good times."

The smile slowly dropped from his face. "At least, until the day that changed the world forever."

I was starting to feel wrong for asking to know more about Hawke. It was clear these memories were not ones he wanted to relive, yet he was still willing to talk about them with me.

"We don't have to talk anymore if you don't want to," I assured him, but Hawke held up his hand.

"No, I haven't talked about this in a long while. It's good for me to get this off my chest. Besides, after our close encounter with a grinel, you deserve to know the truth about them."

"Grinel?" I recognized the word as something Scab Kahlot had said while I was being held captive but just thought it was part of the harsh language of the demons.

"What you know normally as a demon. To be honest, it's not an unfair comparison." His eyes grew dark again. "The terrible things they did to humans more than justifies the term. Grinel is simply their name for their own kind, much like human is the word for our people.

"They appeared from practically nowhere. To this day we've never been able to figure out exactly what they did, but somehow they were able to open portals that led from wherever they came from to our world and poured in by the millions.

It was something straight out of a nightmare, a memory I will never forget: the day of the Pilgrimage." He took a deep, shaky breath.

"I was actually teaching a class that day when the first portals ripped open. Emergency alerts began to sound throughout the town and news reporters – people that gathered information from around the world to tell others that is – were all talking about strange occurrences; massive floods and earthquakes were hitting cities without warning, hurricanes roaring in from seemingly nowhere. It was chaos.

"I sent the students home and started trying to find out as much as I could about what was happening. All the reports had different ideas of what was causing it, but they all agreed that it was a global catastrophe the likes of which had never been seen. Before I could learn anything more than that, the whole town began to tremble.

"Panic gripped everyone immediately. The town was thrown into a frenzy as people tried to flee as quickly as they could. The reports began flooding in of unidentified creatures rampaging everywhere, and there was no telling how long it would be until they made it to our little corner of the world.

"I was keen on leaving too, but I was also worried about Uraj. While everyone else was packing onto the streets to head inland, I forced my way through to the docks, hoping he hadn't fled yet. I found him still inside the warehouse he worked in, apparently expecting me. He had already managed to get hold of a number of survival supplies, as well as a different plan of escape from my own.

"We made to the piers where a lone boat still waited. All the other vessels had already set off, deciding to take the same chance Uraj was banking on: that there would be more safety on open waters than on shore. It turned out the boat still moored there was one he had been working on, but with the situation seeming so dire we didn't think twice about taking it as we cast off the line and took to the sea."

Hawke stopped talking and stretched a little. Twilight was beginning to fall, but even in the dim light, I could see how pale he had become as he told his story. If he hadn't made it clear that he intended to tell it to its end I would've suggested again that we stop. Instead, I waited until he calmed himself. It didn't take long.

"The first few days we spent out there were beyond terrifying. Our only connection to the outside world was a small device that received the occasional news report. All of them told the same thing, though: cities were in ruins, entire countries were being swallowed into the sea, and the death toll was in the millions and growing every day. We wouldn't have believed it if we hadn't experienced firsthand the terrible storms that rocked our little boat so much we feared we would be dead before long too. It felt like it really was the end of the world.

"Our supplies only lasted a couple weeks or so, and we knew we wouldn't last if we didn't brave the shore to scavenge for more. So one night we crept in as silently as we could to the nearest land. The sight that awaited us made us wish we hadn't.

"I'll spare you the worst details, but I can safely say that the reports we had heard did no justice to the carnage we saw. The destruction was so great that it was a miracle we had been able to find any-thing in that mess. I think the only reason there were still supplies to be found was because there were no survivors."

I shuddered at the thought of a whole town re-duced to the same state that the bandit camp we found in the Madness had been left in. Hawke seemed to take my shiver as a sign of cold and took a short break from his story to start a fire in a nearby pit I hadn't noticed until the flames began to flicker to life. The heat that rolled over me did make me feel a little better, and once Hawke had warmed himself to satisfaction, he spoke again, his eyes still transfixed on the fire.

"We spent a couple days scrounging up everything useful we could find. Unfortunately, we had to leave most of it behind when we caught sight of our first grinel. You've seen one yourself, how similar they are to people yet unfamiliar enough to make your skin crawl.

"We bolted for the boat as soon as we grabbed up all the supplies we could carry, but we almost didn't make it back unscathed. The only thing that saved us was the grinel's inability to swim. We vowed then that we wouldn't set foot on land anytime within that foreseeable future. Thus began our life of piracy."

He took off his glasses and sighed as he rubbed his eyes. "It may just be a weak excuse, but let me say that I'm not proud of what we did at that time. Everyone was confused, including Uraj and me, and we were all just desperate to survive. Desperate enough to stoop to stealing from other people."

"I thought you said no one else was…alive, though?" Part of me didn't want to talk about this, but I was finally learning more about Hawke, and I didn't want to stop now.

"We hadn't found any survivors on land, sure," he said with a nod, "but like I said before, we weren't the only ones who thought to escape to open waters. We came across more than a couple boats that were free sailing, just like us. And just like us, they were also low on supplies and looking for any way to get more, even if it came down to robbing others.

"When that first crazed person jumped onto our boat waving around a kitchen knife and demanding our food, I was sure I was going to die. Fortunately, Uraj's career as a blacksmith had forged his body as strong as anything he had worked on, and he clocked the guy out cold before they could make good on their threats. The attacker became the victim, and we took all he had save the tiniest scraps to hold him over a couple days before dumping the poor fool back on his boat and casting off again.

"We lived this way for months, preying off any boats we came across. Thanks to some fishing supplies we 'acquired,' we were able to live off the

ocean itself when food ran low. When water became an issue, though, we had no choice but to
head ashore again.

"Eventually, we became bold enough to make
regular raids inland, avoiding the ever-growing
number of grinel and returning without injury
thanks to their dislike of the water. Food and water slowly became less of an issue, so our raids
started focusing on finding ways to pass the time
when floating out on the blank expanses of sea and
ocean we so regularly saw.

"I managed to collect a small library of books of
all types. Fiction and historical pieces were great
for killing hours, but my favorite by far were survival manuals and instructional booklets. Those
gave me goals to work towards, and I would spend
untold hours practicing how to tie different knots
or proper ways to prepare the fish we caught. With
nothing but time on my hands, I got quite good at
applying the skills I learned from the booklets.

"Uraj, on the other hand, had taken to con-
structing a small kiln toward the back of the boat.
I had concerns about open fires out on the ocean,
where a single mishap could sink us for good, but
he insisted that he could keep it under control. He

kept true to his word and spent his own time working metals and trying new forging techniques.

"Over time, we started feeling a radical change occurring in us. Then first sign of this came from his unnatural control of the forge fire. Whenever the furnace would look like it was starting to flare dangerously, he would simply hold his hand out and it would calm. When I asked him how he did it, Uraj shrugged and told me he just knew he could.

"I started spending less time reading and more time watching him at work, paying close attention when he pulled this stunt. Over time I began feeling a bizarre sensation coming from Uraj whenever he controlled that forge fire and was determined to see if I could do so as well. It took some weeks of study and experimenting, but to both our astonishments, I was able to do so eventually. That was our first brush with essence and a major turning point for our lives."

Hawke had trailed off, and I jumped a little as I saw him sweeping his hand in front of the campfire. The flames swayed back and forth, following his every move. As he lowered his hand, the flames died down to a small flicker before he turned back to me.

"We had lost track of time for the most part, but we had lived on the sea for at least a couple years before we finally decided that we couldn't keep that life up forever. We had to find some place where we could dock for a while.

"Uraj and I had been cruising out of sight of land for weeks, but instead of heading back to where we normally raided, we decided we'd take our chances finding some other land. With any luck, there would at least be fewer grinel somewhere far away from where we were.

"That gamble almost cost us our lives, as we drifted for a month over a seemingly endless expanse of water. When water supplies ran out and we were almost driven mad enough to drink sea water, we caught sight of land. It was a miracle that we managed to make landfall and find something safe to drink. The land we had found was this very continent, what we now know as Astra." He gave the ground a little pat.

"Luck held out for us as we found no sight of the grinel here, but we kept to the shoreline for several months in case they were simply lurking further inland. Once we were able to establish a reliable source of water, we turned our attentions to the strange power Uraj had been exhibiting with his forge.

"It didn't take long for Uraj to discover this power extended to any type of flame, not simply that produced by his furnace. Though he couldn't explain to me how he performed these incredible acts, I was still able to mimic him given enough time and observation of what he did.

"I turned to my archive of books I had accumulated over the years to see if there was any record of such phenomena. The closest I could find were accounts of the inner energy of the human soul, mostly through religious texts from all over the world. We eventually settled on calling it essence, as we found it tied to our state of mind and physical condition – an 'essential' part of living, so to speak.

"We continued to hone this power over time, slowly but surely gaining a better grasp of it while I continued to see if I could find any more information on it. My search ended up ultimately fruitless, but our practice bore results one day when we encountered our first grinel in years.

"The creature ripped through the ramshackle cottage we were squatting in near the beach, apparently looking for nothing other than something to destroy. Uraj had tried his hand at forging blades for our protection, but they were no better than steel rods and proved utterly useless against the demon. As it drew towards us, Uraj and I tried our hand at using our newfound power to burn it alive with the flame from our cook fire, but the grinel laughed off the flames just as easily as it did the swords.

"The creature lunged at me and grabbed my arm, ripping it off with its horrible gnashing teeth. I fell back screaming, and in a last desperate effort Uraj lunged forward and tried to smash the creature with his bare fist. Surprisingly, this worked.

"The grinel hit the floor, its face swelling up and a few of its teeth scattering across the floor. In spite of the searing pain I was in, I could clearly see that our attacker wasn't done by any means. The bruising it had taken was subsiding before my eyes, and new teeth were already growing in where there had been only bleeding sockets before. Through this, though, I also noticed the energy that was radiating: the creature was also using essence, albeit differently than what we were used to.

"Uraj started assaulting it again before it could regain its bearings, but his blows were no more effective than our hunks of steel had been before. As it tried to stand and attack again, I could feel Uraj's essence well in his panic and he threw another punch with all his might. This one did the trick, sending the creature reeling. He seemed to understand at the same time I did that our essence was the only thing that injured these creatures. A few more blows infused with the energy were enough to finally subdue it.

"We tied the grinel up with some spare rope from the boat, and none too soon. It awoke angry, snarling at us in their guttural language. Even though Uraj had worked it over thoroughly, there wasn't a single mark to be found anywhere on its body. Somehow it had completely healed in the short time it took us to bind it."

Sudden thoughts of the grinel Hawke had saved me from in the Madness came to mind. "That sounds a lot like—"

"—Scab Kahlot?" Hawke finished my thought for me. "You're right, this creature we fought and the one who attacked you were one and the same. Watching it heal twice so quickly made something inside me stir, and I had Uraj do something horrific. I had him rip the beast's arm off."

I closed my eyes reflexively, remembering when Hawke did the very same to the demon just days ago. He laid a reassuring hand on my shoulder.

"I'm sorry. I probably shouldn't have told you about that. But just like what you saw, Scab's arm grew back good as new. As it did, I watched as closely as I could, and as I observed, I could feel my essence radiating through me. The next thing I felt was a terrible itching from the stump that was left of my ravaged arm, and in moments I had regrown the limb just like Scab, good as new.

"Both Uraj and I were equal parts shocked and horrified, but it also taught us something new about these still mysterious powers of ours. We had always assumed that the essence and the powers it bestowed were tied to fire, yet my impossible recovery made it clear that there was a lot more than we initially thought. We buried Scab Kahlot alive, realizing that we couldn't kill it, and started studying this power anew.

"It didn't take long to learn that Uraj could not learn how to heal in the same way, no matter how hard he tried. Not wanting to risk a limb, we stuck to making shallow cuts across our palms, but Uraj's wounds acted no differently even when he concentrated his essence as much as he could. On the other hand, my wounds would close up in seconds, even without any conscious thought.

"The only thing we felt could explain it was that our essence reflected our past lives: Uraj's skill with the heat of the forge gave birth to control over flame itself, while my life of obsessive study had given me the power to learn things just by observing them. Even the powers of others."

Hawke had told me about this power of his before, but I had yet to see it in action. It explained why, on our journey to find the pieces of his essence, he had so many powers when he had made it clear most people only had one. It immediately made me wonder, though, who had this original power of his?

"The difference in our powers was an interesting discovery, but we were more interested in the fact that we found something that hurt the grinel. It was clear that average weapons were practically useless, which was probably why mankind's armies failed against them. With this essence, however, we could fight back and maybe start doing something about these monsters that destroyed the world."

"Why couldn't your armies just use essence to defeat the grinel then?" I asked.

"Before the Pilgrimage, when the grinel entered our world, essence was nonexistent," Hawke shrugged. His eyes narrowed in thought. "Uraj and I always assumed that either the power that opened the portals during the Pilgrimage flowed into us and became our essence or otherwise just awoke a power we always had but weren't able to tap into until then. It's strange to think that the event that brought about the end of our world also gave us a tool to try and fight back.

"And that's what Uraj and I did. We started traveling inland soon after, dedicating every waking moment we could to learning more and more about this power. Our first few encounters with the grinel after Scab were close calls, but between my now indestructible body and the raw blacksmith strength of Uraj, we were able to actually destroy the grinel we came across. We were relieved to learn that Scab Kahlot was an exception to grinel physiology – while they are very durable, other grinel don't regenerate in the same way. Our victories emboldened us, and before long grinel began to seek us out in revenge for their fallen comrades.

"They weren't the only ones looking, though. We started to run across small groups of human refugees who, through grit and luck, had been able to avoid the grinel much like we had. They banded with Uraj and me and rallied behind our battles, becoming bolder with each of our victories. Though we tried to teach them how to use essence, it almost always resulted in failure. However, the more faithful of them still followed us into battle, even if all they could do was distract a grinel long enough for one of us to finish them off. It was a tedious and bloody war, and many died, but humans continued to come out of hiding as stories circulated of our victories. Our numbers were swelling every day.

"Eventually, we had crossed from one shore to the other, and our followers were in the hundreds. It was growing more and more difficult to continue wandering with such a massive group, so we decided to take another gamble and attempt to establish a real settlement. It took years of toil, blood, sweat, and tears to put together even the most meagre of housing for everyone, but my power helped as I scoured any book I could scavenge on construction to make things even the slightest bit easier. It was a small boon for us that the grinel had no use for books and so left them alone, though to think of all the useful information that was destroyed during the Pilgrimage..." Hawke winced.

"The years dragged on, and though grinel attacks occurred regularly, we had the power to drive them off each time. A few other settlers showed promise in using essence, and Uraj and I taught them as best we could how to use their power. The abilities they developed further proved our assumption that lifestyle and personality reflected the power. There was a carpenter who could craft incredible things from the most useless looking scraps, a young man with a dozen pets who could communicate with animals, and even a woman who told fortunes for fun but could move objects with the power of her mind alone. Though they weren't the strongest physically, their powers gave us another slight edge in our unending battle with the grinel.

"Their powers also gave us the option to start expanding our settlements further inland. As the numbers continued to swell and more space was needed for our people, Uraj and I started taking groups to find new places to plant roots. With more essence users cropping up here and there, we could leave some of the defense of the new towns in their hands while we continued to explore the more hazardous areas.

"Humanity was beginning to recover, albeit slowly. Years turned into decades, and Uraj's body, once so mighty, began to give way to the march of time. On the other hand, the regenerative properties of Scab's power had halted my age completely – I still looked in my prime, even when I was well over seventy." That reminded me of what the Medicine Man had said the night we came into camp about his own age.

"So you're really over 400 years old then?" I asked.

"That's right. I started aging again when my healing power was taken, but the regeneration takes you back to when your body was at its healthiest. I put on some muscle working on the plantation for all those years, so I'll probably stay like this from now until…" he looked at his hand, still covered in callouses, "…whenever the end does come."

I thought of Hawke's friend Uraj, who he had watched grow old while he stayed the same as always. To watch people you cared about and spent time with die seemed so terrible, just the thought made me clutch at my chest.

"And what happened to Uraj?" I asked.

"He still lives."

We both jumped at the new voice that cut through the night. The Medicine Man rounded the boulder Hawke leaned against, barely visible in the firelight. His eyes were fixed on the smoldering remains while Hawke glared at him.

"Taken to eavesdropping, eh?" said Hawke with an unmistakable bite to is tone. The Medicine Man shrugged without looking up.

"It matters not. Most people in these parts know the story of the Grinel War: we *are* the descendants of those first people you settled here with. Though the tales they tell are a lot more colorful than that dry account you just gave."

"Uraj is still alive?" I asked.

"Quite so," Medicine Man said with a nod.

"I thought he couldn't regenerate, though," I pointed out. Hawke grimaced.

"Uraj found…another means to staying alive for so long."

"Certainly so," agreed the Medicine Man. "That's why our land has always revered the two Old Kings, who drove back the demons and made life possible. One is Lord Uraj Kuznetsov, also known as the Forge. The other is Lord Hawke

Morau, otherwise known as the Scholar." The Medicine Man finally locked eyes with Hawke.

"The people have been waiting for you to return, you know," he said. "Lord Uraj in particular has been constantly sending word looking for any information to your whereabouts."

It was Hawke's turn to shrug. "I've been in the Fertile Lands for at least seven years with my hands tied, so to speak." He stood, dusting off the errant leaves and seeds from his robe. "I still have to find the rest of my essence, but I get the feeling that my road leads back to Uraj. If any scouts come this way asking, you can tell them I'm on my way." With that, Hawke strode away from the conversation and vanished into the dark, without so much as another glance at me.

"Is he gonna leave me behind?" was all I could ask the Medicine Man. He snorted and spat.

"If he tries after telling you all that, he's gonna learn why you don't piss off a doctor."

* * *

As it turned out, Hawke would never have to learn such consequences. The next morning, he came to wake me personally, bringing a large breakfast for us to share. I didn't even notice what we were eating; I was just glad that we were finally sharing a meal together again. He went as far as to make small conversation, asking me what I was up to during the stay in the camp. I told him about the things the Medicine Man taught me, but when I got to all the stuff I learned about weapons from Blake, he blanched a little, though his lips remained shut.

When we finished eating he led me to the western edge of the camp, where I was surprised to find Blake waiting for us. Ze held the reins of a horse, its coat the color of milky coffee. It was already loaded with several weeks' worth of travel supplies,

"See, didn't I tell you Sir Brown Horse would find his way back to us?" Hawke said as he looked at me and smiled. Even I could tell, young as I was, that this wasn't the same animal we had left Sapir with. The horse's coat was too light in color, and it was slightly larger than the real Sir Brown Horse. But Hawke had a look on his face that made it clear he was trying to make me feel better. I decided it was best to just go along with it.

"Yay!" I cried as I ran to pet it. Even if it wasn't our old friend, the horse was still very beautiful, and I looked forward to the adventure we would have with it. "I never got to ride the lumpy camels, though," I pouted as I stroked the new Sir Brown Horse's mane.

"Aw, you can ride those the next time you come to visit!" Blake assured me as ze handed the reins off to Hawke and engulfed me in a hug. "And that better be soon, y'hear?" I returned the hug greedily.

"Can we come back, Hawke? I wanna see Blake and Medicine Man and the camels again!" I looked to him while holding my embrace.

"When we're done, I don't see why not," Hawke answered. "I've got a favor or two I'll have to repay when our business is finished. For one, are you guys sure we can take all these supplies for free?"

"Helping out Hawke Morau and his young ward is my pleasure," replied the Medicine Man, who had just shown up from nowhere as he seemed wont to do.

"Are you talking about Hawke the man who helped you, or Hawke the Old King?" asked my guardian with a wry smile.

"Yes," said the healer, and he guffawed so hard his gut jiggled. That set Blake and me to laughing, and soon all of us were cracking up over nothing.

Hawke swung himself into the saddle and Blake helped him pull me up to sit in front of us. The rest of the Mad Riders had slowly trickled in to see us off, and Jo stood before them all, giving me a small salute.

"Take care out there, wee lass," she said smirking.

"Bye, Micasa!" shouted Blake, eyes growing red and watery. "Come back fast!"

"Yeah!" I nodded, a knot forming in my stomach as I forced myself to smile and wave. Hawke spurred the new Sir Brown Horse forward and started us westward through the forest. As we trotted off, the bellowing voice of the Medicine Man sounded through the air:

"FOR THE SCHOLAR!"

His shout was answered by the entirety of the camp:

"FOR THE KINGDOM!"

Chapter 11

The Legendary Man

After such a long break in one place, it was nice to be on the road again. Even though I spent most of my life in the same area, I had grown to love a life of travel much faster than I expected to. Hawke seemed rather indifferent to our journey as the days passed by, but he was always willing to indulge me when I saw a strange insect I wanted to take a closer look at or a flower I wanted to pick.

I continued pestering him with questions as always, mostly about the things he had talked about during the story of his past. He tried his best to explain concepts like radios and telephones to me, but most of them seemed more impossible than powers and essence.

"Wouldn't you rather hear about the Old Kingdom we're heading into than all that old stuff?" Hawke tried to segue our conversation one morning. He had been trying (and failing) to explain motorized vehicles to me.

"You always do that when you don't wanna tell me about something," I pouted over my bagel. Sir Brown Horse flicked his tail in agreement. When I saw the frown he was giving me, I acquiesced. "Okay, where are we going?"

He brightened a little too quickly and pulled out our map of Astra. "The pull is definitely coming from the west, but I don't think we'll find another part of my essence in the next town."

"Oh, are we close to a town?" I scooted closer to look where he was tapping on the map. Most of it was illegible gibberish to me, but I could make out a labeled dot under his finger.

"Yep, a place called Blanc," he answered. "Been a long time since I've been there, but I don't remember anything of note. With a little luck, though, they might have some news for us."

"They might know where your essence is?"

"Not likely, but things are always changing in the Old Kingdom. Alliances shift, safe zones become embroiled in war, and rulers get overthrown regularly. It's best to keep an ear to the ground."

"Doesn't sound very nice here."

"Unfortunately not." Hawke gave a sad smile. "But it's been my home for most of my life. I know this area much better than the Fertile Lands, and I have many more friends on this side of the Madness too. It might be unstable, but it should also be easier to find a helping hand around here."

"Are your friends more of those 'family' people like in Changirah and Sapir?"

"No, Uraj has little patience for the family doing their work in the Old Kingdom. None of the other lords and ladies like them much either, so they tend to stick to the Fertile Lands. It's part of why the family likes my help so much: I can do things for them on this side, where their hands are tied."

"Other lords?" I barely registered what he had said after that part. "So there's more than just you and Uraj."

"Sort of," Hawke said with a noncommittal wave of his hand. "Most towns have some sort of 'royalty,' and I use that word loosely, that governs them. They listen to Uraj and me for the most part, but over time they've been setting their sights higher and higher. Some even hope to take the place of us should we happen to disappear."

I stopped eating, the bagel halfway to my mouth. "Disappear?"

Hawke snorted and shook his head. "Oh they think they're clever, but these are mostly the type of people who would break down in front of a half-starved bandit. They couldn't so much as annoy a pair of experienced demon slayers."

He shoveled down the last bite of the apple he had been working on and wiped the juice off his hands on his robe. "Now we should get a move on. It's not far to Blanc, but I'd like to get there before sundown so we can relax in town and actually have a bed for a change before we hit the road again."

Our trip was even shorter than I expected, and the first buildings started creeping into view on the horizon just a bit after noon. Unlike the towns we had visited in the Fertile Lands, no archway bearing the town's name greeted us as we passed the first few houses and businesses on the out-skirts of the town. A few people wandered the streets while we trotted down the road leading to the center of town, and more than a few wary glances crept our direction.

Those few glances turned into a few hard stares, which changed to dropping jaws and murmurs of wonder. The people we passed began to follow our progress, still whispering to each other in hushed awe. Hawke's unease was apparent on his face and growing in proportion to the crowd. He tried to brush it off as we approached the central square.

"I remember a fountain in the center of town that I always enjoyed, Micasa. Look, you can see it from here, though it looks like they put something else...oh please no."

There was indeed a fountain in the middle of the square, but a column rose in the center of that bearing two statues. From Hawke's reaction, I could tell it wasn't something that had been there during his last visit to Blanc.

One statue was unmistakably Hawke himself. The robes were a little different from what he usually wore, but the stone visage was almost identical to its fleshy counterpart seated behind me, complete with glasses slipping a bit down its chiseled nose. The statue's hair even went so far as to fall slightly into its face in the same way Hawke's hair often did, though the stony effigy's cut was a sandy color as opposed to Hawke's vivid blonde. The statue was posed with its hand on the hilt of the blade at its waist, a stance I'd seen Hawke adopt on occasion when standing idly about. I had never seen a sculpture so perfectly capture the look of its inspiration.

The other piece was someone I had never seen before. This person's face was as impassive as Hawke's, but there was an undeniable glare shaped to its eyes. A massive scar crossed the right side of its face, from the hair line past its eye all the way down to its heavily whiskered jaw. This man's hair was longer than Hawke's, falling to its stony shoulders and pulled back in a ponytail. Instead of the robes Hawke's effigy wore, it bore a suit of armor reminiscent of the kind the knights wore in picture books. Whereas the Hawke statue stood looking at ease but ready for trouble, this other statue stood with arms crossed defiantly, as if daring trouble to come find it.

"Is that Uraj?" I asked, pointing to the strange figure.

"Without a doubt," Hawke said. He heaved a sigh. "They sure caught his annoyed look well. I don't think he'd appreciate it, but this work really is quite good."

"Yours is really good too," I added.

"Please, the details are all wrong," he grumbled as he pressed his glasses up his nose and swept the hair from his face.

"Look, look, it really is him!" cried one of the peasants who had come to see what the commotion was about. He pointed between the statue and Hawke, like it was necessary to make the connection.

"The Scholah's retuhned t' us!" cried someone else as they bounced a baby in their arms.

Cries of "Scholar" and "Lord Hawke" rose up from the throng as they began to bustle around Sir Brown Horse, trying to touch Hawke or talk to him. Our mount began to snort and prance nervously from the mob, and Hawke's protests went unheard above the din they made.

"Come now, come now, give the man some room!" barked a powerful voice from over the heads of the people. The cacophony slowly died down as they parted to make way for a figure striding forward on a black mare. The voice belonged to a man wearing a white tie and black suit that complimented his steed well. A small curly mustache rested above his lips that pulled into a smile at the sight of my guardian.

"Lord Hawke, a pleasure to meet you." The new figure swept off the bowler hat he wore and bowed his head, revealing his heavily thinning white hair. "I'm Lord Carash, Baron of Blanc, and I welcome you to my little town. It's an honor to have one of the Old Kings stop by our quaint corner of the world."

"Er, it's a pleasure to be a guest here," Hawke said with the slightest bow of his head.

"I assure you, my Lord, the honor is ours," the Baron said somewhat forcefully, his eyebrows twitching with each word to emphasize his point. Hawke looked like he was going to argue, but in the end just let his shoulders slump defeated.

"Sure, okay," was his reply. "My companion here and I were just tired from several days' travel and–"

"–hoping to make full use of our finest accommodations!" Carash finished for him, wringing his hands together and nodding in a way that reminded me of Fern the fence. "Of course! Why I have just the place in mind! If you and your young, um…ward would be so kind as to let me show you."

Even after he finished speaking, Carash continued to nod while wearing his greasy smile. I looked to Hawke to maybe get some sort of explanation, but he merely looked at me from the corner of his eye and raised an eyebrow. The Baron turned his steed around and started trotting through the crowd, and though he hesitated a moment, Hawke finally spurred Sir Brown Horse on as we followed him down the road. Most of the villagers watched with awestruck expressions as we meandered away, while the rest were casting coins into the fountain and murmuring praises at the two statues keeping vigil over the square.

Our journey through town didn't take long as the Baron led us down a long side street to a comfortable looking two-story cottage with a wooden sign above it reading "Blessed Night Inn." He turned his horse around to face us as we caught up, sweeping his hand towards the building.

"You'll find no better bed and breakfast this side of the Madness than the Blessed Night, I'll tell you that much," he boasted. He pulled his horse closer and leaned in towards Hawke, lowering his voice to just above a whisper.

"By the way, glad to see you admiring that centerpiece in the square. Cost the town a pretty ruple, they did; had to be made in Sapir and sent across that damn desert. Ten men lost on that trek, but to be able to see your appreciation of it, I know they're resting easy in the great beyond."

Hawke looked at the man as if he were insane, but the Baron paid no mind as he pulled himself up on his horse, looking more pleased than anyone I had ever seen. It looked like he was about to start another tirade of some sort, but the door to the inn swung open at that moment.

At first, I thought the person who stepped out was a child, but when I got a good look at his face I realized it was simply the shortest man I had ever seen, even compared to the diminutive Medicine Man. He couldn't have been more than a couple inches taller than me, yet the lines in his weathered face spoke of years likely rivaling the blathering Baron. The newcomer's head, deeply bronzed like the rest of his skin, was completely bereft of hair – his was so unnaturally smooth I assumed he must have shaved it. His clothing was nothing more than a sleeveless forest green vest and baggy satin pants, yet despite how basic they were, it was clear to see they were of top quality. Whoever this man was, he was a man of simple taste but went to great lengths to be at his most presentable.

"I heard your prattling from inside, Baron, who are you bothering this time?" The man trailed off as he met eyes with Hawke. "Is that Lord Hawke I spy? Well, this *is* my lucky day." The stranger's hard sneer softened until his face was merely passive.

"Do I know you?" Hawke's irritation cut his words perhaps a bit harsher than he had intended, but if he was sorry for it, he didn't say so.

"Not personally, but you probably know of my associates." The man stepped forward and extended a hand. "My name is Samuel, an acolyte of the Disciples. It's an honor to finally meet you."

Hawke narrowed an eye but, after the briefest pause, reached out and took the proffered hand. They shook, though there was no warmth lost between them. Both released their grip almost immediately.

"I do vaguely remember the Disciples," Hawke admitted. "Don't usually see you just wandering around towns, though."

"True, but that's specifically what I was hired to do," Samuel said. "I've been searching towns near the Madness, trying to find information on your whereabouts. Seems like fortune decided to smile on me, though. I never expected to run into you directly."

"And who hired you to do such a thing?" Hawke asked.

"Lord Uraj," Samuel replied, still as passive as before.

"Of course he did." Hawke groaned as he rubbed his face with a free hand.

Samuel turned to the Baron and gave a stiff bow, his face hardening into a dismissive scowl once more. "With the Scholar here, my business is concluded. I'll be off immediately to report to my client. You've been most cooperative, thank you, Carash." His thanks were somewhat underplayed by his harsh stare, but the Baron seemed too wary of the small man to dare question him. He turned to Hawke once more. "Any messages you want me to pass on to Lord Uraj?"

Hawke pondered this for a moment, then nodded. "Yeah, tell him I said nothing."

For once the man named Samuel cracked something resembling a smile. "If that's what you wish, I'll be off." With that, he stuffed his hands in the pockets of his trousers and took off at a casual pace.

"B-but sir, what about your things?" bumbled Carash as his recent guest sauntered farther and farther away. It was Hawke who answered.

"He's a Disciple. They carry nothing on them but the clothes on their backs, except to bring supplies back for their brethren. I doubt he even used the bed in whatever room he was holed up in."

The strange man had piqued my interest, though I had been afraid to talk with him around. Now that I was watching his back grow ever distant I felt comfortable speaking.

"What do they do?"

"Nobody is sure," Hawke said. "They show up from time to time offering their services as servants to those with influence or power. They work for as long as they feel, and when they're done they take payment. Usually, they only accept actual goods for their services: food, clothing, building supplies, those sorts of things."

"What do they do with it?" I asked.

Hawke shrugged. "Live? It's unclear where they even do that, though. The only thing I know for certain is their leader is some eccentric geriatric."

"A what what?"

"Crazy old person." Hawke sighed. "Which is exactly how I feel right now. Enough of this, Micasa. I need a bath, Sir Brown Horse needs a rub down, and we could both probably use a meal that isn't cold and dry."

As if to answer him, my stomach practically roared. It was so unexpected I jumped, which made Hawke chuckle. I couldn't help but laugh too after that, mostly in relief that he was lightening up a bit.

He vaulted off our horse and helped me down, handing the reins to the Baron. "Take good care of him, my fine fellow," he instructed. "Make sure he's rubbed down, and well fed and rested for to-morrow."

"Uh, yes, Lord." replied the bemused Baron. I doubt he had ever been ordered around so much in such a short time in his life. Still, he held his tongue as Hawke led me inside, waving weakly as the door closed and hid him from sight at last.

The innkeep was waiting behind the desk, a wil-lowy man who seemed to be expecting our arrival. He smiled so wide I thought his head would cleave in two and held out his arms in welcome.

"My dear Lord! The Baron sent someone along to let me know you were coming! Allow me to welc–"

Hawke strode across the room as the man gave his long-winded welcome and put his finger over the innkeep's mouth, shushing him the same way he might a child.

"Draw two baths. Get a meal ready. Tell me which room we'll find these things in." Hawke snapped his orders in monotone, eyes half-lidded with fatigue and exasperation. After a moment he pulled his finger back to let the man speak.

"R-room twelve has already been made ready for you, m-milord."

"Good." Hawke reached into his bag and pulled out a handful of coins, slapping them onto the counter without so much as checking how much he had given him. "Now hush times. Micasa."

He bade me to follow with a twitch of his finger, walking with heavy steps towards the stairs. I looked to the bewildered innkeep with the sorriest look I could muster and gave him a brief bow before running to catch up with my friend.

Lord Carash hadn't been lying about the room; it was easily the nicest one we had been in since our adventure had begun. Resplendent sapphire rugs carpeted a rich mahogany floor littered with beautiful handcrafted furniture. Two beds sat against one wall, covered with deep blue quilts and sheets that complimented the rugs well. Against the other wall sat a large, soft looking couch covered in ivory pillows. Above it hung an oil painting showing a quaint countryside village, possibly even the one we were in now.

Hawke unceremoniously dumped the bags he had dragged in with him on the couch and shuffled to where two doors stood side by side. He peeked in each one, nodding approval before finally turning to me.

"At the least, they understood my request well enough. You can go wash up in that room." He nodded towards the door to my left. "I'll be right over here in case you need me." I smiled and nodded, which seemed to be enough of an answer for him. He returned the smile weakly and trudged through the door on the right.

The bathing room was something of an oddity to me too. The room was nearly as large as our sleeping quarters, but over half the space was devoted to a wooden pit that was currently full of steaming hot water. Against the wall lay various bottles, which upon my exploration were revealed to be full of heavy scented oils and perfumes.

"What are these?" I wondered aloud as I found one that smelled of cinnamon and pine.

"I assume you mean the bath oils."

I was startled by the voice from nowhere but recognized it quickly as Hawke's.

"Where are you?" I looked around for wherever his phantom voice had drifted from.

"The bathhouse next door. There's a slit in the wall so we can speak. You're supposed to put the oils in the water to scent it. Just don't dump too much in."

I did as he said, trying a few splashes of the cinna-pine scent. As it mixed with the water, the soothing fragrance began to fill the room.

"Wow, it worked!" I cried as I prepared to slip into the tub. I could hear Hawke's amused laugh from the room opposite.

"Sometimes I forget how little you've gotten to experience in life so far, Micasa," Hawke reflected. "I've never known someone to get so excited over something like a scented bath."

The water was blissfully hot, helping me to scrub off the dirt and weariness from the road. The water slowly grew murky as I sluiced the last dregs of travel off me. As much as I enjoyed our journey, I equally appreciated those moments when I got to experience what civilization had to offer.

"Are you okay, Hawke?" I finally ventured when I felt he had had enough time to unwind a bit as well.

"Mmm," he grunted. "Odd as it may sound, that kind of reception isn't new to me. It doesn't happen much in the Fertile Lands, though. Not many recognize me by face over there. Guess I spent so long there I forgot to expect this coming home."

I heard a splash and could just picture Hawke throwing water in his face to try and wash away the weariness.

"Everyone seems friendly, though," I said.

"They're expectant," he corrected me. "They're assuming I'm here to do things for them because of my status." Another splash of water. "I've always done what I can to help people, but it gives the impression that they don't have to do anything for themselves. They completely stop trying, and before long I'm shouldered with a burden I never agreed to carry anyways."

"Well, they can do their own work then." I fumed at the unfairness of the situation he described.

"They should, and they'll have to. If they can't stand on their own feet, it doesn't matter what I do." A few more splashes. "Anyways, there's little I can do until I get my essence back. They're just going to have to get along without me for now."

We finished out baths and emerged from the chambers dressed in some wool lined bathrobes they had supplied us. We were greeted with a banquet that looked like most of the inn's kitchen had been dropped in our room, or at least onto a table they had dragged in while we were bathing. Ham, fish, and a quarter dozen different fowls sat steaming in the middle of the table, surrounded by fried potatoes and bowls of fruit and heaps of rice. It was a meal fit for five times our number.

"Wow, overboard much," Hawke agreed with my thoughts as he let out another massive sigh. "Well, we better eat as much as we can stomach. I'd hate for so much food to go to waste."

What should have been a delightful meal was instead reduced to a chore as we stuffed ourselves full to bursting on just about every dish on offer. Only the dried food and fruit lay untouched; we figured we could save that for much, much later.

Retiring to our respective beds, we lay groaning in bloated pain until I slipped into a nightmare-riddled food coma. It was only a few hours later that I was shaken from such a state.

"...on't eat me, potato salad!" is all I remember blurting out as I was roused. Hawke pressed his finger gently to my lips while making shushing noises, and I noticed he had already changed into his white shirt and red kilt.

"Let's not wake anyone else if we can help it," he whispered. He handed my things to me and started shoveling the leftover food from the night before into one of his own travel sacks. "We should get a move on as soon as we can."

"But I'm tired," I grumbled. Nonetheless, I rummaged through my pack and grabbed the first robe I laid hands on.

"I know, I'm sorry. We'll grab a nap later on, but I want to be gone long before sunrise." His gear was already slung over his shoulder, and he stood bouncing on the balls of his feet next to the door. I had barely shrugged into my robe when Hawke cracked the door open ever so carefully, looking around for anyone who might be watching.

"We're good, let's go," he hissed, stepping out the door and impatiently beckoning me to follow. He all but pushed me through the inn as I struggled to wake up, straight out the front door and towards the stables nearby. A heavy padlock held the doors shut for the night.

"If you would be so kind," Hawke requested, tapping on the device. Even as groggy as I was, the lock posed little problem for me and I snapped it open after a few seconds of playing around with a hairpin. Sir Brown Horse was sleeping without a care beneath a blanket draped across his back, and I felt a pang of jealousy for the lucky beast.

Hawke roused our steed and calmed it with a pear from our stocks, loading our things as the horse crunched through pulp and core alike. It was only a couple minutes after we had cracked the door to the stables that we were saddled up and trotting down the road out of town.

"What was the rush for?" I whined as the last few businesses passed us and the road opened to scrubby brush and packed dirt. Hawke rubbed my shoulder apologetically.

"Waiting until morning would have made taking our leave difficult," he explained. "The longer we stayed, the more likely they were to try and get me to do some inane task for them. Better to leave in the dead of night with bleary eyes than try to wade through half a town after sunrise."

I was still half-asleep, and the rhythmic plodding of Sir Brown Horse was making me drowsier. I was too tired to even look at where we were heading, but as I drifted off I did think about how often Hawke must have done this in the past. I thought that everyone adoring your presence would be wonderful, yet from the way he had acted through our short stay in Blanc, I could tell that there was still a lot I didn't know about the life Hawke had lived before I met him.

My bloated stomach growled angrily at me, though, and I decided that those questions could wait. There was still a night of restless riding awaiting me.

Chapter 12

The Half-Man

Scrub and brush. Weed and dirt. That was all that seemed to lay ahead as we continued our travels westward towards whatever pull Hawke was feeling. The landscape was much more barren than the Fertile Lands we had come from, yet it was nowhere as inhospitable as the Madness. Though the plants were scruffy and dry, they were abundant, and there was plenty of evidence of wildlife flourishing in these parts. I spent most of our time on horseback watching as strange animals I had never seen before hopped and trotted around the arid land we wandered through. Occasionally one would stare at our group as we trundled on, but they would scurry for shelter if we so much as drew within a stone's throw of them.

A few days after we had left Blanc, Hawke grabbed my attention and pointed into the distance. Though it was far off, I could clearly see a small lumpy shape on the horizon the color of the setting sun.

"There," he proclaimed, as if that told me anything. When I responded by looking at him mutely, he coughed and continued. "I feel the pull from the Ururu. I get the feeling that's where we're destined."

"The what-a-what?" I said befuddled. He looked at me through narrow eyes for a moment.

"Micasa, you *have* been reading all the books I gave you, yes?" he asked me slowly.

"Of course," I answered just as slowly, though my averted gaze told a different story. He sighed and rolled his eyes.

"I really should be keeping a closer eye on your reading," he chastised himself. "Well, that mountain is the largest natural landmark in the country. It's called the Ururu Mountain, and it so happens that a friend of mine likes to stay near there." His eyes were fixated on the distant shape with anticipation.

"Ooh, what are they like?" Seeing Hawke getting excited at the prospect of meeting with someone wasn't common, so it tickled my curiosity.

"You'll see when we get there. He's something else." Hawke urged Sir Brown Horse to a canter as we started towards the new landmark.

"Do you think he'll have your essence?" I asked.

"Quite possible," he admitted, "but more importantly, he's more likely than the others we've encountered to give me some real answers. There are still too many things I don't understand about my plight. I only hope there aren't any complications."

Complications were just about the only sure thing the holders of Hawke's essence promised, if our previous encounters were any indication. On the other hand, this was the first time Hawke had referred to someone as an actual friend, so my hopes were buoyed that things would be different this time.

With the formation in sight, I assumed that it would only take us a few hours to reach our destination. My surprise continued to grow with each passing day, as the shape loomed ever larger yet still remained beyond our reach. It was only after a week of travel that we finally stood at the base of the mountain. I tried to crane my neck so I could see the top of the massive rock, but I had to lay on my back to have any chance of doing so.

"So where's your friend?" I asked as I reclined on the hard ground and surveyed the towering monolith glowing red in the afternoon sun. Hawke scratched his chin and glanced sideways at me.

"Not terribly sure where he might be, but the pull is coming from the top of the mountain. It might be him, might not. Either way, we're going to have to find a way up." He began to scan the stony walls for some sort of pathway that could take us to the top. I was less than confident in my ability to scale the sheer cliff face, and even less certain of Sir Brown Horse's ability to do so.

"Why don't we just take the ladder?"

"Huh?" Hawke snapped up from his search.

"The ladder. Right over there." I pointed to our left, where far in the distance there was some sort of structure that yawned towards the sky. Without another word, he took the horse by the reins and left to examine it, only pausing to make sure I had time to hop off the ground and catch up.

My assumption that it was a ladder turned out incorrect, but I wasn't too far off. We were met with a series of wooden ramps set in scaffolding that had been erected straight up the mountain's face, crisscrossing upwards. It was difficult to tell, but it looked like it led all the way to the summit.

"Strange," Hawke muttered while prodding at one of the scaffold's wooden supports. "This looks almost identical to those ramps we found in the Madness."

He was right. The same structures that let us descend into that eventful valley were a perfect match for the walkway we now stood before. My companion grabbed the support he had been touching gingerly and gave it a brisk shake with all his strength. It groaned and wobbled ever so slightly, but the ramp held firm.

"I think it's safe enough," declared Hawke. He grabbed a few packs from our mount and shouldered them. "It might not be the best idea to bring Sir Brown Horse with us though. The less weight the better." He tied the horse's reins to the beams and gave him a feedbag of oats to munch. I grabbed a few of my own things and gave Sir Brown Horse one last affectionate pat before we started our march up the construct.

It didn't take long for me to decide that we had made a terrible mistake. This decision came to me after we had cleared about twenty floors and I thought to look and see how far we had come. That moment in my life was my introduction to my fear of heights. I stood bolted to where I was, eyes locked on the ground far below me.

"What's wrong?" Hawke asked, his voice marking him as somewhere part way up the next ramp. I was too transfixed on the precipitous drop before me to turn and answer him. After a few seconds, his hands took hold of my shoulders and turned me gently until my fixed gaze was focused on him.

"It's okay. Do you want to go back down?" he offered, his voice full of concern. I couldn't bring myself to speak, but I shook my head. At that point, I felt I would be sick if I tried to head back the way we came.

"Well, would you like me to carry you then?" he suggested. I thought about it for a moment, but I didn't trust myself not to panic and flail about in his grip. Images of me dragging the both of us over the edge and into the abyss floated to mind, and I shook my head more vigorously than before. Hawke sighed and scratched his head.

"I don't think staying here will help," he said. His eyes were wandering around as he doubtless thought of a way to fix the situation. I swallowed the nausea that was swimming up my throat and gave my own suggestion.

"Lead m-me up there." I was astonished at how badly my voice shook. "Here." I took his hand, my own trembling as badly as my voice was. "I-I'll keep my eyes shut. That sh-should help."

He took a firm hold of me and nodded. "Okay, okay," he cooed, brushing his fingers through my hair. It helped calm me, if only a little. "I'll get us up there no problem. Just stay close."

His promise in mind, I took a deep shuddering breath and exhaled slowly. With my nerves as calmed as I figured they would get, I let my eyelids drop and gave in to the safety of my personal darkness. I felt the wood underfoot creak a bit as Hawke stood back up and tugged on my hand gently, and we started once more up the walkway.

Walking without looking where I was going was not anything I would have called enjoyable. The bizarre disconnect between the feeling of moving and the lack of visual feedback was somewhat sickening and not helped in the least by my knowledge of what lay just to the side. Still, Hawke kept a tight grip on my hand as we wound up ramp after ramp. I tried to keep myself occupied by keeping count of how many floors we were clearing, but I lost track after a hundred or so. Yet still we continued to climb.

A soft, random tune began to float through the air. It took me a second to realize it was Hawke humming to himself. Even though I had no idea what the song was, just hearing his voice as he drifted through the music helped take my mind off of our rapid ascent. Before I knew what was happening, I found myself humming right along with him. Our tunes were completely different, but he didn't falter as we composed our bizarre duet.

"Micasa, you can open your eyes now."

I was so intent on my aimless humming that I hadn't even noticed that we had stopped moving. I took a chance to peek out of my own eyelids, gasping at the sight that befell me.

It looked as if we stood atop a massive floating island of fiery rock, burning brilliant crimson in the early evening sun. All that lay beyond the edge of the mountain's summit was a sea of dazzling sky, streaked here and there with wisps of cloudy islets. I darted further onto the flat peak of the Ururu, spinning in circles to drink in the sight. Hawke still stood at the edge near the walkway, his own eyes wandering across the peak's expanse, until he caught sight of something and let out a noise. I turned to see what he had spied.

Some couple hundred meters away was a tent almost as large as the sick tent from the Mad Riders's camp, anchored directly into the stone with ropes and steel pinions. A mess of blankets, provisions, and other camping supplies lay strewn all about it. A short distance from the mess sat a large lump that appeared covered in burlap.

Curious, I tiptoed closer until I was only a few paces away, where I stopped in shock. The chunky mass was the largest person I had ever seen, dwarfing even the intimidating Apollo by a couple heads. I could only just make out the mess of greasy brown hair that snaked down to its shoulders, crumpling on a back clothed in a worn and weather-beaten poncho. I skipped around to take a better look at the stranger.

Catching sight of his face made it clear that the person was a man, though he bore a face so singularly ugly that it took me some work to reach that deduction. His nose was squashed like an overripe tomato in the middle of his face, taking up most of the real estate. Though his eyes were closed they seemed incredibly small for such a bulbous head, and his rubbery lips parted in a perpetual pout. I put my hands to my mouth when I saw that the stranger was sitting cross-legged on the floor.

If he's this tall sitting, I thought, *just how much taller is he standing?*

Hawke strolled beside me and knelt down, drinking in the strange giant's features alongside me.

"It's always hard to tell if he's meditating or sleeping," he said. Hawke rose and strolled to the man's side. He pressed a hand on one of the stranger's bony shoulders and pushed. The man remained still as the stone he sat on, but Hawke was forced back a step.

"Oh yeah, definitely meditating," concluded Hawke.

"Can you wake him up?" I asked.

"Yeah, but it's not a simple thing. He's in deep concentration right now; he probably doesn't even know we're here. Can you feel it?"

"Feel what?"

Hawke rapped a knuckle on the man's arm. It made a thud like he was knocking on a rock. "He's concentrating his essence," he explained. "It's surrounding him, like a shell. Only way to wake him is to break that shell."

With that, Hawke drew his rusted blade from his side and held it with the point leveled straight at the man. Seconds passed as Hawke stood as motionless as the meditating man. Then, in a whirl of motion, Hawke twirled the sword and brought it into the stranger's side.

I cried out, afraid Hawke would hurt the man, but all that accompanied the strike was a crash like shattering ceramic. His sword pressed harmlessly into the man's side, no more dangerous than a hunk of iron.

"Eh?" came a grunt from the stranger's bloated lips. One of his tiny eyes cracked open, a bloodshot muddy pool. The orb rolled around for a moment, squinting at the sight of me, but when the giant turned his head and caught a glimpse of Hawke both eyes snapped open as wide as they could.

"Aye, Hawke, is it really you!?" His voice was like someone had sandpapered his vocal chords, dusted with an unfamiliar accent, but the grin on his face spoke volumes. Hawke gave a nod and returned a smile of his own.

"Char, it's damn good to see you." He opened his arms in invitation. Without hesitation, the man he called Char accepted gladly and took my companion in a hug that looked capable of crushing bones. As soon as the two embraced, their bodies gave off a radiant burst of light. I had forgotten that this man might have held part of Hawke's essence and so was left trying to blink spots out of my eyes as the brightness subsided. Char still sat holding Hawke, but his face drooped in confusion.

"Wha' the bloody 'ell was that?" he mumbled as he tilted his head to the side. Hawke was trying to wrest himself free from his massive friend's grip as he explained.

"It's what – led me here. I had a hunch – you'd have part of my essence–" Hawke's breath was coming in shorter gasps as Char's grip seemed to gradually tighten. Finally realizing his folly, Char loosened his hold and let Hawke snake free and suck down some much appreciated air.

"Sorry, mate," Char looked away with an embarrassed smile. "Guess ah got a li'l excited there."

"Haha, no harm done." Hawke looked over himself to make sure those words weren't empty. When he was convinced he was still whole, he straightened up and laughed. "Still as brutish as ever, though. One of these days you're bound to snap me right in half." Char guffawed right back at him.

"Aye, and you'll jess stitch yerself righ' back tagether!" For some reason this was enough to set Char off roaring with laughter. Hawke continued to chuckle, and as he did, Char's own laugh slowly faded.

"Yeh feelin' alrigh', Hawke? Usually yer not so reserved."

Hawke's chortle similarly died as his face grew puzzled. "Huh, you're right. Probably has to do with my essence. Speaking of..." Hawke locked eyes with his massive friend. "Who gave you the piece of it that you had?"

Char flinched back. "Ya mean ya don't know?"

"Well, I've had my suspicions, but..." Hawke trailed off.

"Li'l lady Rouge told me ta keep it safe 'til ya came ta get it." Char rapped fingers the size of small logs across one of his comically small legs. "Ah figured it was yer idea, or at least ya knew wha' it was all about. Aye, I was kinda hopin' you could tell me wha' it was all fer."

"So it was her," Hawke fell onto his backside. He sat sprawled out, eyes glazed. "I was hoping my hunch was wrong, but it really couldn't have been anyone other than her."

"Aye, sorry, mate. Ah'm just as confused as you. While we're on the subject of lady Rouge, though," Char's watery eyes turned to focus on me, and I swallowed nervously, "who's the li'lun here? Aye, she's practically a mini-Rouge."

"Oh!" As if suddenly remembering I was there, Hawke bounced up and dusted himself off. "I'm such a dolt."

Hawke took me by the hand and led me over to the giant. Though I was more than a little intimidated by his grotesquely large frame, I was soon standing directly in front of Char, craning my neck just to look him in the eye.

"This is Char Nazval, a dear friend of mine," Hawke said to me. "He's helped me through more scrapes in my life than I care to remember."

"Aye, and more'n a couple o' those were yer own damn fault," Char snorted. "A pleasure t' meet ya, missy." He reached down with one of his pillow-sized hands, making me scrunch up my face and twist away. The appendage only alighted softly on my head, though, and he tousled my hair playfully.

"And Char, this is Micasa." continued Hawke. "She's been accompanying me on my journey pretty much since the beginning."

Char's affectionate rubbing stopped and he stared at Hawke. "What did you say her name was?"

"Erm, it's Micasa." Hawke turned away and coughed awkwardly.

"What sort o' sick joke is tha'?" Char looked to me with eyes full of pity. "Aye, ya better not have–"

"Dammit, Char, she was a slave. What kind of name do you expect her to be given?"

"Is there something wrong with my name?" I decided to chime in. Char's eyes drooped further, which almost didn't seem possible.

"Li'lun," he said softly, "*mikhasa* is a demon's word. It basically means 'worthless.'" When he spoke the word, it came out in the harsh rasp of the grinel language. He stroked the side of my face as if to try and soften the blow of what he told me.

"Oh, like what Scab Kahlot said before," I thought out loud. "I thought it was weird that grinel knew my name when I didn't tell him."

"You know wha' a grinel is? You've *met* one??" Char lumbered to his feet, taken aback by my knowledge. I, in turn, was taken by surprise that, at his full height, he towered over me to the point where I couldn't see the sky without turn-ing around. He glowered at Hawke, which with his imposing stature sent even the seasoned warrior cringing away ever so slightly.

"What've ya been makin' this wee one deal with, Hawke? Exactly what have ya been doin' while runnin' around!?"

"Hey, don't be mean to him!" I cried. I pushed at Char's spindly looking leg, but all it accomplished was sending me tumbling backwards. He looked to me, puzzled. With a sigh, he helped me back to my feet.

"Aye, sorry about that, *mikha* – um, Micasa." Char seemed to struggle not automatically placing the gravelly accent on my name. "Ah get a li'l heated when ya start talkin' slavery, y'see. I was one m'self."

"Really???" I had a very hard time imagining any sort of shackles that could hold a man as stout and powerful looking as Char.

"Sure. 'Swhere mah las' name comes from: *Nazval* is a grinel word for 'garbage.'" He chortled at his admission. "All ah heard most o' m'life was how much trash ah was. But when ah got free, ah promised m'self tha' I'd take ownership o' tha name!" He pounded on his chest and puffed up full of pride.

"So what does Char mean?" I asked.

"It's short for Charles," Hawke explained. "Though I've told him many times over that there

259

are about half a dozen nicknames for Charles already, and Char isn't one."

"Pfuh!" Char spat on the ground. "Ah picked th' name for me, an' ah get to pick how it's shortened! Screw yer 'nicknames'!" He turned to me. "Micasa, yer free t' choose wha'ever name ya want. Don' feel like ya have to keep it jess cuz."

I had never thought that my name had any special meaning, but the prospect of getting to choose what I called myself had a certain appeal to it. It only took a few seconds of considering the possibilities for me to shake my head.

"Nah, I've always been Micasa. I would be confused if I was called something else now." I smiled at Char. "I'm gonna own it like you said you did!"

Char burst into laughter so hard he was practically choking. "Aye, lass, tha's what ah did, innit! Bold choice! Ah like 'er, Hawke! Less have a drink ta Micasa! Ya like coffee?"

And that's how we were roped into dinner with the giant. After disappearing into his oversized tent for a bit, he emerged with enough cookware to make a small feast for the three of us, with a steaming mug of the dark liquid as the sort of crown of the meal. It only took one sip for me to decide most certainly how much I hated it, but both Hawke and Char drank at theirs eagerly as they shared stories of days long past.

"Tell me what about the times you saved Hawke, Char!" I insisted. His expression turned sheepish and he became incredibly invested in buttering an over-crisped biscuit.

"Honestly, Micasa, Hawke's saved me far more times than ah've done fer 'im," he said at last, when he could butter no more. "Might not suhprise ya, bu' ah get inta a lotta trouble when ah'm around other people."

"What could give someone as strong as *you* trouble?" I asked.

"If only bein' strong could solve mah problems," Char muttered, "Ah'd be a man on tha clear an' easy." He suddenly became engrossed in watching his biscuit cool. "Ya can't tell jess by lookin', lass?"

I squinted and tried my best to see what he was referring to, but Hawke jumped in to make it clear.

"Micasa, people don't really grow to Char's size normally. He's half grinel." At Hawke's words Char flinched, and for a while, he looked as if he were remembering days best left forgotten. Of course, I had never encountered someone so large, but I didn't think that had to mean anything peculiar about him.

"Aye, i's true," said Char. "Me pop was a grinel and mum was a human. Betcha never seen such a thing before, eh, lil'un?" He tried to laugh it off, but the sound was forced and hollow.

"So?"

"Eh?" Char cocked his head like he hadn't heard right.

"You don't seem mean to me. What does it matter what your dad was?" I shrugged and took a healthy draught of the soup I had been nursing. Char cackled at my candor.

"Aye, the wee ones always see things so simple. Ah wish more grownups could think like ya, Micasa." He reached across to give me a pat on the head, which resulted in dunking me into my bowl of soup. I scowled at him as Hawke was suddenly overcome with a fit of laughter-turned-coughing. Char tried to look sorry as he dug for a towel so I could clean myself, but he couldn't completely hide the smirk creeping onto his face.

"What about Hawke's essence?" I tried to change the subject from my unwanted bath. "There was a flash when you two hugged. What power did you have, Char?"

"Oy, almost fergot about tha'." Char rummaged through a pocket sewn in his burlap poncho and pulled out a shinestone, which shone a weak green in his palm. He tossed it aside into a pile of rubbish, where it instantly grew dim. "Wasn' a power, jess a simple talent for buildin'."

"That would explain that rickety deathtrap of a walkway leading up here," noted Hawke. Char puffed up indignantly.

" 'Ey now, tha' ramp's sturdy enough ta get mah fat ass up an' down this rock! Watch yer tongue or ah'll rip tha' 'deathtrap' apart an' letcha find yer own way down!"

Hawke seemed to ignore the threat. "Char, did you happen to build something like that out in the Madness too?"

"Ah? Yeah, ah do remember tha' now thatcha mention it." The giant looked off into the growing twilight as he thought. "Had some business out there an' was tired of takin' the long way aroun' tha' canyon. Took a couple weeks bu' it was worth the trouble." The grin he gave flashed a mouth of yellowed teeth the size of small stones.

"The heat didn't bother you?" I asked. The Madness had been, well, maddening for Hawke and I to try and survive in for just a whole day. Trying to imagine someone spending what likely was days standing out in that hellhole to work seemed impossible.

"Ah, i's tha grinel blood in me." Char tapped his chest and winked. "Heat dun bother us a lick. Ah could spend weeks out there withou' a drip o' sweat." He nodded towards the cook fire and raised his eyebrows as if bidding me to watch. With my attention fully on him, he proceeded to place his hand directly into the crackling wood and ashes. He got a good laugh out of my horrified face, stirring the burning pile with his hand a bit for good measure before finally extracting the appendage. Aside from the soot still clinging to his fingers, there wasn't a single mark left from the fire.

"See? Nay a burn on me!" He proudly flaunted the dirty hand. "Guess ya can say I dun char easy!" We both exploded into giggles. Hawke stifled that quickly enough by loudly clearing his throat.

"Char, getting back on track," he said, with more bite to his tone than I expected, "are you sure you can't remember anything else about getting my essence? I still need to know what happened with Rouge."

The laughter died on Char's face as he glared and shook his head. "Ah've already told ya every-thin' ah know. She came, she gave me tha trinket, told me ta hold onto it, an' she left. If yer gonna git so high-strung about it, go talk ta her yerself!"

"I'd LOVE to if I knew where she was!" Hawke stood, his hands balling up in his sudden outburst of anger. I was stunned; he seemed to have a better idea of what was going on than I expected. So why hadn't he told me anything he had suspected yet, if he knew so much?

Char fumed right alongside him but only responded by thumping back to the ground and picking at the remains of his food.

"Ah really can't believe she di'nt tell ya," Char grumbled. "She did say sumtin abou' headin' toward Damkarei. Ya'll see 'er before long ah suppose." Char's answer took the wind out of Hawke immediately, and he slowly unclenched his fists.

"I'm sorry, Char." He turned his back to us and took a few steps away. "You're right, I am high-strung. I have no idea why she did this to me, and it's driving me insane."

There was a tense stillness in the camp as Char and I looked between each other and the quiet, brooding Hawke. Char settled to break it with a sigh and a grunt as he heaved himself to his feet once more.

"Ya said ya can feel the pull, right?" he asked. Hawke turned with a muddled expression.

"Yeah, what's that matter?"

"Jess tell me where ya feel it from now," Char said, waving off the question. Hawke raised an eyebrow but turned for a few seconds before pointing away from where the last vestiges of the sun were setting on the horizon.

"Figgers." Char offered a hand to me, and though confused what he had in mind I let him help me up. Still keeping his grip, he grabbed Hawke by the shoulder and practically dragged us both towards the edge of the bluff. The butterflies in my stomach broke out in full force as I pictured the dizzying height we were standing at, but it was laughable to think I could fight against Char's grasp. He stopped us a scant few paces from the dropoff, my eyes instinctively clasping shut, but Char gave my hand a little shake.

"It's okay, li'lun. Ah won't letcha fall, an' ya gotta see this."

I was certain there was nothing I had to see less than what lay before us, but his hold on my hand reassured me enough to chance a peek. What lay before me was a breathtaking vista of Astra twisting for miles all around, shining a brilliant tangerine hue in the waning evening. Trees were little more than tiny arrowheads jutting out in bunches across rolling hills that looked like tiny dirt mounds from our vantage point. Little strings of road splayed every which direction, and at the end of one of those small threads lay a clump of houses that might have come straight out of a snow globe.

"I don't remember that town being there," Hawke said slowly. Char snorted.

"Ya shouldn't, Liturgy there was settled only a few years ago. An old friend of ours is there, though. If ah was given a piece o' yer soul, Rouge prolly threw one ta tha' smokestack too."

Hawke wheeled on him. "Wait, Kamson lives there?"

"Aye. Ah'm sure he'll be ecstatic ta see ya." Char clapped his shoulder and threw him a thumbs up, turning back to the camp and dragging me off my feet in the process. Several minutes of apologizing from the giant later, we had returned to the fire and Hawke was already starting to grab up our things. Thoughts of trudging almost a mile down Char's walkway in the dark was where I drew the line, though.

"I'm not moving," I declared when he tried to hand my pack to me. To make my point clear, I took my blanket and completely wrapped myself in it, dropping to the ground like a stone. Hawke clicked his tongue but didn't look like he was up to arguing.

"As long as Char doesn't mind us spending the night," Hawke said as if he found it doubtful. Char, meanwhile, had already been pulling out thick pelts and laying them around the fire. With a defeated pout, Hawke flopped down and pulled out his guitar.

As he was wont to do, his fingers danced along the strings to no specific song, choosing to simply play whatever came to him. His gentle improvised lullaby floated through the star-studded night and helped me as I drifted to sleep. With any luck, the ground would be much closer in the morning.

Chapter 13

The Literary Man

As it turned out, my fears of our descent were unnecessary, as I woke to a sudden tremor underneath me. It took me quite some time to gather my wits, only to look up into Char's crooked grin directly above me.

"Aye, welcome to tha world o' the wakin', sunshine," he practically bellowed at me. I clasped my hands to my ears, which elicited a roar of laughter from him.

"So *tha's* whaddit takes ta clear tha sand from yer eyes! Good! Ah don' think ya woulda loved tha trip down!"

It took me several befuddled moments to understand what he was referring to. The boisterous titan was cradling me in my arms, and right behind him towered the walkway leading up the Ururu, which let out an ominous creak as an errant gust of wind sprang up. We were at the base of the mountain.

"Surprised you slept through that," came Hawke's voice from the side. He was busy brushing down Sir Brown Horse and giving him the remains of a half-eaten apple. He chuckled into his hand when he saw my brow knit in confusion. "I came down here early to take care of the horse and was about to head up and try to coax you down. Imagine my surprise when I heard the walkway groaning in agony and this giant lump came clamoring down with you."

"Pfaw." Char rubbed his nose. "Ah just figgered tha lass would 'ave a hard time squirmin' outta me mitts, even if she did wake an' wiggle a li'l." He bobbed me in his arms like a newborn babe, and I could feel my face heating up.

"Just let me down," I fumed, floundering against his grasp. True to what he said, though, it was easier to dream about escaping than doing so. After a bit more laughing at my expense, he deposited me onto the ground with such little warning that I almost toppled face first into the dirt. I shot him one last withering glare before joining my companion, who helped me mount our steed. As far as I was concerned, I had seen enough mountains for one lifetime. The sooner we put some distance between myself and the Ururu, the better.

With some final farewells and a promise to come visit again (albeit closer to the ground), we kicked Sir Brown Horse on towards Hawke's latest attraction. With the sun low in the sky and the trail laid out before us, we blazed a path away from the last vestiges of desert and into the heart of civilization.

"So the next person is another friend of yours?" I asked while the countryside whirled past us at full gallop. Hawke's face puckered like he just shoved half a lemon in his mouth,

"I suppose you could say that. I'd err more towards occasional business partners." Hawke cracked his neck and let out a groan. "Let's just hope things go a little better than they did last time."

"Did something bad happen?" I asked. Hawke's answer was to give a loud and mirthless "HA!" and I got the distinct impression that he wasn't much in the mood to talk about it anymore.

It took only a handful of hours before we were trotting right into the center of the town, but right away there was something terribly unsettling about the settlement. It wasn't as readily apparent from the summit of the Ururu, but all of the buildings in Liturgy were painted a glossy, eye-straining shade of white. In the glare of the midday sun, that would have been bad enough, but to compound things, every threshold of the buildings bore a symbol resembling a ten-pointed star, wrought in some chrome plated metal that only intensified the painful luster of the town at large.

"Ah, Liturgy, now it makes sense," said Hawke with an appraising glance at our surroundings. "An entire town devoted to worship of the Holy Tenet."

"The what?" I was forced to ask as always when Hawke brought up something he had failed to discuss with me before. His mouth twisted as he realized this point himself.

"Explaining religion to you isn't going to be simple." He clicked his tongue and urged Sir Brown Horse a little closer to one of the decorated buildings, bearing a much larger version of those strange stars than the rest.

"The Holy Tenet is a belief people follow that is supposed to help guide them to lead better lives. Back in my time long ago, they referred to such ideas as religions, but in this day only the Holy Tenet exists, so the word has sort of fallen out of use." He reached past me and pointed straight at the massive star symbol.

"That symbol is their mark – the five points on the top represent Honor, Charity, Courage, Discipline, and Empathy. They are the things the belief stresses one should strive their hardest to exercise. The five on the bottom stand for Greed, Lust, Wrath, Sloth, and Envy. These are the things one is supposed to avoid in their pursuit of peace. Five above in light, five below in shadow: these together are the ten points of the Holy Tenet."

While he was explaining the small details of the religion to me, the streets had begun to fill with townspeople who were spilling into the streets nearly simultaneously from all the various domiciles and businesses surrounding us. Nearly every person was dressed in an ivory cloak that matched uncannily with the buildings they poured forth from, heavy cowls pulled up to disguise their features. A scant few wore matching cloaks dyed a startling black, but I had little time to observe better as the ebony cloaked citizens hurried at a greater pace than their white-robed brethren.

Several of the hooded visages turned to regard us silently as we looked at their holy symbol but turned away soon enough once they were satisfied with whatever it was they saw.

"Are they mad at us for something?" I broached after another half-dozen people stopped to peer at us for moments before continuing on their way.

"People who follow the Holy Tenet are naturally wary of outsiders," Hawke explained. "They've been persecuted for what others call 'worthless beliefs' for centuries. Normally people don't openly display their faith – this town is the first I've ever seen so open about it. They must have all migrated here to set up a town to worship without prejudice. It would be strange for them not to be suspicious of us. Don't worry, though, they shouldn't bother us as long as we don't give them cause to fear us."

Sure enough, nobody said so much as a word to us as they milled about on whatever business pressed them onward. It was apparent that they had better things to do at present than worry about a couple vagabonds sitting on a horse in the middle of their town.

"We shouldn't hang around here too long," Hawke said. He pulled back on Sir Brown Horse's reins and steered us down a nearby side street. "If the Lord Ordained were to show up at the church while we were lolling around, we might have been in for some trouble."

The name tickled a chord with me. "Like the one in *The Sandwich Man?*" I asked. "Wait, I thought the Lord Ordained was the Medicine Man."

"He *was* the Lord Ordained," Hawke corrected me. "That was quite some time ago, though. I'm not sure who the new one is, so I wouldn't want to accidentally cross him. Anyways, we have more pressing concerns here. My old… acquaintance is hiding somewhere in this town. Shouldn't take too long to find him, though."

Hawke was trotting us down several alleyways. Every so often he would guide Sir Brown Horse through another sideway, doing his best to keep us off the main roads. We had been traversing for several minutes before I started noticing we had passed by the same shop for about the fourth time. Hawke seemed to notice my confusion because he leaned close and spoke just above a whisper.

"We're being followed. No, don't look around," he cut me off before I could do just that, and it took all my willpower not to do so out of pure reflex. I hadn't seen anything that suggested as such, but with so many people dressed exactly the same, it wasn't really possible to tell if we had passed the same person more than once.

"What do they want?" I asked in a hushed voice. I could feel my hackles rise as I imagined someone staring at our backs, tracking just a few steps behind us. Suddenly I wasn't so keen on taking a peek.

"Not sure, but they've been keeping their distance. If they were trying to make trouble, they'd do it in view of everyone and get the mob against us. Let's head to Kamson's place and see how it plays out."

As it turned out, we had been making laps around our destination the entire time. Hawke pulled up to one of the small abodes situated near the corner of an intersection that didn't stand out particularly from any of the other dozen pure white houses adorned with a ten-pointed star on the streets. A few white-robed drones were still milling on the road when a clanging din broke through the air. I jumped in the saddle, but it was only the sound of a massive bell tolling in a tower several blocks down in the center of town.

Immediately, the silent figures evacuated into one building or another. In seconds, the streets were completely abandoned save for Hawke, myself, the horse, and a lone black cloaked character standing not three strides from us.

"So," Hawke shot a sideways glance at the figure, "are we just going to stand out here or are you going to invite us in?"

After a quick peek around to make sure we were well and truly alone, the figure strode swiftly to the door and unlocked it with a key stowed in its sleeve. Our pursuer slipped inside, motioning with a single finger for us to follow before shutting the door behind itself just as quickly as it had opened it. Without a word, Hawke tied up Sir Brown Horse, brought me down, and led me by the hand into the now open house.

Never before had I seen living conditions in such disarray as the one we had crept into. Stacks upon stacks of papers and books lay strewn among furniture that at one point might have been nice, but clearly had been in use for a very long time. A thick acrid smell filled the room, making my nostrils itch so fiercely I couldn't hold back a multitude of sneezes. The only light in the room tried to squeeze through a window being blocked by a pile of tomes each as thick as a dictionary. Yet there was no missing the robed person who sat on a scattering of documents littering the couch.

"Lock the door," a high-pitched voice issued from the hood. With a shrug, Hawke reached back and turned the simple latch. Once that was done, our new companion stood and tore the robe off, tossing it onto a nearby coat rack with indifference.

The now revealed figure looked to be a girl not much older than myself, with soft pale skin and brown almond-shaped eyes that danced over us. Her hair was black as charcoal and cut shoulder length as was popular with younger women, shining with a brilliant sheen even in our dingy surroundings. She eschewed the robes that were popular among most people in favor of a form fitting black tunic and pants that showed her slim figure, tucking into pointed boots with inch-thick heels. The way she carried herself, though – hands on her hips and head cocked sideways – gave the impression that she was much older than her initial appearance suggested. She gave a brazen chuckle as she regarded my guardian.

"Wow, Hawke, you've definitely seen better days. I thought a king would be more mindful of his appearance." She flashed a brilliant smile that crinkled her face cutely.

"Certainly have seen better ones. Glad to know my friends can still recognize me, though." Hawke allowed himself a smile.

"Shut up for a second," she snapped. Her eyes locked onto me. "Who in the world is this adorable thing?" Without warning, she bounded across the room and engulfed me in a hug. "She is the best, ah!" It was difficult to mind her enthusiasm while she was screaming directly into my ear, and I tried to fight her off. As usual, my strength was insufficient to the task.

"Come on, Winter, don't smother the poor girl." Hawke knelt and pried the woman's grip from me, allowing me to regain the breath the woman had just crushed out of my lungs.

"Fine," she pouted. "You're here to see Luke anyway, right?"

He nodded. "I assume he's expecting me?"

"Yeah, he's already hiding somewhere in our room." Winter jerked a thumb towards a very short hallway with a lone door at the end. "Go fetch him. I'll go get some tea ready for all of us." She jaunted into the hallway and turned to the right through an open passageway.

Tenderly, Hawke stepped around the towers of scattered written debris and made his way to the suggested room. I managed to carve my own way behind him, although more than once I sent a pile of clutter shuffling to scatter on the ground; fortunately, it didn't affect the decor by any great leaps.

Hawke cracked the door open to a musty bedroom that reeked of the same biting odor that the living room possessed. A large bed took up most of the floorspace, only challenged by the similarly large desk shoved into one corner underneath a window as lonely as its counterpart in the den. Like the rest of the house, scattered papers seemed to be the most prominent furnishings, though the bed looked to be carefully overlooked in their placement. No one was visible in the room, and the only noise we could hear was Winter's humming and the sound of running water coming from the kitchen behind us.

"Did Winter make a mistake? There's no one here," I said at the sight of the disheveled mess. Hawke was about to answer when something long and pointed shot from the table, its tip aimed straight at Hawke's neck. I had barely the time to cry out in surprise and try to warn him before it struck him full force.

"Ow."

The dull pencil bounced off him and landed on the hardwood floor, rolling away nonchalantly. The only indication it had struck Hawke at all was a small red dot on his neck that faded almost instantly, but he still rubbed the spot on reflex and glared around.

"Seriously, Luke!? Get the hell out here!" he barked. A response came from one of the cabinets built into the desk, which began to cough violently. The door to the storage space flew open and deposited a lump of rumpled clothing that looked to contain a man somewhere within. The fellow stood up and stretched his back, which popped several times.

The man himself was stranger than the lady, who had already struck me as quite bizarre compared to what I was used to. His own clothes were not dissimilar, though whereas Winter's tunic was dark as her hair and well cared for, this newcomer's was a wrinkled, faded blue mess that looked as if it had seen much better days. Over his tunic he wore a frumpy navy blue coat that was clearly a couple sizes too big, making him seem bloated and ungainly on his feet. His face was even worse for wear than his clothes, covered in several days of uneven dark stubble peppered with white.

Pale blue eyes that verged on grey glared from dark, sagging sockets. Complimenting his sleepless eyes were sunken cheekbones and a head of rapidly thinning bronze hair streaked with silver. Everything about him spoke of a man who rested rarely and unwell.

"Alright, alright, no need to be so irritable!" The man, who was undoubtedly the Luke that Hawke had called to, snarled irritably at us. He dusted off a black wide-brimmed hat he had been holding to his chest and flopped it on his head before plunging a hand into his coat pocket and chucking something directly at Hawke. My companion snatched the object out of the air, which brought forth an all too familiar flash of light. As the room faded to normal, it became easy to see the shinestone that Hawke had caught, still shining a radiant turquoise in his palm.

"There, now piss off and leave me be!" snapped Luke. He turned to sit himself at his desk.

"Don't be that way Luke, they should at least stay for tea," Winter commented from right behind him. Mr. Kamson jerked in surprise, but Hawke and I practically leapt back in shock. At no point had we heard her enter the room or walk past us to reach the other side of the bed where she currently stood.

"Fine, fine, if you'll refrain from popping around like that," the scruffy man said.

Winter giggled a bit and planted a kiss on his forehead. "Oh hon, you know that's impossible."

She handed a saucer with a thick glass of cloudy liquid to Hawke and me, setting Luke's on one of the steadier piles of documents on the desk he sat at. I blew on the steaming contents of the cup and took a sip, recoiling at the bitter taste. Still, it wasn't as strong as the coffee Char had served. I took another tentative sip. When I looked up to thank her for the drink, she had vanished.

"Don't let it bother you, girl," Luke wheezed out as he watched my surprise. "She likes to do that a lot. It's practically a hobby at this point."

He produced a small silver container with curling inlays from his coat pocket. It snapped open to reveal a row of thinly rolled cigarettes. My old master had been fond of smoking them in his parlor with guests on the rare occasion we had them, and instantly I understood what the smoky odor that befouled the entire house came from. Luke slipped one between his lips before unearthing a fancy looking gold plated lighter. A flick of his thumb brought a flame to life, and he raised it to his face to light up.

"Hey!" Hawke exclaimed. He reached towards our reluctant host and clenched his fist in the air. The lighter's flame snuffed out, and the barely smoldering tip of the cigarette extinguished with a feeble puff of smoke.

"Hey, yourself! What's the big idea?" complained Kamson. Hawke jerked his head in my direction and shot a dirty scowl at Luke, who regarded me for a moment before letting out a frustrated hiss.

"Criminy, alright! I'll just bite on it, if that's okay with you, *my Lord*." Luke spun in his chair and let out a series of hacking coughs. "You and Winter both nagging at the same time is going to be the death of me."

"You're still smoking like a chimney and you say nagging will be the death of you."

"Is there a reason you're still here!?" Luke peered over his shoulder. "You got your trinket back, just leave me be!"

"I need to know if Rouge said anything to you about this." Hawke waved the shinestone at him.

"Winter's the one you should be talking with then. The gypsy is her friend, not mine."

"Talk about Rougey like that again, and the only thing you'll be eating or warming your bed with for the next month will be this ocean of papers you refuse to throw out," said Winter.

Once more I jumped as I whirled around to find the young woman leaning against the opposite wall, sipping on some tea of her own.

"How do you do that?" I cried. "You just appear and keep scaring us!"

She gave me another toothy smile. "It's an old habit, moving around without people noticing." She took a swig of her drink and looked away while doing a failing impression of not being proud of her ability. Remembering how she had tailed us through the town, I didn't get the notion she was shy about doing it whenever it struck her fancy.

Hawke sighed and took a seat on the bed, taking another sip of his tea. I hopped up beside him; it looked like we might not get our answers for a while. Might as well make ourselves comfortable.

"What's the black robe for? I couldn't tell the difference between it and white robes," Hawke asked her. She laughed and slapped her knee.

"Oh, it's the best! People who have 'strayed from the path' of the Holy Tenet are forced to wear the black ones as a form of penitence by the elders. The good little girls and boys in white keep away from them like lepers, and these 'sinners' are forced to wear the robes nonstop until the elders give them leave to change. Usually, that doesn't happen for months, so black robers end up reeking something awful and looking generally disgusting by the end of it!"

"Uh, how is that the best?"

"Because nobody who follows the Holy Tenet would dream that someone would wear one of the robes on *purpose*!" She tapped the side of her head. "Think about it! I can walk around town pretty much anywhere I want and people avoid me like I'm diseased. Makes it simple to take a casual stroll without getting bothered by someone to join them at church or whatnot – the rest of the townspeople want nothing to do with me!"

She looked between us with her wide grin, looking for some sort of reaction. All I could manage was a mute glance at Hawke, who returned it looking just as confused. Somewhere behind us came the scratching sound of Luke working wildly at his desk, punctuated by the occasional cough.

"Yeah, that's great," said Hawke finally, looking desperate to change the subject. "Soooooo about Rouge…"

"Oh yeah! Rougey gave me that shinystone a while ago and said to have Luke hold onto it until you came for it!"

"She didn't tell you what it was for?"

"Nope!" she beamed.

"Why Luke though?"

"Beats me. Maybe because he looks so grumpy all the time no one would want to get near him to steal it." I looked back to see Luke glowering over his shoulder at Winter. She flashed him a wink.

"Don't let his tough guy act fool you," Winter continued. "He's sweet as a teddy bear. One time some guy made some rude comment about me. He wrote a three-page letter to the guy basically saying he'd murder the guy if he ever even thought about treating me poorly."

There was a snap, and the head of Luke's pencil went tumbling into the air as he whirled. His face had flushed considerably. "H-how do you know about that!? I never even sent that letter!"

"Hon, you think I don't flip through all the papers in here just because there's so many?" She giggled. "You can't hide things from *me*, of all people."

Luke grumbled some obscenity under his breath. "Should've burned it..." he growled, turning back around and fishing for a new pencil to work with.

"So are you going to introduce me to this little cutie here," Winter said, switching gears, "or am I going to have to wring it out of her?" She flexed her fingers at me in a way that made me wholly uncomfortable.

"Oh, it completely slipped my mind. This is Micasa." Hawke gave me an affectionate rub on my arm as if sensing my discomfort. "Micasa, you probably already gathered that this is Winter Kamson. Luke is her husband." Winter responded with a small curtsy, looking pleased as punch.

"So Rouge abandoned you with the kid after shattering your essence like fine china?" came Luke's voice from behind us.

Hawke whirled on Luke angrily, but our host only gave him a cool glare and chomped on his cigarette.

"She's not our child." Hawke's words were ice in his throat. Luke didn't flinch in the least, instead shrugging and rolling his eyes.

"Either way it seems you got screwed on this matter."

Hawke was on his feet and at Luke before I could blink, holding the scraggly man by the collar and looking ready to kill. Still, Luke didn't make a move.

"You're acting irrational," crooned Luke in a frighteningly soft tone. "That's not something I expected from you."

Hawke was all but baring his teeth at him, yet he let go and threw himself down beside me once more. He let go of the shinestone he was still clenching in his hand. It clattered to the floor and went dark.

Winter was looking furious with Mr. Kamson, but he held up a hand. "Fine, I do know something that might interest you," Luke sighed. "Some of my contacts have told me that there's been a gypsy camp staying for an unusual amount of time outside of a major city a couple weeks from here." Hawke looked taken aback at Luke's sudden generosity, but the writer held up his hand again.

"I don't have any idea why this crap happened to you," he continued, "but Uraj and you have a lot to answer for. Get your shit in order fast and start doing something worthwhile." With that, he turned back to his desk and started writing again.

"We should go." Hawke stood and straightened his robe. I looked back to Luke, but he made no move that he heard him. Winter still looked frustrated with everything in general but tried her best to soften her expression.

"Okay. Be careful on your way out. Drop by sometime for dinner," she tried to offer.

"Yeah," was all he replied. He took me by the hand and led me back through the messy house in silence. The quiet persisted even after we had saddled up and crashed through the streets at full gallop. A few curious hooded heads popped out to watch us tear out of town, but if they cared they showed no signs of it.

Before long we were flying through the countryside again, with the luminous town quickly shrinking behind us. I was afraid to talk to him, with his face chiseled into a dirty look, but I didn't want to just leave him to fester with his thoughts.

"What was wrong with Mr. Kamson? He seemed really angry for some reason." I attempted to broach the subject as best I could without setting him off. He winced like he had forgotten I was there, but he still answered me.

"Luke writes informational articles for various newspapers and other publications to try and educate people about the world. We've worked together in the past – I would travel to places too dangerous for him to go and get him the info he needed to write his articles."

It wasn't an answer to my question, but it sounded like he had been holding this in for a while and was desperate to let it out to someone, anyone. Sure enough, he kept going.

"One day he released an article titled 'The Old Kings: Humanity's Greatest Threat.' It was a piece that completely smeared Uraj's and my reputation, accusing us of wasting our talents and power on ourselves while civilization slowly crumbled. When I tried to talk to him about it, he told me to…well, he told me to leave with some colorful language involved. This is the first time I've seen him since then."

"Well it couldn't have been that bad," I said. "Everyone looked like they liked you on our adventure."

Hawke fixed his gaze forward, focusing on nothing at all. "You're right, Micasa. The problem is, sometimes I feel like he's right. And I hate it."

Chapter 14

The Wandering Man

I had seen Hawke in many moods along our adventure; some high, some dark, and even some rather humorous ones. Yet no matter what whim took hold of him, the one thing you could never claim him to be was quiet. Whether it was explaining aspects of a world I had little knowledge of or simply discussing something that caught his fancy, he always had something to chime in on. Now, I was stuck with a Hawke who would have readily passed as a mute as we ambled down the winding country road.

While at first I enjoyed the chance to simply enjoy the scenery as we passed by, soon I started wishing he would try a little harder to get me interested in the details of our surroundings. Even my attempts to prod him into conversation rarely elicited more than an affirmative grunt or a shrug of indifference. It wasn't long before I started worrying he actually *had* gone mute.

This behavior continued for over a week of travel as we trekked over flowing fields of knee-high grass and wove a path through a verdant forest that had begun to tinge with copper. The dropping temperatures of the day and the growing clouds started whispering of the coming fall.

It shocked me to realize I had been traveling with Hawke for almost an entire season. With all the unique events that had comprised our journeys, I couldn't even fathom anymore how I had lasted so long in such a dull and painful life in the shackles of someone like my old owner who had worn Hawke's name falsely.

It was for this reason that I had grown so terribly worried about the genuine Hawke Morau. Time and again he rebuffed my attempts to speak to him while he continued to stew in whatever thoughts milled in his brain. It wasn't until another half a week passed that he finally spoke a real sentence, and it was due to no effort on my part.

"That man looks like he needs help."

I had been tending to Sir Brown Horse's coat, using some of the tricks Blake had taught me back at the bandit camp, and nearly dropped the brush in my surprise, so accustomed I had become to his silence. His gaze was fixed down a small dirt road that split off from the main causeway we had been blazing since we left Liturgy. The tiniest of figures was skulking ever so slowly towards our small camp. At such a distance, I couldn't see how Hawke knew the traveler needed help, but once they drew a deal closer, it was plain to see the heavy limp they suffered through, aided by a stout looking wooden cane.

For as many strange people I had encountered on our adventure, I thought I had seen all manner of oddity there was to see, yet this newcomer broke that expectation once again. He was a man about of height with Hawke's lengthy frame, though far more heavily muscled. His ebon skin was cloaked in a tattered beige robe with a faded grey cloak wrapped around his shoulders, a small travelsack slung over his shoulder. Most noticeable was his hair, which was such a startling bright shade of red it looked as if the man's head was on fire. The only indication we got that he wasn't was the glacial pace he made as he marched on steadfastly.

"Hoy, there!" Hawke cried whilst waving his hands over his head. The traveler raised his eyes from the monotony of the path and took us in, though he didn't miss a step as he marched onward. He did grace us with a friendly smile and a wave of his own.

"Well met, friends!" the man said cheerfully. I returned the wave, refreshed by his upbeat attitude, and Hawke bade him to come join us at our little respite from the road. The stranger put a bit of spring into his step and hobbled directly towards us, plopping to the ground with a contented sigh between my companion and myself when he at last reached our grassy clearing.

"Don't suppose you got a sip of water to spare an old beggar, do you?" our new acquaintance asked softly without hesitation. Hawke was already digging through our things, quickly depositing a waterskin, a hunk of bread, and a sharp wedge of cheese at our guest's feet. The vagabond snatched them up all eagerly and tore into the food, only pausing to wash it down with copious draughts from the flask. We let him eat in peace until he had destroyed our small offering, leaning back on his hands and letting out a satisfied belch.

"Needed that more than I thought," he said, "thanks mightily." The man's eyelids drooped in contentment. "Name's Anonce. To whom do I owe the pleasure of meeting?"

"Erm, the name's Hawke," my guardian responded slowly. When Anonce made no sudden motions at the name, Hawke let out a small breath of relief and swept his hand towards me. "This is Micasa. We're both just traveling the countryside, taking in the sights."

"Sightseers, eh?" Anonce let his gaze slowly float towards Hawke. "Picked a bad spot to wander, then. Been lots of demon sightings in this area and more than one attack. Place I just came from suffered such a fate."

The news rattled Hawke visibly, but he did his best to shake it off. "That's unfortunate. We can't quite turn around, though, so I guess we'll have to take our chances moving forward."

"Oh, I'm sure you'll be fine. Nostromos is just down the other road, and they've always been a safe bet for a weary tourist to rest up."

"Oh, are we that close to Nostromos already?" Hawke whipped out our map and pored over it. "Wow, we might have completely missed it if you hadn't mentioned that. Thank you, Anonce."

Hawke turned to me as he tucked the map away. "You'll like Nostromos, Micasa. It's a quiet little village that stocks up on all sorts of odds and ends from around the country. It's sort of like the Changirah of the Old Kingdom."

Memories of our stay in the bazaar town brightened my mood considerably, and seeing how animated Hawke was becoming helped me relax more than I had in a long time. "That sounds great! How soon will we be there?"

Anonce took it upon himself to answer. "Aw, it's less than a day's walk from here, I figure." He scratched his chin and glanced down the long road, where it disappeared into a thicket of trees. "Say, you both have been so hospitable so far. Mind if I put you out for one last request?"

"What would that be?" asked Hawke.

"Hearing both of you talk about Nostromos with so much excitement has given me the urge to pay a visit myself. Might you allow me to be a bother to you both for just a little longer and tag along to town?"

"Well, the horse only seats two..." Hawke began, but Anonce chuckled and shook his head.

"No no no, these old feet of mine get me around plenty fine. You two keep the horse, though I hope it won't trouble you too much to keep the pace casual. My hooves are sturdy, but don't quite match the speed of the real deal." He let out another chuckle, and this time Hawke joined in.

"I think we'd both be delighted to have your company, wouldn't we, Micasa?"

"Yeah!" I nodded.

"Then I'm ready whenever you are," declared Anonce. The friendly vagrant helped us pack up, and before long we were back on the road with a new traveling partner in tow.

We quickly learned that Anonce was just as chattery as Hawke, as he regaled us with story after story of the people and places he had encountered during his wanderings. His exploration of the ruins of the lost kingdom of Corellia; his encounter with the grinel known only as the Giant's Shadow; his night of gambling with Bronco Ballard, a man who claimed to never lose, and proved those boasts true. Each of his tales grew more fantastic than the last.

As entertaining as he proved to be, there was a hint of desperation in his voice that spoke of his loneliness. It was plain to see it had been a long time since he had spoken to other people, and having someone to listen to him was what he really wanted. I was enraptured by his stories, but Hawke only grew more tense with each one. He had yet to fully relax since he had heard about the demon attacks.

"Been to Changirah recently, have you?" Anonce said, changing subjects halfway through a story about a small hamlet he had stayed in the year before.

"Yep! And we saw a concert in Sapir!" I replied.

"Haven't been to the Fertile Lands myself for quite some time. Crossing the Madness is always risky business. It must have been quite a harrowing journey across, yes?" He raised an eyebrow towards Hawke, who returned the gaze coolly.

"We managed," was his only reply, the smile he wore pulling at his face tightly. For a second I thought I saw Anonce's eyes narrow, but the look flitted away in a blink.

"Sorry, didn't mean to pry. Just been a while since I've met people coming from that way. Any news to share…from…oh."

Anonce was looking down the road, where a small wisp of black unfurled into the air. Something was burning in the distance, and we didn't need to make a huge leap to figure out what it likely was. Without a word, Hawke set his heels into Sir Brown Horse and urged us to a gallop, leaving our traveler friend in our dust.

Charred husks of buildings were all that greeted us as we passed into the town. The sign that once welcomed people to Nostromos dangled limply off a post by a blackened, crumbling chain. Scorched bricks lined the streets we plodded down as we passed smoldering crates that once held goods. Ashen faced citizens were still pawing through what remained of their ruined belongings, or perhaps someone else's. A few men were eyeing our pristine supplies with hunger, but one look from Hawke sent them grumbling back to the filthy, garbage-strewn alleyways.

"This doesn't look like what I thought it would," I helpfully pointed out as I watched two children fight over what could have been either a stuffed animal or a shoe.

As it turned out, the people we had been passing so far were the lucky ones. One of the buildings stood out from the others, not only for the diminished damage it had taken in whatever befell Nostromos, but for the massive white tarps laid out in front.

One side of the tarp had dozens of people laid on it in various states of injury: burns, lacerations, and missing body parts and limbs were all in attendance. Healthier bodies rushed between them, desperately trying to tend to the wounded. Some of them sported blood-stained bandages of their own.

On the other side, large misshapen lumps lay beneath the coverings. A couple families hesitantly peeked underneath, looking for something they recognized amongst the innumerable bodies. More than once their findings resulted in a rush of tears and consoling embraces.

"We stumbled into a damn warzone," Hawke muttered under his breath as our path took us right towards the ramshackle hospital. A couple young men bustled forward with cooking pots on their heads and kitchen knives in hand.

"Can't you see the road's closed here!? Turn around and get out of here if you have half a brain!" one of the boys barked, brandishing his cutlery towards Hawke. Even from where I sat, I could see how badly his hand shook.

"What was it?" Hawke asked, ignoring the warning.

"What does it look like? Demons, you moron," the second boy answered flippantly, though he seemed keen on keeping his friend between us and himself.

"This just happened?"

"What do you care? Get lost already!" The first boy waved his knife around again.

"Let them do what they want, Boris, they don't have the look of bandits." The second one took his friend by the shoulder and yanked him towards the pavilion where the injured lay. "We got more important things to worry about." He spared us one last glance. "My friend is right. If you want to live, go back the way you came as fast as you can." With his piece said, both young men rushed off to find some way to help.

Everywhere we went the reception was similar. Hawke would try to get more information from the people on the street, but no matter where we searched we were met with little more than suspicious eyes and cold shoulders. The bustling little town I was promised had been reduced to a ruined husk filled with paranoia and death.

"Hey, haven't we seen that before?" I said, pointing at a landmark in the middle of what was once a town square. A fountain of cloudy water sat amidst scorchmarks and burnt piles of rubble. With no better leads to go on, Hawke steered Sir Brown Horse in its direction. The crumbling stonework had been smashed up at the top, leaving behind two pairs of expertly carved legs that looked terribly familiar.

"Seems like other towns took a page from Blanc's book," Hawke said dejectedly.

"I think it's a marked improvement from the genuine article," came a familiar voice from the other side of the fountain. Hawke urged our horse forward to find the speaker.

Anonce was lounging against the cracked lips of the fountain, his cane propped against a shoulder. His smile was cloaked behind condescending eyes. By Hawke's expression, they hadn't gone unnoticed.

"While you were running around getting snubbed by the populace, I've been chatting up the town about what happened," said the traveller. "One of the few perks of being a no name vagrant: people are a lot more willing to share their grief with someone who looks as bad off as they do."

"I already know they've been attacked by a demon," Hawke shot back at him.

"Merely a symptom," Anonce dismissed immediately. "The question is if you understand the problem?" When Hawke had nothing to retort with, Anonce huffed and pulled himself to his feet with the aid of his cane. "Can't blame you entirely

I suppose. Kings can't know everything going on in their kingdom all the time."

"You knew from the start," said Hawke.

"You're not a face that's easy to forget." The fiery-headed vagrant nodded towards the broken replica of my friend. "The people look up to you more than you might realize. Makes it all the harder for them when they need your help and you aren't there."

His words struck similar to what Luke said before and, likewise, elicited a similar response from Hawke. Silence blanketed the small square, aside from the occasional sob or holler in the distance. Anonce took the quiet as allowance to speak some more.

"A lot of demon attacks have been happening around this part of the country recently, but Nostromos has been suffering through a string of attacks, they tell me." His eyes swept across the town, filled with sadness. "Specifically, one demon has joined with a gang of bandits and sweeps through every couple days or so. They take little, but they destroy anything the townsfolk try to rebuild. If this continues for much longer, supplies will run out and doom everyone to a slow, painful death."

"What about the guards?" I asked. "Changirah had a bunch of them! I thought this place was the same?"

"Sweet child," Anonce said, looking at me with sadder eyes than before, "this town has two major cities for neighbors: Damkarei, where the Two Kings rule from–" his eyes flickered to Hawke for the briefest moment, "–and Val'Hala, a place also called the Lonely Kingdom. The man who rules there, who calls himself King Othenidus, does not get along well with Uraj or your friend there. Nostromos is supposed to be a neutral ground between the two; neither can claim it part of their territory, and any conflict that comes between the two cannot involve the citizens. Normally, this means that the town is at peace, but it makes problems when other dangers arise."

I looked to Hawke to confirm what the wanderer said, only to be met with a grimace.

"Nobody can get out of town to ask for aid from either city," Anonce further explained, "and even if they could, neither would come. Their laws forbid it. The town is doomed by the same rules that keep civil war from spilling over."

I waited for Hawke to respond, to come up with some retort that would dispel the horrible truth

Anonce had laid bare. Once again, only silence met my expectations. Anonce, too, seemed to assume my guardian would say something, watching him closely. Hawke didn't stir a muscle but must have realized he had to break the stillness and took a deep breath.

"Thanks for the heads up. If that's the situation, there's nothing more that can be done here. I hope things go well for you on your travels, Anonce." With another kick of his heels, he spurred Sir Brown Horse forward, towards the other end of town.

I was floored.

"We – we're going to get help for them, right, Hawke?" I managed to stammer out. Surely that was why he would be rushing off so soon.

"Our journey isn't over yet, Micasa. We need to keep moving forward."

This was beyond my comprehension. After everything I had seen Hawke do for others, it was impossible for me to believe he would just leave these people to the fate that had befallen them.

"I have to say, I really expected better, even from you, King Morau," Anonce said without looking at us, his voice dripping with disdain.

Hawke didn't slow as he responded. "You expect too much of a broken man."

My protests froze in my throat, even as we passed out of town and back onto the road, leaving the broken remains of Nostromos behind us to a dark future.

Chapter 15

The Raging Demon

It was beginning to seem like a rift was growing between Hawke and myself. I thought we had grown closer since our short stay with the Medicine Man and the brigands who called themselves the Mad Riders, yet aside from our stay with Char, the Old Kingdom appeared to hold nothing but dark tidings for the man that had freed me. Now I was forced to watch him turn his back on people who had been counting on his assistance. It left a bitter taste in my mouth to have to go along with his decision. It was the angriest I had ever been with Hawke.

He tried to strike up small talk with me as the distance between us and Nostromos grew greater, but my rage held my tongue. Any time I thought to tell him off, the words turned to acid in my mouth, and my lips stayed sealed. It didn't take long for him to get the hint that I had nothing to say, and once more we lapsed into an uncomfortable tolerance of each other's company.

We had apparently been pushing Sir Brown Horse quite hard, since by the time we stopped to make camp we were already out of sight of town. The path had been rising upward, growing steadily rockier until we found ourselves in the middle of a dried out ravine. We managed to find a small cave nestled between two thick shelves of rock that managed to fit both of us and the horse. We quickly set to unloading necessities for the night, anything for an excuse not to talk.

Our steed was well lathered from the hard ride. Hawke went to brushing him down and feeding him once we had unpacked. I was left to my own devices, which boiled down to hunkering inside a small crevice between two boulders and watching the remains of twilight creep away outside the mouth of the cave. I barely registered when Hawke handed me my portions of dried meat and fruit for dinner.

"We'll have to be careful tonight," Hawke said to me while he served. "Those bandits are likely still nearby. We can't risk a fire until we're closer to one of the cities, unfortunately. Hopefully, they won't wander by here tonight, and we can head out early tomorrow before any of them awake."

I barely heard what he was saying, focusing determinedly on the unappealing meal instead. I ate only a bite of each portion before the roiling in my stomach forced me to shove away the rest and roll over to try and get some rest. Hawke draped some blankets over me and patted my shoulder, but I pretended to already be fast asleep, and he made no further attempt to get a response.

This was the first time I seriously wondered if I had made the right choice in coming so far with him. Not that I thought for one second that being a slave would be better than the way things were now, but I started considering if perhaps I should have given more thought to staying behind in Changirah or one of the other towns we had passed through in the Fertile Lands. The Old Kingdom was so unfamiliar and filled with more ghosts of Hawke's past than I had ever dreamed. Memories of the faces of the Nostromans, filled with pain and grief, mingled with images of Hawke walking away as they pleaded toward him with palms outstretched. The thoughts swirled in my head until they were screaming, threatening to drive me mad—

I awoke with a start, disoriented and unsure where I was for a second. A quick shuffle of my body reminded me of the rocky floor I lay on, and after a few seconds, my eyes properly adjusted to the darkness. Hawke sat near the edge of our little shelter, his sword leaning against his shoulder and his gaze fixed on the lone path leading through the ravine. I was too rattled from my nightmare to return to sleep, so I lay still and watched Hawke as he kept his vigil without so much as a twitch for hours.

The dead of night was still on us when he looked back at me, as if to ensure I was still out. I hastily closed my eyes at his first shuffling movement, feigning sleep, which seemed to convince him well enough. From my cracked eyes, I saw him remove a folded piece of paper from his cloak and laid it near my head. He favored me with a lingering glance for a moment before exiting the cave.

He spent some time rolling a couple large rocks in front of the entrance, the blue-black wound of an opening in the cave going even darker. I almost cried out in protest, but my intrigue kept me still enough to see how it played out. Once the mouth was mostly obscured by the boulders, the blur of color that was Hawke disappeared from sight up the mountain path.

After waiting a few seconds to see if he came back, I rose quickly and snatched up the paper he had left, which turned out to be a note. His handwriting was bumpy and coarse, as if scribbled out as quickly as possible. It simply read:

Micasa
Have something to do
If you're up before I'm back, eat something and wait for me to return
-Hawke

Of course, I immediately rose and headed for the cave's exit. The rocks he had placed there so hastily helped hide the cave adequately enough, but there was more than ample room for me to squeeze over them and outside. Once free on the path, I wasted no time plodding up the same direction I had seen him head, my bare feet slapping hard against dusty stone as I struggled to catch up.

It took only a couple minutes at my pace before I caught a glimpse of Hawke's cloak fluttering up ahead. In a sudden burst of realization, I threw myself behind a nearby boulder right as he started to wheel around. My hands were clasped to my mouth, and I silently chided myself for not being sneakier on my ascent. If he caught me tailing him, he'd undoubtedly take me back to the cave, and I might never figure out what he was up to.

Expecting him to round the corner and discover me any second, I risked a peek from my hiding place. Luck held on my side, though, and he already had resumed his trek. Giving him another few moments to get ahead of me, I resumed my tailing, this time keeping my footsteps as inaudible as possible.

This lasted for over a quarter of an hour as he continued marching along, sometimes forsaking the path altogether and scrambling over piles of rocks instead. This made following twice as hard as I struggled to keep to the same route and simultaneously keep myself from making even the slightest noise. One misplaced step or jumbled rock would have easily spelled the end of my investigation, and I knew Hawke wouldn't have left me behind for some trifling business. Whatever the reason, something out here was deadly serious, and I wouldn't know what unless I continued.

Eventually, a faint glow came into view atop a rocky outcropping, and my guardian picked up his pace considerably as he headed towards it. This, thankfully, gave me the chance to speed up with less chance of discovery as he crested over a ledge and out of sight. I was able to sidle right to where he vanished and peek over, gaining a perfect view to his destination.

A roaring fire had been erected in the middle of a large clearing, surrounded by no fewer than a dozen hardy looking men and women. Their dirty leather armor and chipped, rusty weapons immediately made it clear that these were no ordinary travelers and certainly not strangers to trouble. Closest to the fire sat a hooded figure bulkier and taller than the rest, wearing a chainmail vest over their cloak and crude cotton breeches with leather cuisses. The figure was polishing a worn-looking longsword with a scrap of cloth, its edge gleaming in the firelight.

Hawke was standing some ten feet away, his own tarnished sword already drawn from its scabbard and hanging loosely from one hand. The entirety of the camp had frozen, their eyes glued to their unexpected guest.

"Got ourselves a 'ero it would seem," one of the scruffy bandits growled as he dropped the hardtack he had been eating and stood, dragging a club off the ground. He smacked it against his hands a couple times as he approached my companion, a sickening grin cutting across his face. "Wager yous a lawman 'ere for our 'eads?"

Hawke's back was to me, so I couldn't see whether or not he met eyes with the ruffian, but he didn't so much as twitch a muscle as the man stepped with his reach. Without another word, the marauder swung his weapon two-handed square at Hawke's chest with enough force to break ribs.

The club cracked in two as it made contact as if Hawke were made of stone. The bandit's eyes went wide in shock, before widening even further as his own chest was cleaved open from a single stroke of the sword. Droplets of his blood glittered through the air like burning jewels, and the bandit screams broke the night air for but a moment before he crumpled to the ground and stirred no more. For all his efforts, Hawke stood as if nothing had happened.

Immediately, two more bandits stood, notching arrows and letting them loose at him. The shafts struck dead on and splintered like twigs on contact. Hawke stepped forward, completely unfazed by their attacks, with his sword leveled towards the hooded figure who had yet to stir.

"Looks like a live one here," came a rasping voice from beneath the hood. The stuttering tone and high pitch brought back terrible memories and sent a shiver down my spine. All the remaining bandits had already jumped to their feet, weapons at the ready, but the figure took its time standing. The bandits looked hesitantly between the swordsman who had already cut down one of their own and their apparent leader, as if waiting for some sort of instruction. Unperturbed by its companions' discomforts, the figure lowered its hood and laughed.

I had been somewhat expecting what hid beneath the cowl, but it didn't lessen the fear that welled up inside me at the sight of the grinel's twisted face. There were similarities between its own grizzled sneer and Scab Kahlot's: the lipless maw, the leathery skin that looked more like a grotesque mask, the almost lifeless stare in its unblinking eyes made it clear this was something far beyond human. However, it was equally distanced from its counterpart we met in the Madness, from the lime coloring of its flesh to the carpet of stubby horns that covered its bulbous scalp. Two catlike pupils fixed on Hawke, the slits narrowing further as they focused.

"Been wondering when one would show up," it hissed between pointed teeth so thin they were practically needles. "Almost expected to have to destroy another town before one would."

All the bandits looked as if they had been holding their breath when the grinel removed its hood, but they let out a collective gasp when the creature's gaze flickered over them.

"Maim it, but don't kill. That pleasure is for Killer Mapta."

Every member of the gang was covered in a visible layer of sweat and looked as if they wanted nothing more than to put some miles between themselves and the two monsters in their midst. It only took another glance from the horrific figure to send the message: *do as I say or you're dead anyway*. Weapons raised, all the bandits roared a battle cry and charged Hawke all at once.

There was a whirlwind of movement from the center of the bandit horde, accompanied by shrieks of pain and a shower of crimson as limbs and viscera were sent flying in all directions. My mind went numb at the sight, trying to process what I was seeing, while bodies rapidly collapsed in wet heaps. It took Hawke less than half a minute to disassemble the entirety of the gang, leaving only the armored grinel standing there, laughing.

"Humans call *grinel* monsters, and look at this one!" It let out a shrieking cackle. Hawke spat in the dirt at its feet and raised his sword, still miraculously clean.

"I hate killing people," my companion muttered just loud enough for me to hear, "but I have no problems cutting down you filth. Just tell me one thing before I rip you apart: why torture that town? What did you gain from ruining their lives over and over again?"

The creature raised the sword it had been polishing while drawing a second one from its back, crossing the blades in front of itself. "Killer Mapta's been waiting for the one standing here, or the fiery one." The demon circled around the fire, facing off against Hawke with a raised guard. "Scholar and Forge are known for killing *grinel*. Slaughtering enough humans seemed easiest to draw one out."

"You did all this just to bring us here?" Hawke's voice was deadpan, disbelieving. The demon nodded and laughed, looking very pleased with itself. A convulsion pulsed through Hawke.

"'Killer,' you say. That's quite a name you chose," said Hawke. "There really is no redeeming quality to you monsters. Come on, then." He gripped the hilt of his blade with both hands, "I'm here. Do what you came here for."

"Glad to," replied the grinel naming itself Killer Mapta, twirling the blades in its grip. With an unearthly roar, it lunged at Hawke and attacked.

My experience with the grinel as a whole was very limited, but it was clear even to me that this foe was a magnitude more dangerous than the vermilion demon that had kidnapped me. Scab Kahlot was ready to kill, sure enough, but it was with an animalistic ferocity, clawing and biting recklessly. With this one, there was calculation and rhythm to its violence. Each swing of its swords cleaved graceful arcs that threatened to rend flesh and sever muscle, to spill blood and end lives. It was amply easy to see why the townsfolk of Nostromos feared this creature's wrath.

And yet for all of its ferocity, my companion seemed indifferent to the onslaught bearing down on him. When he faced Apollo before, Hawke had been able to barely avoid harm through careful steps and weaving, but now he practically danced between the demon's blades. Where any normal person would have been reduced to a pile of gore, Hawke instead made Killer Mapta look like a flailing child trying in vain to swat a fly, and the frustration on the grinel's face was growing visibly greater by the second.

"You seem to be having some trouble hitting me," said Hawke, just barely audible over the grunts and curses of his attacker. "Allow me to help you out here."

With that, he planted his feet and stood fully upright. A flash of depraved glee crossed the demon's face, and it accepted the invitation Hawke made without delay. Both its swords crashed into him simultaneously, and it was all I could do to keep from shouting in dismay.

Instead of watching my friend's body fall as so many bandits had, I was forced to clasp my hands over my ears as a painful ringing filled the air. Killer Mapta's excitement quickly bled from his face as the shattered remains of his swords tumbled through the air and disappeared into the night, leaving him holding but a pair of crumbling hilts. Hawke brushed off his robe with the air of someone who had been traveling a dusty road all day.

"You've grown lax with all the innocents you've been murdering." Hawke's tone was like ice in my veins. "A body coated in essence is as strong as a suit of armor. That holds just as true for humans as it does for the grinel." His eyes fell on his adversary, who was still staring blankly at its broken weapons in disbelief. "It's too bad; if you had fought me even a month ago, things might have gone much worse for me." Hawke's sword rose as he spoke until it was poised high above his head. The demon turned his eyes upward, slits narrowing, and its mouth dropped open.

Hawke's own lips twitched. "Let's see how your essence matches against mine."

The old sword blurred through the air, almost too fast to follow. The shriek followed so closely behind you might have sworn it was the blade that made it in its descent, but the noise quickly melted into a burbling grunt. Most of the demon's torso fell away from the body, each half of the creature hitting the ground at near the same time. Then silence ruled over the night once more, broken only by the occasional pop from the fire still burning away.

Hawke stood, engulfed in that eerie quiet, for what felt like hours without moving a muscle. His sword hung limp at his side in one hand, and his breathing had slowed until he could have been mistaken for a statue. Eventually, he did stir, bending over and grabbing the upper part of the body that had been cleaved away by the arm. He set off in the direction of the main pass, dragging the carcass behind him and leaving a ghastly dark trail in his wake.

I broke from my stupor and realized that he would likely be heading back to the camp before long. I quickly scrambled from my hiding spot and made haste back towards the path to try and beat him to camp. For a few minutes, I was left skittering over rocks trying to retrace the steps we had taken to get to the location, fearing I had lost all sense of direction. Thankfully the main path was not too far off, and from there it was a simple matter of sprinting as fast as I could back down the mountain until I came upon a familiar pair of boulders.

My chest was heaving from all the running and I could feel the sweat running down my face, and once I had scurried back into the cave, I had to take several deep gulps of breath to try and calm myself. A few quick wipes of my blanket to hopefully clear away my perspiration later, I was huddled back where he had left me earlier in the night with eyes clenched tight.

I don't know how much time passed before I heard the sound of shifting rock coming from the entrance. Still more time passed when a soft orange light filtered through my eyelids and the air warmed.

"Micasa."

Hawke's voice was so unexpected I opened my eyes instantly. He had lit a fire close by and was staring into the flames with a blank face, his eyes hidden behind the glare of his glasses.

"Why did you follow me?" he asked. I had no clue what had given away my shadowing, but I couldn't bring myself to deny his accusation. All I could do was stare at him.

"Did they all have to die?" I finally responded. It was the only thing I could think of. His head turned away from me so slightly that I wondered if he even realized it had moved.

"If I hadn't done what I did, even more people would have lost lives at their hands," was his answer. It wasn't enough to convince me.

"Is it really that simple?"

"No," he replied after some thought. "Nothing is ever that simple."

"Then how do you figure out if you did the right thing?"

He turned and looked at me, the light of the fire still obscuring his eyes. "You do what I said back in Nostromos. You keep moving forward."

Chapter 16

The Neglectful Man

To say things grew awkward between Hawke and myself after that bloody night would be a gross understatement. Our conversations were nothing more than one-word questions and nods or shakes of our heads. It took little time for us to fall into the same tired routine: wake, eat, ride, rest, ride again, eat, sleep. Days upon days passed with this monotony. Even the landscape echoed our feelings, with quiet stretches of dusty brushland only occasionally interrupted by a tree or boulder.

The only thing that I could find to take my mind off our predicament was the ready supply of books Hawke normally kept on hand. Most were full of words I couldn't decipher for the life of me, with titles like Astronomy of the Modern Era, Applied Mathematics, and The Lusty Sapirian Maid. In spite of my best efforts to make any sense of them,

I quickly tired of trying. The remaining handful of books were the children's stories he had acquired for me, but I had already read those twice over long ago and had little desire to revisit them so soon.

All that was left was the map, which until now I had barely given more than a couple glances. At first, the dozens of tiny lines crisscrossing the outline of Astra seemed overwhelming, but it didn't take long to suss out which ones represented rivers and which were boundary lines for cities. Hawke even noticed my sudden interest in navigation and offered a couple tips, most helpfully teaching me how to tell our direction from the position of the sun.

Once those details were made clear, I started tracing out the path our journey had taken since the night we escaped from the false Hawke Morau's estate. It was incredibly strange to think of all the places we had been to, only to see them as tiny labeled dots on that massive piece of parchment. For once I started understanding the scope of how far we had come, and all the things I had gotten to experience along the way, for better or worse.

We stopped one day by a little brook running through a thin grove of trees. Their red leaves were rapidly thinning, carpeting the sodden ground and crunching underfoot. Hawke was busy filling our canteens and waterskins while I sat with the map near Sir Brown Horse, who was enjoying his own fill of the deliciously clear water. I had just about caught up to our progress on the map, the line I had been tracing our path with just passing out of Nostromos and through the hills marked near it. It was only now that I started looking where that line was leading us.

"It looks like Val'Hala is next," I mumbled to myself, wondering if I pronounced the town's name correctly.

"What was that?" Hawke asked, freezing with one of the canteens halfway towards the creek.

"Oh, sorry," I apologized, "I just noticed we're almost to Val'Hala."

Hawke capped the canteen and brusquely walked over to look over my shoulder. His eyes darted over the parchment for a second, then he clapped me on the shoulder.

"Wow, Micasa, I'm impressed. You learned how to read this much faster than I thought!" He smiled down at me, and just like that, I felt some of the tension that had been growing between us over the last several weeks melt away.

"You think I did okay with this?" I beamed. He gave me a nod and pointed down towards where my last mark had been made.

"Yeah, here's the woodland we're in right now. We just have another day and a half or so before we reach Val'Hala." He turned an eye to me and raised an eyebrow. "Micasa, will you do me a favor and be our navigator for the last few stretches of our journey? It would help me out a lot."

Having Hawke tell me that I could have responsibility over something important to our travels made me well up with gratitude. Finally, I could feel like I was contributing something, rather than just being a passive rider. I nodded my head enthusiastically to his request.

"Wonderful! Thank you, Micasa." He gave me a brief hug and walked back to Sir Brown Horse to feed him, now with a slight jaunt to his step that hadn't been there before.

An hour later, after we had eaten and had a bit to relax, we were back on the road heading northwest towards the city. Hawke hummed a little tune to himself while I pored over the map with a newfound enthusiasm, looking for landmarks to mark the progress we were making.

"Hey, Micasa, it's been a while since the last time I saw you working with the locks," said Hawke some hours later. "Why don't you put the map away for a while and do some of that?"

"Oh, the ones we have are too easy for me," I told him.

"Eh? Really?"

"Sure, lemme show you." I folded up the map and put it in a saddlebag, trading it out for three of the padlocks we kept on hand for me to play around with. Holding them forward so Hawke could see, I proceeded to snap them open and close with my bare hands.

"When did you learn to do that without your hairpin?" Hawke's voice was full of amazement. I shrugged and tossed the locks back in their bags.

"A while ago. I just kept fiddling with them until eventually I could do it. What I want to know is how you weren't hurt by those swords and arrows from the bandits. Was that the power you got back from Mr. Kamson?"

"No, actually it's something anyone who can use essence can do, though it's not easy." Hawke pulled out an apple from his knapsack and held it in his hand. "Essence is your life energy, you re-member? Well, it's possible to channel it through your body to reinforce it." His grip tightened on the apple until the fruit splintered and exploded in his hand. "With enough practice, you can make yourself several times stronger or turn your flesh tough as steel."

"So even I could learn that?" It was an exciting prospect to get to do something other than open and close locks with this power of mine.

"Maybe, someday. It's not the same thing as honing your power, though. Would probably take years, at least."

"I don't care! I wanna learn!"

Hawke laughed at my insistence. "Okay, okay, when all this is over, I'll try and teach you."

It was as if our discomfort over the last month had just evaporated, and I couldn't have been happier that things were starting to return to the way they were before. My companion seemed to be trying his hardest to keep the tone light, and even though I couldn't completely forget what had happened with the bandits, I also couldn't ignore the effort he was taking to make things right between us again. That alone made me feel that there was reason to put my trust Hawke once more.

The dirt path we had been traversing opened to a cobblestone road wide enough for two carriages to ride abreast. Other travelers started appearing on the way, carrying sacks full of belongings or driving carts packed with wares to peddle. Hawke tried to make some small talk with a few, but most were heading directions different from our own, and grew quiet or laughed when he mentioned we were heading towards Val'Hala. Eventually, they would take some turn at a crossroads and slowly shrink away while we forged onward down the main road.

Our own destination was already growing larger by the minute, though that was no great feat; the city easily dwarfed even the largest ones I had seen on our adventure to date, with gargantuan stone parapets creeping above a towering curtain wall of brick and mortar. The closer we drew, the more it seemed the blockade was bearing down on us until even the early afternoon sun disappeared prematurely behind its berth.

A mob of people was gathered near where the road met the wall, and it was only when we had ventured closer that I finally caught sight of a pair of bronzed gates set in the stone, just large enough to let a single cart in at a time.

"Is the pull coming from anyone here?" I asked Hawke. He shook his head.

"No, it's definitely coming from inside the city. The real question is whether or not we'll even be able to make it in."

"We can just follow everyone else in, right?" I asked.

"I doubt any of these people will make it in. Val'Hala has a strict policy on letting people enter the city without some business to conduct. You see the guards patrolling the crowd?" He pointed towards several heavily armored figures wielding simple but dangerous looking lances. "They're here to keep people from just stampeding inside. Only those with the right paperwork will actually be let through. This may be a problem."

One of the guards turned and looked at us, his gaze lingering for a long moment. I could understand why: we were a couple of the only people who weren't on foot and stood out readily on horseback above the throng. He started to turn away, then suddenly snapped his head back and took a long stare. After a few seconds, he started pushing through the crowd, casually elbowing aside anyone who was even remotely in his way. Hawke noticed him by this time too and was watching his approach with mild curiosity.

When he was but a few paces from us, he froze, eyes narrowing like he was trying to make sure what he was seeing was real. "Oy!" he finally roared over his shoulder. "Bates, come take a look here!"

Somehow his voice carried over the din of the mob, as a second guard quickly appeared beside his comrade.

"What is it, Horace? Someone causing trouble?" asked the new guard.

"No, no, look you fool! The guy on the horse!"

Bates the guard turned his focus on us, scowling a bit as he made his own inspection. A moment later his expression turned to shock and he let out an audible gasp.

"Could it really be? 'Ey you!" He pointed to Hawke. "What's your name?"

"Er, I'm Hawke Morau," Hawke said hesitantly. The two looked at each other and laughed.

"Well well well!" exclaimed Bates the guard. "Fancy that! The Lady wasn't off her head after all!"

"Who'd have thunk it?" cried the one named Horace. "Guess we *weren't* pokin' around here for nothin'!" The guard turned back to us and beckoned with a hand. "Come on then, the Lady's been waitin' fer ya!"

Hawke and I looked at each other mutely and shrugged. So much for getting in being a problem.

The two guards immediately began jostling the crowd aside to make room for us to proceed. Anyone who tried to argue changed their mind quickly when the spears started pointing, and soon enough we were making way straight through to the bronze doors. Other guards noticed the commotion and came running, but a few muttered words from Horace or Bates and a quick glance at Hawke were all they needed to join the effort of moving the congregation aside. With their combined efforts, there was effectively a road that cut right down the middle of two masses of very confused people.

"Oy, who's the girl?" asked Bates as he and Horace fell in step next to Sir Brown Horse. They seemed to have taken no small pride in our discovery, shooing away other guards who tried to follow as if they were personally responsible for us.

"My ward. Anywhere I can go, she can go too."

"Fair enough," the guard acquiesced, "though if the Lady says for her to go, she has to go. No offense, Lord Hawke," Bates quickly amended with a slight bow of his head.

"Who's this Lady you keep talking about?" I asked him. Horace let out a guffaw on the other side of us.

"Oy, th' lass needs a bit more time in school!" he snorted. His laugh turned into a cough at Hawke's icy glare, and he looked away. "Beg pardon, miss. What I meant ta say is, th' only Lady in all these 'ere lands is Lady Lheona. She rules 'ere with 'er husband, Lord Othenidus, in this prosperous land of ours Val'Hala." He hazarded a peek at Hawke, who gave him a small nod of approval. The guard's shoulders relaxed.

"What has the Lady requested my presence for?" Hawke asked them. Both the guards shook their heads in unison.

"That's the thing. Our dear Lady won't tell a soul – not even her Lord husband," explained Bates. He leaned in closer and dropped his voice to a hush. "And if I may say in your confidentialness, she's been in a right state about it for years. Not a day has gone by where she hasn't asked if you've been sighted and regularly punishes the city guard for damn near nothing! Practically in hysterics all hours of the day, hardly sleeps even."

"Hysterics? Lady Lheona?" Genuine confusion laced Hawke's words. "That's not the same woman I remember. As long as I've known her, she's been, er..." Hawke fumbled with the last words, but Horace picked them up.

"Th' Iron Maiden? Nah, don' worry about that ol' name. Course no one here would call 'er that to 'er face, but we know she's been tough as nails since, 'ell, forever. No one knows why she became like she is now, but," he nodded towards Hawke, "whatever it was, it has something to with you, milord."

Our discussion had lasted all the way to the gate, still closed firm against the masses who were just now being parted by the few guards posted there to let us through. Horace paraded straight to the doors and gave them a series of sharp taps with his spear. A second later, a peephole slid open, occupied by a pair of suspicious eyes.

"Oy, some trader 'ere to peddle their crap?" came an irritated voice from the squinting eyes. Horace leaned in and whispered something, causing those eyes to bolt open in shock. The eyelet slammed shut, accompanied by the sound of something heavy sliding on the other side. With a mighty groan, the doors began to creak open, and immediately chaos started bubbling up as people pushed and shoved to try and get it.

"Quick, before it turns into a damn riot!" Bates barked at us, rushing to help his fellow guards in holding back the buzzing mob.

Without wasting another moment, Hawke urged Sir Brown Horse through the doors, which had scarcely opened wide enough to encompass us. The instant we had passed through, a group of guards on the inside started shoving the gates closed again. At one point, a dirty arm broke through the threshold, but a few jabs from the blunt end of a spear quickly prodded its owner away as the doors slammed shut with a bang. A large wooden crossbar was dropped into place, and the gates were secured once more.

The city residing inside such imposing walls was much plainer than I had been expecting. All the buildings were constructed of the same sandy stone that the city's walls were, with hardly a decoration to be found among them aside from the odd sign. The central area consisted of little more than a communal well and a couple empty benches. A few people wandered the streets, clad in dusty tunics and breeches, but aside from the occasional cursory glance, no one paid any mind to the newcomers in their midst.

"Sir, Lord Hawke is it?" One of the guards had approached us as I took in our surroundings, a woman wearing the same armor as her fellows outside and donning an iron helm. "I am Sergeant Diane Farhel. You are expected at the keep."

"Expected?" Hawke blurted. "How could she? We just got here."

"She's been expecting you every day for the last several years, sir," Sergeant Farhel said matter-of-factly. "It seems today is the day those expectations are met."

"Alright, but I won't meet her unless my young friend here is allowed also," he said, motioning towards me. Farhel gave a curt nod.

"The Lady said nothing about you having to come alone. I have no reason to disagree. Now, if you'd be so kind as to follow me."

The guard turned on her heels and marched down the street, pausing with a glance over her shoulder to see if we were indeed following. Hawke quickly nudged Sir Brown Horse into action, and soon we were traversing deep into the heart of Val'Hala.

Or at least I would call it the heart if there was any real action going on. Most of the town seemed to be practically deserted, with only the rare elderly citizen meandering somewhere or a child dutifully batting at some object with a wooden sword.

"Where is everyone?" I wondered aloud.

"It's drill time currently," Farhel replied, not looking back as she walked on. "You'll see most of them when we reach the courtyard." She pointed down the main street, where a tall keep stood in the distance, enclosed by yet another stone blockade. Sounds of clashing steel and the occasional shout could be heard from that direction, growing increasingly loud as we approached.

I sucked in my breath as we passed the arch leading towards the keep and entered the open grounds. What must have been thousands of people were grouped off into pairs and seemingly engaged in combat, wielding mostly blades with the occasional lance or mace or axe spotted here and there. Their movements were slower than what I had seen in previous fights I had beheld, rigid and practiced as each fighter seemed to take a turn attacking while the other blocked or parried before taking their own turn. Every so often a cry of pain would rise from somewhere, though there were so many people it was impossible to see from where it came.

"What are they doing?" I gasped.

"Training," Farhel answered flatly.

"Everyone except children and the old serve in the military here," Hawke further explained. "They practice here to hone their skills."

"But some of them are getting hurt!" I exclaimed. Farhel let out a snort.

"The Lord and Lady believe live steel helps us take our training seriously. The only ones getting injured in such basic exercises are simply learning to be more alert the hard way."

We strode through the training grounds to a flight of stairs leading straight to the doors of keep. A guard near the bottom took the reins of our steed while Hawke helped me down.

"Your horse will be well kept in the stables while you're away, Lord Hawke," assured the guard before turning to lead Sir Brown Horse back through the training grounds. Hawke took me by the hand and started up the stairs, Farhel still leading the way as we climbed higher and higher. I fought the urge to look back, knowing all too well how far we had ascended, but I could picture the throng of trainees looking like ants from where we were.

At the top stood another pair of doors, wrought in dark studded iron this time. A pair of guards flanked the entrance but readily opened the doors with a short gesture from Farhel. We started to make our way in, but Farhel stood fast near the threshold. As Hawke passed her, she leaned in and whispered sharply.

"Watch yourself."

Hawke paused for the briefest moment but only to give her a small nod before urging me to head in.

I was expecting the foyer of the keep to be barebones utilitarian, much like everything else in the city so far. You can imagine my surprise, then, as my sandaled feet sunk into a plush carpet lining the hallway lined with polished marble columns that shone in the light radiating off of several crystal chandeliers hanging far overhead. The walls of the passage were adorned with paintings of the same grim looking man dressed from the shoulders down in a bronzed suit of armor, his greying hair cropped short and face set in a perpetual sneer.

A lone hallway led out of the foyer straight ahead, weakly lit by wallmounted candles. The end of the corridor was nowhere in sight. With only one way to proceed, we made our way through the passage in silence.

The walls seemed to slowly close in on us the further we walked, a growing feeling of claustrophobia creeping inside me. I let out an audible sigh of relief when I saw the bright lights coming from a room just ahead. As we passed into the chamber, a voice cracked the stillness.

"Attention!"

A contingent of over a dozen guards snapped to the ready, spears held at their side. They stood in rows to either side of us all the way to a raised dais upon which two great thrones stood, carved from some beautiful polished wood. In one of those thrones sat a woman clad in a dress of the deepest blue I had ever seen, her face hidden behind a hand she was leaning upon. The guards made no move, so Hawke took my hand once more and cautiously tread towards the dais. I had time to marvel at the brilliant torches that lined the walls, set inside crystal orbs that diffused the light until the room was bright as day – exceedingly useful, considering not a single window adorned the walls to let in even the barest sliver of sunlight.

As we drew close to the foot of the throne, I got a better look at the woman sitting there. Her golden flaxen hair had been done up in a complicated braid that draped over her shoulder. Her dress was simple yet immaculate, perfectly tailored to showcase the gentle curves of her body. As she raised her head from her hand to regard us, I could see lines in her face suggesting her to be a fair bit older, yet there was no denying the beauty in her high cheekbones and small sharp nose. Her eyes, a gentle jade green, would have been lovely too had they not been puffy and red, and tears were still visibly streaking down those elegant cheeks of hers as she looked between the two of us.

'You've...you've finally come!" she managed to choke out, her voice wracked with emotion. "Quickly! Come here and take this wretched thing from me!" She pulled at a thin cord draped around her neck that disappeared into the neck of her dress. Hawke took a step forward, then halted.

"First, my Lady, I ask if you would please answer some questions," he said. Her eyes practically bulged from her head.

"NO!" Lady Lheona screamed. Her guards visibly started but remained at attention, while her fingers began to dig into the armrests of her throne. Hawke remained stoic, though.

"I need some simple answers, my Lady. Until you do, I can't help you."

I didn't understand what Hawke was trying to do. Obviously, this woman had part of his essence, so why he would suddenly play this game was beyond me. Lheona also seemed confused, biting her lip as she began to rock back and forth.

"Fine, you have three. Then you take this thing away or so help me…" she snarled, looking as if she'd lose control at any moment. Hawke agreed with a slight bow.

"Three is plenty. First, where is Lord Othenius at the moment?"

"Away on training," she dismissed immediately with a wave of her hand. "You know how rare it is for him to be here; things are no different now than they ever have been. Question two," she demanded.

"Okay, I've heard a group of gypsies has been seen nearby. Is that true?" This time the Lady recoiled in her seat and blanched.

"Yes, they're a couple days or so to the west, just off the main road!" Fear overtook her countenance as she started rambling, "You tell her I kept my end of the deal! Every day for all these blasted years, I never once removed it! She has no reason to place her curse on me! Promise me you'll tell her!"

Hawke blanched at her words but composed himself quickly. "I promise I'll relay your message, my Lady. My last question is, may I approach?"

She looked confused for a second, but when she realized what he was getting at she nodded with enthusiasm befitting a child.

"Yes, yes, by all means, take this already!" Her eyes fluttered towards me for a second before she quickly added, "She may not, though. Only you." Hawke looked at me from the corner of his eye.

"You'll be okay, Micasa. Just sit tight, alright?" he said. I nodded, uneasy with having to be near so many armed strangers. All I could do is trust that we'd be on our way quickly.

"Okay then." Hawke took a deep breath and marched straight up the dais to the mad woman. She was looking at him with such feverish antici-pation her whole body trembled.

"If I may have your hand," Hawke requested softly, offering his own. In a flash, she grasped his arm with both hands, giving me just enough time to clamp my eyes shut before the room was filled with blinding light.

The guards cried out in surprise, and when the light faded it was obvious I was the only one who was expecting this as the guards furiously rubbed at their eyes in an attempt to clear them. For that, I was the only one who saw as Hawke slowly withdrew his hand, sucking in deep breaths while his eyes flickered around wildly.

Lady Lheona, on the other hand, had made a complete turn in demeanor. She calmly brushed an errant tear from her face and looked at it, as if trying to understand what it was.

Slowly the guards around us were starting to blink the glare away, looking expectantly towards their liege and my guardian. The Lady closed her eyes and took a deep breath. When they opened, she was staring straight at me, her expression like stone.

"Seize her."

Chapter 17

The Wild Man

The manacles were on me before I even had time to register what she had said. No matter what else was thought of these guards, the one thing you couldn't call them was slow to follow orders. I hadn't noticed them step up in the slightest, nor did I even see where they had kept their cuffs hidden. Now I could feel the cold iron biting into my wrists as my arms were locked rigidly behind my back.

"Micasa!" Hawke cried out from his place near the Lady. He took a step forward, stopping when the rest of her contingency formed up in front of him as a barricade, with two of them remaining behind to watch over me.

Their mistress stood from her seat and straightened her dress. She brushed away the last of the tears that had been covering her face with indifference, leaving scarcely a trace of the hysterical person who had been shrieking at us just moments ago. Her face was a mask, passive yet terrifying, and she regarded the both of us as if she wouldn't have cared if we dropped dead on the spot.

"Now that all that's been dealt with, there's still the matter of what to do with you, Morau," she droned. Hawke's eyes flickered to her but returned to me promptly. His breath was coming in heaving gasps, and even from where I stood I could tell he was sweating hard. Never before had I seen Hawke look so irritated, neither when I had been tortured by Scab Kahlot nor when he confronted the murderous Killer Mapta. It was a look of desperation.

Something inside me snapped when I saw how he worried. I was done with standing back and watching Hawke try to solve all of our problems. There had to be something I could do, even in these manacles.

The manacles! It was like a fire sparked in my heart when I realized my fortune. I had been wriggling myself free of them since before I knew what my power truly was, and now the opportunity had come for me to make use of my practice. I shifted my arms a bit, getting a feel for the bindings. Yes, they were well made, but nothing terribly intricate or altogether different from what I had worked with before. It would only take me a second to shrug them off. I could already feel the latches begin to loosen even as I thought about it.

"MICASA!"

A roar came that stopped me in my tracks. The guards, too, stepped away in surprise, and even the Lady's countenance broke as she struggled to compose herself. Hawke was staring at me like a mad beast. I was completely taken aback; the man I knew as Hawke Morau was composed at all times, even in the most dire of situations. The man who was looking at me now was full of anguish and looked like he might strike out at the slightest provocation.

"REMEMBER THE SANDWICH MAN!" he shouted again, so loud and strained I might not have believed he had said it if I hadn't been watching his lips move.

Remember the Sandwich Man? I tried to remember what the saying meant. In the intensity of the moment, it took a few seconds to recall what he had told me so long ago: don't use your power recklessly. Somehow, he had known what I was about to do and was adamant that I didn't free myself from captivity. Why would he bring that up right now, though?

It only took a little consideration to understand what he was trying to tell me. If I unlocked the shackles now, I still had almost no chance of escaping the guards flanking me, and knowing that I could free myself they might do something more drastic to keep me under control. In the worst case, they might kill me. My desire to take action almost put me in an even worse situation than we were already in.

My eyebrows raised at my realization, and Hawke slowly nodded once. It seemed like he had a plan. Once again, to my frustration, I had to wait and watch and hope that he could find a way out of this mess.

Lady Lheona had recovered from her brief shock and crossed her arms. A slight smirk played on her face at Hawke's distress. "I don't know what you're babbling about, Morau, but this girl obviously is worth a lot to you. Is she the gypsy's whelp? She certainly has the look of it." One of her graceful hands rose into the air. "With a snap of my fingers, my soldiers would end her life right here. What do you think I should do?"

"I think you should consider your own position," Hawke snarled. I didn't even know he could snarl. "I'm right here next to you and armed. If anything happened to Micasa, your own life would be forfeit." His hand already hovered over the hilt peeking out from his side.

"True, I know how quick you are with a blade. I'm no fool to think I'm stronger than you, but will you risk this Micasa's life over it?" Her hand quavered as if she meant to snap, and Hawke visibly flinched. This elicited a cold chuckle from the Lady.

"Oh, how easy it is to read you now. Fine, I'll make you a deal. If you promise to toss your sword aside, I'll call off the guards from your little follower. Fair enough?"

Hawke seemed to think this over for a good while, his eyes darting feverishly over the guards while his mind seemed to be working something out. At last. he nodded.

"Fine, but call them off first."

"Of course." Lheona waved her hands at the soldiers beside me, who broke off at once and joined their fellows around Hawke. Once he seemed assured of my immediate safety, he slowly pulled the sheathed sword out of the sash where it hung.

"No stupid moves now," warned the Lady, poising a hand towards his head as if it were a weapon.

"Wouldn't dream of it," he said. He dropped it at his feet, and a quick nudge from his foot sent it skittering across the stone, where it came to rest a few yards away.

"Wonderful," cooed Lheona. She turned to her guard. "Keep your spears trained on him. Attack at will if he shows any sign of resistance." The squadron approached my companion with trepidation, the tips of their weapons converging on his throat until they formed a deadly collar around his neck. Lady Lheona seemed content with this and stepped off the dais towards me.

"Now the question remains of what to do with you," she said. I thought she was talking to me, but she cast a glance over her shoulder at Hawke before returning her focus to me. "My dear Othenidus would surely love to have a few words with you, but I've been considering some ways to try and kill an immortal. I'm sorely tempted to try a few. What do you think–"

Lheona was interrupted by a collective grunt resounding from the guards surrounding Hawke. She and I both looked over just in time to see the guards stumble back from Hawke as if shoved by an invisible force. My friend barreled his way through in a flash, running straight towards me.

"Get him, you fools. He's unarmed!" the Lady bellowed while she stepped forward herself to try and intercept him. As if it heard her words, Hawke's sword leapt from the ground and soared into its owner's outstretched hand. Lheona went rigid with incredulity, but Hawke seemed to be expecting this.

"Micasa, free yourself!" he cried out. It took me a couple seconds to get what he meant. With the shackles already partially loosened from my previous attempt, it took only a small shake of my hands to send my bonds clattering away.

Meanwhile, Hawke had bull charged Lheona head on with his sword bared. She cried out and threw her arms up for protection, keeping herself from seeing Hawke lower his weapon and ram into her shoulder first. Our captor was knocked prone, but Hawke continued his mad dash. I started running towards the door too, but Hawke scooped me up by the waist with his free arm before I had taken a dozen steps.

"Sorry, we gotta go fast," he apologized in such an off-handed way I almost suspected he wasn't sorry at all. We were already flying down the corridor we had just been taking, the gate in front of us rapidly growing larger.

With a bestial grunt he shoved his foot into the doors, which flew open like they were made of particle board. A couple pained bellows rang out from behind them both, followed by a pair of similar sounding thumps. Hawke planted me on the ground and whirled around to slam the gate shut again.

"Micasa, a little help here," he snapped with a pointed look at the door. Caught up in the heat of the moment, I took hold of the handles and locked it without really thinking.

"Good, good," Hawke muttered to himself. He knelt to check on one of the two guards who had the misfortune of being behind the gates when he had burst through. The poor soul was still clearly dazed, so Hawke helped himself to the short-sword the guard wore at his hip.

"What are you doing?" the soldier muttered as Hawke undid the belt clasping the weapon to his body. Hawke's response was to punch him in the face.

"Do me a favor and stay down," he asked the obviously unconscious guard. With that, he turned back to me and secured the sword belt across my shoulder.

"You said Blake taught you a bit about sword-play back at the bandit camp, right?" His words were breathless, and his frenzied attitude was making my heart race.

"Yeah, a little," I said. I was startled as a loud pounding sounded from the gate I had just locked, followed by a steady flow of choice expletives.

"Okay then, listen close. We don't have much time." Hawke leaned close and stared me straight in the eyes, his voice a deadly whisper. "We need to get to Sir Brown Horse and make a run for it, but all those people down there are going to try and stop us. I'll protect us as best I can, but if you have to, use this." He ripped the short-sword from its sheath and placed it in my hands. As small as it looked compared to other swords I had seen, it felt tremendous in my tiny grip. "Only as a last resort. Can you do that, Micasa?"

The idea of swinging a blade around myself was almost enough to paralyze me with fear. Practicing with Blake was one thing, but using it in a real fight was something I had never considered. At the same time, I knew Hawke wouldn't do this unless things were worse than I thought. A few more bangs sounded behind me, and the other gate guard was beginning to drag himself back to his feet. Hawke was putting his trust in me in a way he never had before.

"Okay," I answered, tightening my grip on the pommel. He smiled and patted me on the head. Then it was back under his arm for me, and with a leap, Hawke took to the steps leading back to the training ground three at a time. My stomach dropped into my feet as I finally caught sight of just how high up the stairs had taken us. A tiny insane voice in the back of my mind rejoiced to see I was right about how the trainees below looked like ants.

The other guard had recovered enough to stand, but we were already halfway down the stairs by the time he managed to stumble to the edge. Instead of chasing, he opted to bellow down, "Stop them!"

It was a surreal sight to behold as over a thousand faces turned and stared straight at us in unison. A thousand faces attached to a thousand armed soldiers who were just practicing optimal ways of killing people. I couldn't stop the nervous giggle that bubbled up.

"Hang on!" Hawke advised, though what he expected me to hang onto I have no idea. The closest trainees collapsed in on him with spears and daggers as he touched ground, all striking as one. He pulled me close to his chest and balled up, forcing their steel to crash into him. Their attacks had as much effect as the bandits outside Nostromos, bouncing off his body with all the lethality of soft rubber. Hawke stood and swung his sword in a wide arc. The soldiers jumped away to avoid, but in midair they were suddenly catapulted backwards by an unseen power, sending them flailing to the dirt.

Several dozen more were already stepping around the prone bodies ready to lash out, but Hawke was sprinting at full speed past them before they could reach him. A handful of soldiers in the distance reared back and hurled their spears with frightening accuracy, but they clattered off Hawke without slowing him in the slightest. A dozen more thunks behind us indicated what was likely a hailstorm of javelins following our progress.

The trip towards the keep hadn't felt terribly long, but with an entire army closing in like two murderous walls, the exit seemed to shrink away the faster Hawke ran, even at his breakneck pace. A mass of warriors now fell upon him on all sides, striking anywhere they could reach with spear and sword alike. A few noticed me tucked against his breast and attempted to spear me through his arms. Hawke's blade danced around to deflect most, but a few managed to slip through his guard. It was all I could do to wave my own blade in a desperate attempt to stave those few off, and though a couple came perilously close, the worst I suffered for it was a spearhead piercing through my robe and striking Hawke's impervious body.

My guardian let out a battle cry, and just like that, the dome of attackers was hurled away from him in every direction. They collided with their fellows who were trying to join the fight, giving Hawke an opening to make a break for the exit once more.

Finally, we exploded through the archway into the town proper, but our pursuers were still hot on our heels. Hawke wove through the abandoned streets, storefronts and residences blurring by. He turned onto a wide central road that ended at a large stone building with sturdy wooden gates. A pair of soldiers guarding the gates hollered at the sight of us, but Hawke plunged straight towards the door. A few flicks of his sword deflected their attacks, and with a sweep of his hand, both guards were sent flying backwards into stone walls, where they crumpled unmoving.

"Get it open!" he shouted, setting me on my feet. From the other side of the gate, I caught the smell of horses and hay, realizing we had reached the stables. Off in the distance, I could hear the muted shouts of our chasers growing louder each second. For a moment my mind blanked.

"Micasa!" Hawke cried urgently. I snapped back to reality and fumbled with the door for a second. When it didn't budge, I ripped a hairpin from my head and jammed it in the keyhole. There was a pop, and with Hawke's help, we wrenched the doors to the stables open.

The building was packed with a number of the largest horses I had ever seen before, snorting and stamping nervously at the sudden intrusion. Sir Brown Horse was lounging in a corner munching on hay contently, looking particularly small in comparison to his war-bred brethren. We hurried to saddle our mount and load our things onto him as the din outside kept escalating. By the time we had climbed onto his back, a number of fighters had run onto the road and noticed the stable doors open.

"Whatever happens, don't let go of the reins," Hawke advised me. Without waiting for an answer, he kicked Sir Brown Horse immediately into a full gallop, firing out of the stables at top speed. Several soldiers were running at us, but a few jumped out of the way at the sight of us charging headlong into them. Those gutsy enough to take a stab as we passed were parried by Hawke's quick blade work.

Back and forth Hawke steered our mount through side streets and main thoroughfares, sometimes completely backtracking around as we attempted to avoid clusters of roaming soldiers. Those that couldn't be avoided were blocked time and again by Hawke when they weren't hurling themselves out of the path of Sir Brown Horse's pounding hooves.

At last, we reached a long stretch of road leading straight to the gates we had entered. It was strange to think that, for everything that had happened, we had come through those same gates only maybe a half hour before. Now all that was standing between us and freedom were those doors, the guards standing at the ready next to them, and about a hundred trainee soldiers pouring out of alleyways and side lanes straight toward us.

"Micasa, remember what I said about holding onto the reins," Hawke reminded me. "Trust me, it'll be okay."

"Mmm," I managed to grunt. I found it hard to focus on anything other than the small army charging at us.

"This part's gonna suck for me." he moaned wearily. With a kick of his heels, we were off at a gallop again. Then, just as we hit full speed, Hawke rolled off the saddle. If he hadn't been so adamant about telling me to keep a tight hold, I might have very well fallen off at the sheer sight of what he did next.

Hawke rocketed forward on the ground faster than anything I imagined was possible, easily breaking Sir Brown Horse's pace by threefold. As he raced forward, the soldiers barring the path were tossed aside just being in his proximity, weapons scattering from surprised hands. He reached the doors well ahead of me, ripping the crossbar away like it were a stick. The guards who had been watching the gate were long gone when they caught sight of Hawke's unbelievable feat, leaving him free to shove the gates open. Sir Brown Horse and I were fast approaching, and now I could see the mob of refugees still bustling on the other side. In seconds we would barrel straight into them.

Hawke wasn't done yet, though. He clapped his hands together, holding them for a few seconds, then whipped them in a wide arc to either side of his body. There came an uproar of screams from the frightened crowd as they were flung to either side of the road, leaving a wide path that I was more than happy to ride straight down.

I managed to slow down Sir Brown Horse just long enough to let Hawke haul himself up, then we were off like the wind. Innumerable shouts were raising behind us but we dared not look back, riding so hard that Sir Brown Horse's breath came in steamy bursts. We rode like that for as long as we could, turning off-trail and cutting through open countryside whenever possible. The sky darkened so quickly I thought we had been riding through the whole day, but it only turned out to be heavy black clouds that had rolled in, unnoticed by us in our escape.

Eventually, we slowed to a trot as we reached a grove of firs that we hoped to catch our breath behind. Hawke, Sir Brown Horse, and I all were panting mightily, the horse from exertion, and myself from the sheer adrenaline coursing through me. A few errant raindrops began to pelt us, followed shortly by a veritable torrent. Hawke tilted his head back, looked to the sky, and let out a bellowing laugh like nothing I had ever heard from him.

"Even Mother Nature's on our side, Micasa!" he exclaimed, wrapping an arm around me in a tight hug. "You were incredible back there. They'll be telling that story for years to come! Let's find a place to settle down for a bit."

We managed to find a spot where the branches grew thick enough together to mostly shelter us from the rain. Hawke gathered up some tinder into a pile and, from a single spark off, his flint had a campfire roaring in the blink of an eye. I was content lying on the ground, trying to piece together any part of our escape so that it made sense.

"What in the world did you do?" I managed to wheeze out after some time. "People were flying away without you touching them. Was that the power you got from the Lady?" Hawke had propped himself against a tree, still panting like he had forgotten how to breathe. He shook his head a little and shot me a twisted smile.

"That little trick was courtesy of Mr. Kamson. Lets me move things just with the power of my mind and some essence. Don't use it often, though, very tiring to use it too much." His heavy breathing was certainly testament to that. I had never seen him so exhausted before.

"So what did she have of yours?"

"My…how to put it…my emotions?" He snorted and rolled his eyes. "Tell me honestly, did you ever think I acted a little, um, too calm while we've been together?" Thinking back on it, it did seem like Hawke often underreacted to things most people would have flown off the handle on.

"I guess so," I said. "You're saying you haven't felt anything the whole time we were travelling?"

"Not *nothing*. But my feelings have been, I guess I'd say, muted this whole time." Hawke let out another chuckle that grew into a cackle I found unnatural for him. This new Hawke was going to take some getting used to.

"Man, I feel better than I have in ages," he said, still cackling. His laughter forced a smile out of me in spite of my exhaustion. A tiny worry in the back of my head was still burning, though.

"Are we safe here?" I asked. Considering how hard they tried to keep us from escaping, I was skeptical that the whole city of Val'Hala wouldn't be out searching for us.

"Well, Lheona is a very proud woman," Hawke mused. "She'll probably send a couple small squads out to sweep the immediate area around the city, but I don't think they'll stray too far. She's too dignified to risk her Lord husband finding out someone pushed around their entire army and escaped without a scratch. Plus, with all this rain, most of our tracks should be covered before they have a chance to track us."

He read the unease still on my face and scooted over to sit next to me. "You go ahead and take a nap. I'll keep watch, okay?"

A little sleep sounded like a great idea, but as hard as I tried I just wasn't sleepy after all the excitement of the day. I tossed and turned for a few minutes on my blanket before giving it up and sitting up.

"It's no use, Hawke," I started telling him. To my surprise, he was completely out, still sitting with his arms crossed over his knees. For all the time I had known him, I had never actually seen him sleep. He always seemed to be awake when I went to bed and was always up before I awoke. Considering the spectacle Hawke put on for us to make our escape, it was no wonder he had no energy left.

I took some time to feed Sir Brown Horse and brush him a bit, taking a bite to eat for myself as well. Then I took a seat next to my companion and tugged my new little short-sword free, laying it at my side. After all he had done, the least I could afford Hawke was to take one night of watch.

Chapter 18

The Regretful Man

As luck would have it, Hawke's prediction that nobody would come for us was mostly true. Somebody did come poking around in the wee hours of the morning, but it only turned out to be the homeowner whose land we had accidentally stumbled onto in our flight. He blew up just a bit when he caught sight of our little camp. This in turn woke Hawke immediately, who was so quick to draw his sword that the poor fellow was sent scampering away in terror.

Hawke apologized several times for falling asleep on watch, even after I repeatedly made it clear I understood how tired he was. We decided it would be best to pick up and get moving, just in case our unwitting host was off to alert the authorities to our location. Once the fire was well and out, we were back on our way west, following the moon as it occasionally peeked out from the clouds on its own journey to the horizon.

We kept well south of any main roads, sticking instead to the cobbled streets the locals likely used to visit their neighbors or head into the city. When there was no path that led where we needed, Hawke stubbornly pushed our horse through yards and fields in any attempt to avoid drawing closer to Val'Hala. Even as far as we strayed from course, the sandy line that was the city walls was still visible just on the northern horizon, standing vigil.

A whole day passed before Hawke felt comfortable turning towards the main road again. The last glimpses of the Lonely Kingdom were long gone by then, and now I switched my attention back to our map. There was a morbid enjoyment for me to cross our path through the dot labeled Val'Hala, to the point that I added a few extra scribbles over it for good measure. Tracing the way ahead following the main road, I found that there was only one city left along that path; one that sat right on the coast of Astra.

"We're going to Damkarei, right?" I asked. "Is that our last stop?"

Hawke let out a weird, shuddering exhalation. "It is, but we have one place we're heading before that."

"But there's nowhere else on the map," I argued, looking over it twice just to be sure. Hawke's whole body shuddered this time.

"No, it's not a town. It's where Lheona said I'd find the gypsy camp." I remembered Hawke asking about that from the Lady and finally put two and two together.

"We're going to see Rouge!" I cried with excitement. Just saying her name made Hawke yip awkwardly. I was confused by his reaction. "Don't you want to see her?"

"Eh, well, yeah and no." He scratched the back of his head so hard his hair frizzed up. "I haven't seen her in so long, and I still have no idea why she...did what she did."

I had almost forgotten that it was because this mysterious Rouge broke Hawke's essence that our adventure had begun in the first place. All the great times I had with him, and all the near-deadly escapes, and even Hawke didn't know why this had happened. I couldn't figure out if I wanted to thank her or yell at her when we finally met.

Finally, we came upon the main road once more, built out of huge chunks of granite expertly fitted together so snugly you'd think the road had been carved from one giant hunk of stone that stretched for miles. Hawke grew positively twitchy as we set back onto it, constantly throwing glances along the side and jumping at the slightest noise, only to grow sour when he realized it was just a bird or some rodent scurrying about.

In the late evening, we found a woman with a travel sack heading the opposite way. She fawned over Hawke when she recognized who he was, and he in turn paid her some passing courtesies that elated her. When he asked her if she noticed anything on the road, she bristled and told us about the band of heathens who dared to nestle just off to the side. She was raving about their "barbaric rituals" and "honeyed words meant to lure in unsuspecting souls," even blushing a bit as she admitted she was almost swayed by their charming ways. Her words made him break into a sweat and pale.

"Please, Lord Hawke, promise me you'll take care of it," she implored.

"I was, uh, actually on my way to do just that," he lied terribly, unable to look the woman in the eye. "Just tell me where the, er, heathens are and I'll make sure to take care of it, or something."

"Oh, bless you, milord!" she said, oblivious to his unease. "They're just a few hours off! I'll let everyone in Val'Hala know of your gallantry as soon as I arrive!"

"Oh please, don't," he chuckled nervously. "It's all part of being a king."

"Oh, bless you mightily! Strong, just, *and* humble!"

She refused to leave until she could kiss his hand and finally started back her on her way with a happy tune on her lips. Hawke looked ready to fall off the horse.

"I don't think I'm ready to see Rouge like this," he moaned. "Let's call it a night. We can catch them tomorrow."

All through the evening, Hawke was a nervous wreck, spacing out when I tried talking to him and not touching a bite to eat. I had hoped that perhaps a good night's rest might do him some good, but it seemed that his brief encounter with narcolepsy had already passed. When I awoke in the early hours before dawn, he was still sitting where I had left him, wide awake, looking even worse than he had the night before. I forbade him from doing anything else until he had washed up and made something more presentable of his gaunt, haggard complexion lest he be mistaken for a grinel. After a long morning intermission of tidying up the nervous sod, we struck out again.

We were greeted with a cool, temperate morning. Aside from a few wisps of cloud floating carelessly about, the sky was opalescent against the sun's rays. It was the perfect day for travel.

At least, it would have been if Hawke didn't continue to jump and flinch at every little noise that cried out in the distance. I thought I was in for another tiring haul, but the woman's estimate held true. It was just a few hours before there came a commotion that made Hawke convulse uncontrollably.

I wasn't quite able to make it out right away, but the closer we drew the more I was able to start picking out the sounds of musical instruments and laughter. Over the brush and scattered trees to our right, I caught brief glimpses of brightly painted wagons and draw carts, with the occasional impression of someone wandering between them. A well-worn footpath opened in the foliage a bit down the road, and we were finally able to take in fully what we had stumbled upon.

It looked like someone had erected a town fair in the middle of the wilderness. People dressed in garish motley and flamboyant tunics milled around a camp filled with carts bursting full of oddities. Multiple campfires burned cheerfully in a multitude of colors that changed sporadically. One individual was juggling an assortment of balls, weapons, and lit torches with an almost bored look on his face. Occasionally a comrade would toss a new bauble into the rotation. Another gruff-faced fellow was chucking throwing knives at a man leaning lazily against a tree, the weapons burying in the trunk a mere hair's width from the lounger. There was even a woman covered in satin scarves standing atop a horse as it cantered around the site while the rider appeared to read a book.

One of the performers noticed us watching the chaos ensuing and bounded over to us with a friendly grin plastered on his face.

"Good morn to you, sir and lass!" he exclaimed warmly. "What brings weary travelers such as yourselves to our little slice of paradise?" I was struck dumb from the absurdity of everything I was seeing, but Hawke's silence seemed intentionally weighted. The man looked between the two of us, waiting for some sort of reaction. Then his eyes slowly rolled back to my companion. The smile dropped from his face much quicker.

"Triumph, it's me. Hawke," my companion said softly. Our greeter took a step forward and gaped.

"By the Lord Ordained, he's actually done it," he breathed. Another performer, much older looking than the others and donning a bright yellow robe and deer antlers on his head approached, laying a hand on his friend.

"What's the matter, Triumph? Have our new friends really impressed you so?" the geriatric cackled.

"No, you blasted codger, look with your eyes!" Triumph actually grabbed the man's head and turned it towards Hawke. The old man peered hard, smacking his lips a couple times, but it took only a second before his toothless jaw was agape.

"He's here! He's here, he's here!" the man rambled with his arms in the air. He continued this way as he shuffled into the camp and out of sight, the other campers now turning their attention towards all the fuss.

"I'll be right back with everyone! They won't believe it!" Triumph cried as he sprinted off hollering wildly. "Hawke's returned! Hawke's finally returned!"

My friend let out a groan so drained it made me tired just hearing it. He slowly dismounted and helped me off, just as the scarfed woman I had seen before approached us, still on the horse.

"Hawke, I'm so glad to see you again," she said, though her passive face didn't impress much joy. Hawke put on a weary smile.

"I'm glad to see you too, Chestnut. You mind taking care of our friend here? His name is Sir Brown Horse." He gave our steed an affectionate pat.

"Sir Brown Horse. A knight worthy of legend, to be sure," she praised. "I will see to his every need." She snapped a couple times and snorted. Sir Brown Horse's head swung to face her, and she gave a sharp whistle. Her own mount turned and trotted away, and to my surprise, Sir Brown Horse followed close on their heels.

We barely had time to start walking into the camp when a flood of colorful strangers began converging from everywhere, stepping out of tents and swinging in from the trees, and I swear one even tunneled in from the ground. They engulfed us in a circle and stared in rapture as if they had never seen anything more incredible in their lives.

A lone figure emerged from the cluster, considerably more normal-looking to me than the others. He wore a plain scarlet vest with polished gold buttons done up all the way to his throat. His satin grey pants hung loosely over well-worn moccasins that curled at the toes, which drew attention to the limp he walked with. His hair was heavily thinned and mostly white with thin streaks of bronze, though it grew long enough in the back to be pulled into an absurdly tiny ponytail. Hazel eyes regarded us, watery and swollen, and his bushy mustache crinkled as he smiled.

"I couldn't believe it when they told me," the old man said. "I thought we'd be waiting here until we all turned to dust. Come here, little one." I thought he was referring to me, but Hawke strode past and embraced the elder for a moment.

"You're looking well, Mirth," Hawke commented as they broke their grip. The man gave a single hearty guffaw.

"Ha! If only looks were enough to keep up with this lot," he said. There was a round of laughter from the group, but it was scattered and half-hearted. In fact, nearly all of the gypsies were looking somber and trying their best not to look at Hawke, which seemed strange compared to how they were acting just minutes ago. Even Mirth's mustache seemed to droop as he turned around and walked through the parting curtain of onlookers.

"So... where's Rouge?" Hawke asked in a higher voice than usual. The old gypsy stopped his gait mid-step.

"She's waiting in the same place she has been for years. I'll show you," he said before shambling off again. Hawke started following, the color draining from his face.

"What do you mean she's 'in the same place'? Why didn't she come here with you? Hey!" Hawke's voice cracked as Mirth walked on without replying.

The crowd around me began to disperse, the atmosphere thick around them as they went back to their original tasks with none of the enthusiasm they showed before. I realized I had just been standing there without moving the entire time and rushed to catch up to Hawke.

"...on't make me say the obvious, child," Mirth was finishing saying as I reached earshot of the two. They were just passing out the back of one of the tents and into a small forested area. Hawke was nearly pacing circles around the old man.

"*You* need to stop playing word games and tell me what happened!" Hawke was now yelling straight at him. Mirth turned left near an overgrown willow and stopped, pointing straight ahead of himself.

"There's your answer."

I just managed to reach them, peeking around Hawke's legs to see where he had been led. A couple dozen yards ahead was a large patch of land that had been cleared of plants and stones, save for three distinct rings of rocks that stretched about six feet long and two feet wide. The dirt underneath the rings looked like it had been disturbed, and at the end of each formation, a wooden marker stood erect. There was no mistaking what we were being shown.

"Two taken by mobs, and her by illness." Mirth sighed and shook his head. "I've done this so many times you'd think I would be used to it."

If Hawke heard him he paid no mind. With shaky steps, he approached the graves and stopped before the middle one. He let out a choking sound and his knees buckled out beneath him. I cried out and tried to go to him, but Mirth placed a hand on my shoulder. As soft as his touch was, I felt like I was rooted in place.

"Let him be for a bit, lass," he said. "He needs some time alone with her."

"But–!" I stammered. I didn't just want to leave him there, stewing in whatever he was going through at that moment. It was Hawke who spoke up.

"Just for a bit, Micasa. It'll...be okay." He sounded completely unsure of his own words, but Mirth gave me a gentle tug back towards the camp. Unable to think of a decent argument, I reluctantly let myself be pulled away.

It was impossible to think that after all this time, after all the fighting and effort Hawke had put into coming this far, that we'd be met with such an ending. My eyes started to itch fiercely, my vision blurring. Then the tears started to flow, tracing hot rivulets down my cheeks.

Mirth mopped them off my face with a handkerchief and made soft shushing noises while he took me back to the main clearing. The kindly gypsy brought me to one of the several rainbow strobing campfires and bade me sit. I assumed he would leave me to my own devices, but the old man instead took a seat beside me and gestured to no one in particular.

The juggler I had seen before appeared keeping five swords aloft, handling them by the blades without once so much as nicking his fingers. He hurled one high into the air and tumbled away as another performer bounded in and opened his mouth wide. The blade went straight down his throat, eliciting a horrified gasp from me. After a second the gypsy tugged out the sword, which was for some reason now covered in bright pink flowers. He plucked one off and held it towards me. I flinched away, not sure I wanted to handle something that had just been pulled from his mouth. With a flick of his wrist, the flower changed into a dove that fluttered into the sky.

From what might as well have been thin air, other gypsies continued jumping in one by one and putting on dazzling displays of skill and trickery. In spite of my dark feelings, I couldn't fight my amazement at their performance, each one as fantastical as the last. At some point, Mirth handed me a plate of food, and I had eaten half of it before I even noticed it had been given to me.

For a finale, Chestnut rode in standing atop Sir Brown Horse, who reared back on his hind legs and hopped backwards comically. The gypsy woman stepped off his head and leapt into the sky, somersaulting as she landed kneeling before me. The dove from earlier alighted onto her outstretched hand, and a quick snap of her hand turned it into a rose she held for me. I couldn't fight the smile creeping to my lips, and this time I took the flower. As she stepped back to bow, the other performers all rushed out to join her. Mirth and I both broke into applause.

"They're incredible, aren't they?" he murmured to me as he clapped.

I nodded. "Who taught them to do all that?" I asked. Mirth let out a chuckle.

"Nobody taught them. They're simply using talents of theirs to do what they love to do: make people's lives a little brighter." He looked at me with a raised eyebrow, and I realized I had completely forgotten my foul mood.

"Everyone who's talked about gypsies on our way here said you were monsters and evil," I told him, "but why would they hate you if all you want to do is make them happy?" His brow furrowed.

"Quite a thoughtful question from one so young," Mirth hummed. "I suppose people fear us because, for all the things we can do, they only think of how such skills could be put to darker purposes."

"Like stealing someone's essence?" I ventured. The wizened gypsy's face slackened at my question.

"So you've heard about that. Yes, of course you would. Traveling with Hawke for so long, it'd be impossible not to." He nodded to no one but himself.

"Hawke told me she stole his powers, but I still don't really get it," I said, casting my eyes to the ground. We sat in silence for some time before Mirth spoke up.

"Micasa, is that right?" he asked softly. "Let me share something with you." He stood and offered his hand out to help me up. Slowly, Mirth hobbled through the camp, his leathery grasp leading me along.

"You said Hawke told you about essence, yes?" he started saying. When I nodded, he harrumphed. "We gypsies don't think of such energy in so cold a manner. That strength is a person's *soul*, and that is what we strive to touch when we perform for people and connect with them. All living things, plant and animal, have a soul coursing through them. Reaching a person so intimately that we can touch their very soul, I suppose you could say that's the gift we gypsies have; what Hawke would call a power." He rolled his eyes.

"Touching a soul?" I repeated aloud, confused. Mirth smiled.

"It must not make much sense, but as strong as a soul is, it's also very delicate. Even small things in life can change a person's soul so dramatically they become like someone else. Gypsies can forge bonds with people so quickly that we can learn secrets about them they never knew they had. We can see that soul in all its glamour, and thus learn a person better than they know themselves." A sad expression crossed his face.

"Because of that, we also understand just how fragile a soul truly is."

Our walk had taken us towards a large carriage where several gypsies were loitering about, looking ready to die of boredom. At our approach, they perked up considerably.

"What's up, Mirth?" asked one of the troupe members with a relieved grin. "Taking the little lady on a tour?"

"In a manner of speaking," he replied without smiling back. "Do me a favor and get the trunk." The cheer faded from the bunch almost instantly.

"O-okay," the gypsy replied hesitantly. He looked at a couple of the other stragglers pointedly, and the three together rushed inside the carriage.

"On rare occasions, Micasa, a gypsy does something selfish that endangers the troupe," he kept talking like our conversation had never stopped. "Our lifestyle is already one where we live in fear every day. For one of our own to threaten our ways, there is only one punishment."

A large door swung open in the rear of the vehicle, and the three that had disappeared inside struggled to lug a bulky footlocker outside. They carefully deposited it on the ground, something inside clinking as it came to rest. Their work done, the gypsies split away and took position close by, looking far more alert than before.

Mirth approached the chest and undid a half-dozen clasps holding the lid in place. He beckoned me closer and lifted the top slowly. I inhaled sharply at the sight: hundreds of shinestones were piled inside, blazing in all colors imaginable. Mirth looked sick at the mere sight of them.

"We do not kill those gypsies who endanger their fellows," he told me. "We break a piece of their soul off, one that holds whatever they cherish the most. It may be a talent of theirs, or a fond memory, it matters not. Once done, they are exiled from us, never allowed to return. We place that part of their soul in one of these stones and keep them here where they usually sit, forgotten." He closed the trunk as if he couldn't bear to look at them anymore and turned to regard me with heavy eyes.

"A broken soul is a terrible thing, lass. The wound left is invisible but never heals. It is a pain unlike any you can imagine. Most who suffer this can never sleep, so great is the agony, and in the end are driven mad by it. It is abominable for us to do this, and yet without such a deterrent we might very well die out completely."

I was thunderstruck. Somehow I never thought just how terrible it was for Hawke to have his soul broken so. And his had been shattered into so many pieces! Just how much had he been suffering this whole time?

I couldn't leave him alone to deal with all that pain by himself. Ignoring the rest of what Mirth was saying, I rushed off to find Hawke at once.

Doing so proved simple enough, since he hadn't moved an inch from where we left him. I was afraid he'd be mad that I was interrupting his thoughts, but when he noticed me out of the corner of his eye, he actually beckoned me over with a hand.

I knelt beside him, but his focus was turned back to the grave marker, where 'ROUGE' had been carved roughly into the wood. Not wanting to disturb him, I contented myself with putting my hands in my lap and preserving the stillness of the moment.

"It's funny," Hawke said suddenly. "When I gained the power to heal, my bad eyesight from the old days vanished completely. It felt so liberating not having to wear glasses anymore. Then one day, Rouge and I are talking about nothing in particular when she looks me straight in the face and says, 'You know, you'd be cute with glasses.'" He took the pair off his nose and flipped them over in his hands with a sad smile on his face. "Been wearing fake ones ever since." His smile tightened into a wince.

"I'm sorry," was all I could think to say to him. I scooted closer and wrapped my tiny arms around him. They didn't even fit all the way around his chest, but I squeezed as tightly as I could. His arm snaked around me and pulled me closer.

"It's like everything I look at reminds me of her," he wheezed, his eyes growing watery as the first tears began to sneak down his face. "You know, you do look quite a bit like her. Same hair, same olive skin, nearly the same eyes even. Maybe deep down, part of me wanted to bring you along because you reminded me of her, even if just a little."

"Do you…want me to leave?" I said in a tiny voice, my heart like lead. He replied by pulling me to his chest and hugging me as tightly as I did him.

"No, Micasa. Not ever," he sobbed. Together, we cried in silence until well after the sun had disappeared.

Chapter 19

The Nostalgic Man

Neither Hawke nor I felt that leaving the gypsy camp in such spirits would bode well on the last leg of our journey, and decided that some down time would do us both some good. This delighted the gypsies, who hadn't had any guests partake of their hospitality for a long while. They cleared out a tent for our use with astonishing speed, furnishing it with foldaway feather beds and a personal bath so quickly I suspected that they were betting on our extended stay the whole time.

Life around the camp seemed to be a neverending whirlwind of action. All of them rose at the first peep of sunlight, milling about with fierce energy that for the life of me I couldn't muster straight out of bed. Everyone had a hand in cooking breakfast for the camp, led by their head cook who called himself Porridge and seemed to perpetually have flour covered hands. While all the gypsies did their best to make food for the lot, Porridge moved so quickly in their slapdash kitchen it made wonder if he really needed the help in the first place. When I made an off-hand reference to the Sandwich Man, he chortled.

"I love that story!" he exclaimed, but he added with a wink, "The Sandwich Man doesn't have anything on me, though!" He scooped up a seemingly random assortment of ingredients he had just been preparing and started rolling them in his hands while whistling. After a couple seconds he held out his palm towards me, presenting the most elaborate breakfast biscuit I'd ever seen. One bite was all it took to see he wasn't just idly boasting.

"Uwa, it's so good!" I squeed through a mouthful of egg and salsa. He puffed up proudly and talked about cooking while I finished my food, then sent me off to help serve the others.

Everyone ate in a great tent that had been purposed into a sort of mess hall, where a nonstop cacophony of stories, jokes, and arguments clashed together over their meal. Once they finished, quick work was made of cleaning the dishes before everyone scattered to begin practice for the day.

Rehearsal was a vital part of their livelihood to them, for they never knew when their next performance was, as evidenced by the show they had given me the other day. Most of the time they simply honed their various expertise in solitude, but there were always at least one or two groups of gypsies who were discussing ways to fit their acts together. Fires were started, objects were sent flying, and arguments boiled into near fistfights everywhere you looked, and by the way everyone else reacted, it was clear that was simply the norm for them.

Hawke popped up one late afternoon after lunch looking for me. Before he could start talking, though, he was beset by a small mob of gypsies that surrounded him.

"Hawke, do something with this fire I need for my new trick!"

"Hey Hawke, can you do that mind lifty thing on me? I got a great idea!"

"Hawke, tell me what you think of this song I'm working on!"

He was pulled every which way and gave me an apologetic look as he let himself be dragged away to tend their requests. With all his power, it seemed he was well equipped for a life of entertainment. An image of Hawke in jester's motley and facepaint flashed through my head, and I had to fight hard to contain a fit of giggles.

When he had finally accommodated everyone an hour later or so, he found me again, looking like he had just been hauled through mud.

"I was afraid I'd never get away," he grumbled. He took a deep breath and tried his best to recompose himself before asking me if I was interested in starting swordplay lessons.

I was taken aback by the offer, mostly because Hawke had always seemed reluctant about the idea of me handling weapons. I still had the short-sword from Val'Hala, though, and it was the first lesson he had offered in something that didn't involve reading a book or playing with locks.

So, while the gypsies spent each day honing their acts, we found our own little corner of the grounds to practice in (relative) peace. He tried to introduce me to the proper way to grip a hilt, which way to attack when certain openings were made, and how to perform parries against an opponent.

The problem was that Hawke was, in fact, as terrible a teacher as he told me he had been long ago. He explained things too quickly for me to grasp, got irritated when I didn't pick it up right away, and would just as quickly skip to another lesson before I had any decent understanding of the last one. It was so bad we started drawing a crowd who would openly laugh at his attempts.

"Wow, this is beyond terrible!" cried out one young boy, only a few years older than myself, during a practice where Hawke was failing to explain how to disarm a foe. Hawke's face went rigid, and he turned on the boy with a wicked gleam in his eye.

"You're right, son. Perhaps a practical demonstration would help Micasa learn better," he crooned. "Would you be so kind as to grab a training sword and help me?" The boy flinched but, seeing that I had his attention, tried to make a show of bravado.

"The name's not 'son,' it's Darkfire!" he declared. Hawke slapped his palm to his face as the boy stammered, "O-of course I'll help!" He flounced away and returned shortly with a dulled metal blade. Hawke was already standing at the ready with his usual sword poised, still splotched as ever with rust.

"H-hey, I thought we were just training!" the boy calling himself Darkfire whimpered when he caught sight of the curved blade. Hawke put on a reassuring sneer.

"Oh, this old thing is even duller than yours," he promised the lad. "Now, you've been taught the basics, I'm sure? Good. Micasa, you signal when to begin."

The two squared off, Darkfire with knees trembling and my companion looking ready to fall asleep. At my call, the boy launched at Hawke. In less than a second, the training blade was on the ground and Darkfire was yelping in surprise. Hawke looked like he had barely twitched.

"And that's the proper way to disarm someone," Hawke declared with a smug look.

"You went too fast. I didn't see a thing," I said. Someone coughed behind me, and I turned to see Mirth looking angrily at the two of them.

"Are you really baring Symphony at children now, Hawke?" he said, his tone cold. For once, Hawke had nothing to retort with. Mirth turned his gaze on the boy. "And, Darkfire, you know better than to make a nuisance of yourself to guests! Now go find something useful to do!" He looked back to Hawke. "Both of you!" And with that, he was gone.

The boy muttered some apologies and skittered off with the training sword. The few who had watched their quick scuffle shambled away, some still snickering or shaking their heads. Hawke had turned a deep shade of red.

"Sorry, Micasa, I did something really stupid there." he muttered.

"Kinda. What did Mirth call your sword? Symphony?"

"Huh, I thought I had mentioned that before," he said bemusedly. "Yeah, Rouge gave it that name long ago. She said watching me practice with it looked like I was conducting a symphony, and the name just sort of stuck."

"Ooh, did she give you that sword?" I asked.

"No, Uraj made it for me. That was a long time ago, though." The color drained from his face as his stare trailed off into what I could only assume was a distant memory. When I asked him if he was okay, he blinked and shrugged off the question.

"I think we've practiced enough for one day. I'll take Mirth's advice and go find something else to do," he said. He gave me a little wave as he trundled off.

Of course, when Hawke said he was going to do something, it was a sure bet that he was going to sit at Rouge's grave. When he wasn't sleeping, eating, or trying to teach me the way of the sword, it was the only other place he spent time. Sometimes I would join him, and we would sit for some hours without a word between us. He never complained when I was there, but I knew that there were times when he likely just wanted to be alone and sort his thoughts. This seemed to be one of those times.

My sword "lessons" were the only thing I really had to look forward to during the day. Without those, I was left to wander around camp and find ways to pass the time. Mostly this boiled down to watching the performers at their craft or trying to strike up conversations with those who were taking a break. They were friendly to be sure, but I had little idea what to say to them other than talking about what they were working on.

The only one who seemed interested in seeking me out to talk was Mirth himself. He would frequently show up when I was sitting by myself, and we would talk about whatever popped into our heads. That was how I found out he was more or less the de facto leader of the gypsies, though I had gathered as much by the reverence the others showed him on matters around the camp. He would ask at length about my adventures with

Hawke, taking a keen interest in my growing talent with locks.

"Hawke's told me you were once a slave, is that right?" he brought up during one of our conversations. I nodded, trying my best to suppress the memories that came flooding back at the mention. Mirth nodded sadly.

"You may not believe it, but many of us here have been down that path too," he confided in me.

"Really?" I found it hard to believe with how upbeat everyone seemed all the time.

"Indeed. Very few children are born into our ways," Mirth explained. "Almost all our numbers are runaways: some from slavery, others from the army, and some who were just tired of the life they were living." He gave me a meaningful look. "We're always willing to take newcomers into our ways, if you need a place where you'll be accepted for who you are."

I wasn't expecting the offer. Of all the places I'd been, it certainly was one where I felt most at ease. Still, I shook my head.

"I want to keep traveling with Hawke," I told him. "But I'd love to come visit you all again someday!" His mustache scrunched up as he grinned.

"Of course, child. You and Hawke will always be welcomed like family." He gave me a gentle pat on the back and stood with a groan to leave. Before he left, he added, "Oh, speaking of children, I haven't seen you playing with any of them around here. Maybe you should introduce yourself?"

I hadn't thought even once about trying to reach out to the kids of the camp. I had seen them from time to time playing games or watching the adults practice from afar, and a couple times they even yelled at me, trying to get me to join them. Truth was, I was uncomfortable around children my age. I spent basically my whole life only speaking to and interacting with adults, so I had no idea what to say to or do with other kids.

I decided that maybe it was time to take that plunge and went to go find some to talk to. It didn't take long to find a few of them squatting in a circle and cheering. As I approached with trepidation, one of them noticed me and waved wildly.

"You're just in time! The race is almost over!" she cried out, pointing excitedly at whatever they were watching. I ventured close enough to see a pair of snails were gliding languidly along the ground. They were going completely different directions, and I couldn't make out any point in either one's path that would constitute a finish line.

"Uh, who's winning?" I broached. They all tried to exclaim over each other.

"I am!" "No, I am!" "I picked both!"

I was almost overwhelmed by their enthusiasm for something so ridiculous, but my curiosity once again got the better of me. I stuck around until one of the boys hopped into the air with fists held up triumphantly.

"I knew it, yes!" he bellowed, running to me. "You came here with Hawke, right? I'm Shrub!" He pointed to the girl who had waved me over. "That's Goggles, and he's Potato!" The boy he pointed to looked dejected, though I couldn't figure why: both snails had barely moved from where I last saw them.

"I'm, uh, Micasa," I introduced with a nervous chuckle. "I like your names."

"Thanks!" exclaimed Goggles. "Everyone here gets to pick their own!" She turned back to their other friend. "Stop being a baby, Potato! Micasa is here to play now!"

As if just noticing me, the boy rubbed the snot from his nose and bounded to his feet. "Now we have enough for leaf racing!" Potato declared, which sent Goggles and Shrub into a fit of cheers.

So that's how I was dragged along into their games, which they jumped between without a moment's notice most of the time. We skipped between racing leaves on tiny streams, hunting for the biggest pinecone (in a forest bereft of pine trees), seeing who could throw a stone farthest, and hide and seek. They barely bothered to explain the rules, and when they did usually broke them almost immediately. Yet by the end, I was laughing right along with them and making up my own rules along the way, to their delight as well as my own.

I decided to have a bit of fun with them by showing them my talent, pretending to close a padlock with the key and challenging them to open it. They scoffed, but soon all were throwing the lock on the ground in frustration and saying I broke it. I answered them by picking it up and shaking it open with one hand. They exploded in applause, making my face burn in humiliation.

"Can you do that to *anything*?" Potato asked in awe. When I nodded sheepishly, the three looked at each other with devilish intent.

Suddenly we were sneaking into Porridge's kitchen, with promises of some great treasure being whispered in my ear by the trio as we stealthily made our way to the cook's pantry. I saw what they had in mind the moment I laid eyes on the massive latch securing our target's bounty.

I felt guilty about sneaking behind the chef's back after he had been so nice to me, but the other kids were so excited I couldn't bring myself to disappoint them either. It took hardly an effort to break in, and in a flash the kids grabbed handfuls of sweets and cakes and were off, beckoning me to hurry. I took another second to secure the pantry again before we were all bolting away, running as if our lives depended on it.

Their unadulterated joy at our success seemed completely overblown to me when all we got away with was a bunch of junk food. That didn't stop me from joining in on their excitement as we reveled over our spoils.

And so the days passed in a whirlwind of watching the performers, training with Hawke, and spending time with my new young friends. Thinking about it now, it was perhaps the longest time Hawke and I ever stayed in a single place, even years later. It was the only place that ever really felt like a true home to me.

* * *

The cold fall nights often brought everyone into the largest tent during the evenings, where they built a great fire to warm themselves with after dinner while entertaining each other with grand tales and bawdy songs. It was during one of these little get-togethers that Hawke, who had avoided them for the most part, slid into the tent at some point and quietly watched from a little corner of his own. He had already been there for some time before even I noticed him, and I bade him join me as I roasted a marshmallow over the flame. He did so reluctantly, to the jeers and hollers of the gypsies berating him for hiding so long.

"Oy, Hawke, you're the only one who hasn't performed for a night!" Chestnut slurred at him. Her face had been steadily growing redder as she downed tankard after tankard. Shouts of agreement roared all around us.

"Yeah, even li'l Micasa put on a show with her locks! You gonna let her upstage you!?" cried Edge the knife thrower. Hawke gave me a sideways glance and smirked.

"Did you now?" he asked, making me turn away embarrassed. He chuckled. "Well, I guess you're right then. What should I do?"

A dozen suggestions were thrown at him, but he ignored them as his eyes scanned the crowd.

"Hey, Four Chords!" he finally shouted, getting the attention of a gypsy who was never seen without his acoustic guitar in tow. "Lend me Sheila for a bit!"

"Ah, a solo it is then?" the musician cackled as he slipped the instrument to my companion, "Be gentle with her, though, or I'll have yer head."

His warning brought a few laughs, but the look in his eye was deadly serious, and he only let go after a long hesitation. Hawke carefully strapped it to his shoulder and struck a few notes, reaching to the tuning pegs. He stopped short when Four Chords shot him a venomous glare.

"Write anything new while on the road?" Mirth asked while tending to the fire. Hawke shook his head.

"Well, this song is a bit of an old one, but only one other person has heard it before," he explained. The room itself seemed to dim as everyone grew somber. He looked up with a tiny smile. "We're leaving tomorrow, so I thought I'd make one last memory of Rouge to share with the troupe."

He strummed a couple chords, nodded to himself and took a deep breath, then began to play. The melody was surprisingly tender, yet not nearly as sad as I was expecting. When he began to sing, it was with a high, unusual twang I'd never heard him speak with.

I hear you whisper quietly you wish to soar away
escape from cold translucent nights and hollow pallid days
Yet even as your breath escapes and captivates the air
The only thing I notice is the passion in your stare

And oh! To watch a raven fly
without a place to land
all I can do is try
to catch her in my hand

Along a stretch of golden sand aside a shallow shore
Or to a kingdom tall and proud we've never seen before
No matter where, you're dancing, twirling, all the world's a game

But dazzling sights just can't compare to when you
call my name

And oh! To watch a raven fly
without a place to land
all I can do is try
to catch her in my hand

A thousand miles you've dared to roam
Yet there's still no place you call home
With fingers clasped in prayer I ask
to lift your eyes, remove your mask
Then maybe you'll come to rest at last

And oh! To watch a raven fly
without a place to land
all I can do is try
to catch her in my hand

And oh! I've borne each restless night
for what tomorrow brings-
The hope its morning light
may finally stay your wings

As the final notes slowly ebbed away, the room
was left in numb shock. The gypsies looked at one
another, none of them sure how to react. Hawke

gingerly gave the guitar back to its owner, who wore an unreadable expression as he hurried out into the night. Just when I thought he had struck them all speechless, a torrent of different reactions came pouring in.

"BAHAHAHA! I never struck you as a hopeless romantic, Hawke!" roared Chestnut at the top of her lungs. She looked to a few of her nearby friends for backup, but several were blushing furiously and fidgeting as they looked at the ground.

"Hey, Hawke, you need to teach me that ditty," Edge whispered as he leaned in close. "There's this little cutie in Val'Hala I've been sorta talking to that would flip for it. Oh, she's a blonde, though, you think it'd matter?"

All around us they were either laughing or looking with amazement at my friend. Mirth actually wiped a tear from his eye and clapped Hawke on the shoulder.

"Thank you for that," he said in a husky tone. "It's good to know that Rouge was loved so."

Hawke had turned almost purple from the flush creeping up his face, but he shrugged and laughed. "Truth be told, I always thought it was a silly song. I just sort of made it up one day while we were lolling around and bored. She was crazy for it, though, so I sung it all the time. As goofy as it was to me, it was worth playing a thousand times over for how it made her smile."

"No better reason needed, child," Mirth said with an approving nod.

As the gypsies started to mill about again and business went back to usual, Hawke turned to me. I thought he was going to ask how I liked the song, but something else was bothering him.

"I hope you don't mind heading out tomorrow," he said. "I just feel like I've done what I can here and am ready to finally finish what we started. Are you okay with that?" I nodded vigorously.

"Whenever you're ready, I am!" I exclaimed. He ruffled my hair and smiled.

"Great! We should get some shuteye then. We can head out right after breakfast." He stood and started to leave but halted mid-step.

"Oh, one last thing." Hawke turned and leaned in close, staring me straight in the eyes with a lifeless look that sent my spine tingling.

"If I hear again that you're using your power to steal from people, you will be punished. Is that clear, young lady?" he hissed. I was barely able to nod.

"Y-yessir."

* * *

It was hard to believe we had spent almost half a month with the gypsy band, and yet as we finished loading our bags onto Sir Brown Horse and saddled up again for the first time in weeks, I felt like I wouldn't have minded staying just a bit longer. Not a person was missing from the crowd as all the gypsies came to bade us farewell and best wishes on our journey. Mirth approached and clasped hands with Hawke.

"Will you be staying much longer?" asked Hawke. "When all this is finally done, I'd be glad to come stay for a while longer. I'm sure Micasa would, too," he added.

"Yesyesyesyesyes," I chimed in. Mirth howled with laughter.

"And we'd be delighted to have you again, but we'll be picking up roots and heading out soon. We stayed here to fulfil our obligation to you, and now it's time we get back to our ways. Gypsies weren't meant to lay down for so long." Hawke gave a small appreciative bow.

"Of course. Here's hoping our paths cross again soon," he bade Mirth, clasping hands one more time. Shouts of goodbye rained on us from the troupe, and I waved at all of them as I returned their farewells. With a last glance over his shoulder, Hawke nudged Sir Brown Horse to a canter and led us onto the main road. Their cries seemed to follow us even long after they had vanished from sight.

"I really want to see them again," I told Hawke, "and Blake, and the Medicine Man, and Winter, and Char. I really hope we can see them soon." Hawke's sights were firmly fixed on the road ahead.

"I do too," he said, "but first, I have one last piece of unfinished business."

Chapter 20

The Dead Man

Damkarei.

After hundreds of miles of journeying through seemingly endless expanses of fields and mountains and forests, to behold a place where the land itself stopped stole my breath away. The city looked much as the others we had been through did, but I couldn't tear my eyes from the ribbon of sparkling blue glittering in the sunlight, stretching completely across the horizon. Somehow, its mere presence bolstered the town into something unto a dream: the City of Two Kings.

"I forgot, this is probably the first time you've seen the ocean, isn't it?" Hawke asked. I sighed in awe.

"It's the most beautiful thing I've ever seen," I whispered. I didn't want to ruin the moment by making too much noise. I would have gladly stared at it for hours, but Hawke tapped me on the shoulder.

"When we're done, we can go right down to the beach, how about that?" he offered. I twisted in my seat to look at him with my most pleading expression.

"Yes, please!" I cried to his amusement.

"Okay, okay, it's a promise. Hopefully, things won't go too roughly." The humor vanished from his face. "Nothing is ever simple with Uraj, though."

"You don't think he'll give your essence back?" I asked him.

"Hard to say. The Uraj I used to know would have never gone along with something like this. Rouge wasn't there to answer my questions, and she didn't tell her troupe anything about this whole mess, but I *know* Uraj knows what's going on. And I'm not leaving until I find out."

The land gently sloped downward as we approached the seaside city, the aroma of salt spray lingering in the air. High above us, white gulls circled lazily overhead and screeched to one another. A few followed our progress down the road, perhaps smelling our food and hoping for something to scrounge. The late morning sun reflected off the sea, the two fiery orbs casting a white glare over everything for miles.

I was still enjoying the splendor of our destination when my body lurched forward. It felt as if someone had placed a sack of bricks on top of me, my body growing so heavy that I couldn't even straighten myself. A low rumble filled my ears as the pressure built. Sir Brown Horse shrieked in terror as his knees buckled, nearly toppling him over.

Hawke swore loudly. As quickly as it had come, the feeling subsided. I gasped like I had been submerged and just allowed to come up for air. Hawke's breathing sharpened too, but it was his face, now contorted in anger, that had changed the most.

"What was that!?" I said, still struggling to catch my breath.

"Uraj, of course," Hawke growled, placing a hand on my shoulder protectively. "Sorry, Micasa, I should have expected this."

"But what did he do!?" I looked around but could see no signs of anyone else near us. If Uraj was hiding, I thought, he was good.

"He's not here," Hawke explained when he saw me frantically searching the area. "It's a trick you can do with your essence. Basically, you surround yourself with it, and you can tell when something enters or moves inside the area. For people who can't use their essence to protect themselves, it feels like a terrible pressure surrounding you. Uraj himself is likely there–" He pointed past me towards a jagged shape that dwarfed the other buildings of the town, "–our old castle. He always did have a fondness for it, even as it crumbled around us."

It looked to be another mile at least before we even reached the edge of the city proper. It made me shudder to think, how strong was Uraj if he could reach this far with his essence?

"At least he didn't keep it up," I said, trying to think positively. Hawke laughed dryly.

"Oh no, he's still scrying. I've just put an aura around us like a bubble, so you and the horse won't feel its effects. Thing is, he knows I'm here now; he's definitely already sensed my essence. Surprise won't be an option anymore."

The town itself was larger than I had assumed from a distance, at least rivaling Val'Hala in size. The biggest difference between the two, aside from the lack of walls guarding Damkarei, was the assortment of people milling about the streets as we rode in without incident.

Right away it was clear that something was wrong. Despite the number of citizens we saw going on with their business, it was eerily quiet. There were no idle conversations being held, vendors and customers did business with curt hand gestures and broke away as soon as they could. Even the occasional barking dog or screaming child I had heard time and again in other towns was nowhere to be found here. I turned to Hawke, only to see he had pulled the hood of his cloak over his features and kept his head held low. He held a finger to his lips, telling me to hold my tongue for the moment.

Hawke rode straight to an inn and paid for a room and stabling for Sir Brown Horse. The entire transaction consisted of nothing more than a handful of coins shoved into the innkeep's hands and a terse nod. Once our things were loaded into a room and locked, we spent some time trying to placate our steed now that it would have no shield from Uraj's presence. When at last we calmed him enough to hopefully leave him be for a while, we set to the streets on foot.

I expected Hawke to head straight to the castle, but instead he led me inside a small tavern situated down a secluded alleyway. The room was nearly empty, save for a lone patron drinking alone at the bar and the proprietor leaning against a banister with a foul mood etched in his features.

Hawke bade me to sit at a booth in the far corner while he approached the barkeep and started talking to him in whispers. I had barely situated myself at the table when Hawke returned, still not speaking. Shortly after, the barkeep returned with a mug for Hawke and a small glass of milk for me. He nearly slammed the containers down before spinning around wordlessly and returning to his favorite brooding spot.

"Keep your voice down as much as possible," he murmured out of the corner of his mouth. "We don't want to arouse too much suspicion."

"What would they be suspicious of?" I whispered back. Hawke gestured with his head towards the door.

"You saw how everyone was acting. They can feel Uraj's essence too. Imagine having to go around feeling that pressure on you for long periods of time. All of Damkarei is on edge, and seeing me might set them off."

"Seeing you?"

"The city knows who I am, Micasa," he pointed out. "All they think is that Uraj is angry right now and is taking it out on them. They've probably heard he's looking for me, and if they realize I'm here, it might start a riot. It's best to just take care of this as subtly as possible."

"So why are we here?" I asked.

Hawke sighed. "I was hoping to get some information about what Uraj has been up to these past several years. The barrister here I've long known to keep his ear to the ground, and I'd hoped he could tell me something I could use. I just learned now how strained the situation is."

As he was talking, what looked like a child entered the bar and glanced around. He was greeting the barkeep when his eyes landed on us. Without hesitation, he marched over and took a seat next to Hawke, to my friend's astonishment. It was only now that I remembered having seen him before.

"Samuel," Hawke put voice to my thoughts, "I had forgotten you were working for my old colleague."

The diminutive man looked between us with all the passivity he had shown in our first meeting. "Uraj has requested me to come escort the both of you to the castle. He informed me I would find you here," he explained.

"The both of us? Micasa too?" Hawke looked shocked.

"He was very clear that the girl was to accompany you," said Samuel. My friend shook his head.

"I don't like this. Micasa won't be safe there. She has to stay behind," he protested. I had assumed I was going with him regardless, and was going to argue his decision, but our guide spoke up first.

"Uraj also asked me to tell you that if she didn't come, he would make things worse for the townsfolk." At this, Hawke bit his lip. A growl rumbled in his throat, and a moment later he threw his arms up in defeat.

"Fine," he hissed, then adding, "Micasa, don't leave my side for a second." I nodded, not interested in the least to experience that pressure from before. Samuel stood and walked to the door, waiting while Hawke and I quickly finished our drinks and rose. Without so much as a glance spared between the three of us, we were out the door and on the winding road leading towards the far edge of town.

A large stone bridge spanned a considerable moat that surrounded our destination. The trench below our feet seemed to feed directly from the ocean, and in the receding waters of low tide, a carpet of sharp barbs peeked out from the bottom. A few strands of seaweed and the occasional unlucky sea creature could be seen clinging to them.

The castle itself looked as if it had once been a grand edifice that had reached towards the sky during days long forgotten. A few towers still yawned upward, casting deep shadows in the waning daylight. The outer courtyard, full of weeds and overgrowth, was littered with crumbling statues and fragments of the curtain wall that had cracked off over who knows how many years.

Samuel led us through the ruins, past rotted wooden stables and what may have once been a chapel to the Holy Tenet, to the castle proper. He stopped next to a pair of heavy iron doors and crossed his arms.

"In here," the disciple said, not meeting our eyes. "I go no further."

Hawke snorted impatiently. "The audience room. Of course he would make a show of all this." He yanked on the handle, and the heavy gate groaned open with reluctance. Taking me by the hand, he took one last breath of the outside air and led me over the threshold.

The corridor was dark as night, the slip of light from the door like the moon trying to cut through the clouds. Once we started inside, even that disappeared and we were left sightless. I could hear Hawke scrabbling along the walls, and a few seconds later a torch flared to life in his hand, blinding me momentarily. When the spots cleared away, I could just make out the dusty stone walls and floor, with dozens of unlit torches sitting idly in their sconces.

We had only ventured a scant few yards further into the long hallway when a great whooshing sound filled the air. All at once the dormant torches sprung to life, their flames leaving our passage awash in an orange glow. Hawke sneered and tossed the light he had been holding to the ground.

"He's playing with us," he said slowly. Maybe it was my imagination, but the torch fires seemed to flicker up and down. His hand found mine again, his grip tightening uncomfortably as we made our way towards the blackened square at the end of the hallway.

Even with all the light pouring into our path, the chamber we stepped into was a blanket of shadow smothering our eyes. Hawke held me back with a hand, bidding we should continue no further into the room. Somewhere in the inky depths came a hissing sound, and again the darkness was banished from a multitude of fires roaring into existence.

The room was vast enough to hold a hundred people comfortably, carpeted in moldy rugs that had forgotten what color they were long ago. Aside from the half-dozen large braziers that illuminated the room with their crackling flames, the only furnishings were a pair of chairs hewn from granite standing atop a single large step. The throne on the right was smashed to pieces, its remains scattered about the base as if it had just been destroyed and nobody could be bothered to clean it up.

The second throne was clearly occupied.

It looked like someone had laid a suit of mottled grey armor into the chair and arranged it to resemble a person sitting in it. As we cautiously crept closer, though, it was clear that *something* was nestled inside. A mop of stringy white hair poked out of a dark shape just visible from the armor's collar, and as I peered to make out its owner I nearly shrieked in fright.

The face that gazed at us was almost identical to the ghoul that had accosted me on the old plantation. Leathery flesh stretched across its skull, its mouth devoid of teeth and perpetually hanging open.

It was the eyes staring at us now, piercing silver, that drew the only difference between this creature and the lifeless being from days past. This was something that should have died long ago, yet the spark behind those eyes said that it wasn't ready to see the other side. The curious hiss from before escaped from its leathery lips, and now I could barely make out the words.

"*Hawke, you're looking well.*" it spoke, its mouth barely moving as the words slurred out.

"I've heard that more than once on the way here," Hawke said. His words were sharp, but there was no mirth in his features, no warmth to his tone.

"*I thought you'd never make it here.*"

"How could I not? I can feel the pull coming from you even now. You have it," he accused.

"*Scholar,*" it breathed. Hawke tensed at the word, but the figure broke contact with him as its eyes darted to fix on me. My blood froze in my veins.

"*Who is the girl?*" came the forced words from the husk. Hawke looked between me and it, confusion etching lines across his face.

"Micasa? Didn't you tell Samuel to have me bring her?"

"*I assumed Rouge would be with you. I meant her.*" The suit of armor rattled as its wearer shifted slightly.

Hawke's eyes darkened. "Rouge is dead, Uraj."

A wisp of noise passed out of the effigy, the barest excuse of a gasp.

"*This... isn't what we planned.*" it breathed. A jolt ran through my friend's body.

"You didn't *plan* this? Then what DID you plan, Uraj!? What was this all about!?" he screeched at the desiccated remnants of the king. Uraj remained silent for some time. "TELL ME!" Hawke bellowed even louder. The figure sucked in a shuddering breath.

"*Not yet.*" Its head tilted to the side. "*All would go to waste if I simply told you.*"

"Then what do you want!?" Hawke roared with clenched fists. In response, a low rumbling started to fill the room. The flames danced wildly as if caught in a wind storm, and a cascade of dust rained from the roof. Slowly, so slowly that I thought I was seeing things, the figure of the Forge rose from the throne. The suit of armor clanked noisily against itself, hanging off a frame ill-suited to wear it. The withered face turned to regard Hawke, and its silver eyes sparkled in the flames.

"*I want what's yours.*" Those horrible deadened lips pulled back into a mockery of a smile. Hawke's own lip curled in disgust, and in a flash, he was gone.

Hawke was on Uraj with his sword drawn before I had noticed he had moved. The blade was a reddish blur aimed straight at the Forge's shriveled head, but it stopped short with a crack of thunder. Undeterred, Hawke stepped back and whirled around to bring his sword up towards one of the joints in the loose armor, point first. Again, it jolted to a halt inches from its target with another resounding crash. Hawke's assault was relentless, and yet it was like an invisible wall had been placed all around Uraj that deflected any attack made on him.

I was so transfixed on their struggle that I gasped when a bead of sweat stung my eyes. I thought the tension was making me perspire, but no – the room had grown unbearably warm during the last few seconds. It was also considerably brighter than I remember when we had entered. Tearing my attention away from the fight, I blanched in horror at the sight of the braziers surrounding the room. Their flames stretched toward the ceiling, fingers of heat twisting and grasping upwards.

On some unseen cue, the scorching pillars swayed and descended as one, like snakes striking out. Hawke glanced upward a split second before they would engulf him. In a single bound, he catapulted himself backwards and out of harm's way. The combined force of the flames scorched the very stone black, their impact sending a wave of shimmering heat directly towards the both of us. Hawke screamed an obscenity as he put his hands together and swept them apart as he did in Val'Hala.

It was something like out of a dream, the inferno splitting into two tempests that raged completely around both of us. It dissipated quickly, revealing Uraj still standing right where it had been before. The emaciated visage looked down at the burned dais and let out a dusty chuckle.

"*Close*," was all it had to say. Hawke glanced back at me as if to ascertain my safety, before whirling back on his foe.

"If you're intentionally trying to hurt Micasa…" he started, letting the venom in his tone finish for him. The Forge's head turned shakily to one side, then the other.

"*Only you,*" it insisted. The braziers began to burn fiercely again.

"Micasa, keep back a bit," barked Hawke with a wave of his hand. "I can't trust that you'll be safe if you stand this close to him."

I scuttled off until I was practically at the door, but I could hear the clap of their attacks already starting again before I had turned around.

My companion was striking out in a fury of blows, each landing with a louder peal of thunder than the first. They still refused to make contact, but even with his essence shielding him from harm, Uraj was rocked back and forth with every strike. His flames struck individually now, firing from the braziers and lashing out like hellish whips. Hawke paused his charge only to duck or pirouette out of harm's way. The few tongues of fire that did find him rolled away harmlessly thanks to his own essence, but even when dodging, he would flow right back into his strikes the moment he was out of danger. I understood then what the name of his style – "Sword Tempo" – truly signified.

They might have fought for hours. In the heat of the moment, literal and figurative, there was no telling how long their powers would hold out. It seemed that Hawke was gaining the upper hand, though, as Uraj staggered more and more with each deflected blow. Its conjured flames began to sputter as if sensing their master's predicament.

With a mighty swing, Hawke brought his sword into the breastplate of the burnished armor where it finally made contact, burying deep into the steelwork. Uraj slumped to his knees and the living fire receded until the braziers were left with little more than glowing coals that filled the room with shadows. Without hesitation, Hawke lashed out his free hand straight towards Uraj's cadaverous, unprotected face.

There was a snap, and a lobstered gauntlet met Hawke's grasp. Uraj's arm bent at the elbow in the wrong direction. Their fingers entwined, steel on flesh. Hawke grimaced, pulling back like he was trying to break the grip, but Uraj somehow managed to hold firm.

A sucking sound emanated from the hollow that was the Forge's mouth, and his mailed hand began to glow an angry orange. Smoke curled from between their hands, a heartbeat before Hawke's hand burst into flame.

I shrieked at the same time as Hawke. Their grip released, and my guardian went stumbling backwards off the dais while holding his burning hand over his head. Uraj was staggering to its feet, a steady hiss still emitting from its frozen mouth, Symphony still lodged in its plate. I watched on, horrified, as the flames consuming Hawke's arm slowly crept towards his shoulder. Uraj's focus was fixed on that flame, the air warping around him as he bade the fire to engulf my friend.

Hawke finally recovered from his surprise and held the arm in front of himself, concentrating intensely. The flames stopped climbing, but still burned fiercely. Hawke grimaced and knit his brow in effort. The smell of cooked flesh was filling the room and making my stomach lurch. Finally, the fire began to flicker and sputter, and then at last die down completely.

The relief was short lived when I saw why the flames had vanished: there was simply nothing else to burn. Hawke's arm had been completely incinerated, to the point where even the bone had been reduced to ash. Hawke panted, sweat and tears streaming down his face, as he surveyed the blackened stump that remained.

The sight was enough to curdle my blood, but before I had a chance to grieve, the stump twitched. A tangled mess of flesh, muscle, and bone sprouted from the wound and writhed. Like some morbid artist at work, the shape twisted and folded until landing on the shape of an arm, where it tightened and lay still.

Hawke took a few seconds to flex the fingers of his new appendage. His breathing slowed, and his body relaxed as the last of the pain subsided. For all that had happened in those couple minutes, the worst he had been left off with was a missing sleeve from his robe.

Then Uraj laughed.

Chapter 21

The King of Men

It was like someone was sawing through green wood. The hollow man threw its head back and the sound poured out, echoing against the stonework walls. Then came the choking noise. Its whole body began to convulse and shudder. The armor rattled like it was alive. Even so, the thing that was Uraj continued to laugh its macabre laugh.

Then its face began to swell. The greyed, leathery flesh brightened, the eyes rose from their sunken sockets. Teeth erupted from desiccated gums. Platinum hair burst forth from its scalp to join with what wiry remnants had been there before. Its broken arm jolted and snapped back into proper shape.

The suit of plate that had before been hanging limply ballooned outwards, filling with bulging arms and stocky legs and a barrel chest. No more did the figure slump with the weighty steel's encumbrance. It stretched upwards to a height akin to Hawke's, and still it laughed. Now, though, there was music to this laughter. It sang a song of feelings long forgotten and warmly remembered.

When at last all grew quiet, a man stood where before was only an abomination. He lowered his head, loose strands of his newly grown hair falling around his shoulders. His eyes, more alive than they had been in decades, danced over us. Stout fingers caressed the side of his face that once held a scar, vanished with the last traces of the husk we had met. He let out a throaty chuckle and held out his arms as if to welcome us for the first time.

Uraj Kuznetsov, the Old King, the Forge, had been revived.

"It's more than I had dreamed," his voice rumbled in a polished baritone. He bounced a little on the balls of his feet, swung his arms, twisted his neck. Each little move made him titter like a child. "I never thought I'd feel this good again."

Hawke's face was aghast. He looked mutely from his arm to the man before him.

"This was what you wanted all along," he said.

Uraj smiled amicably at him. The look came across as patronizing on his face. "Of course. You think I enjoyed being a shriveled prune of a person? I thought observation was supposed to be your expertise, 'Scholar.'" He chuckled a little. Hawke bristled, his fists clenching until his knuckles turned white.

"Oh, that reminds me," the Forge added. He held up his left hand asking for patience while his right reached underneath his breastplate and rummaged a bit. With a tug, he dislodged the largest shinestone I had ever seen from the depths of his armor. Large as a grapefruit, it pulsed a dark purple in his grip.

"Catch," he called out, tossing the stone underhand to my companion. Hawke snatched it out of the air with both hands. Light flooded the room, and even with my prior experience with the phenomena, I was caught unaware and rendered blind. My eyes watered, and I desperately blinked to try and clear my vision. When at last it returned, Hawke was standing where he had been before.

He looked no different than usual, and at the same time, it felt like I was seeing him for the first time. When he looked back at me, I saw I was only partly right about his unchanged appearance, for where he once had pale blue eyes, they had turned a glittering silver.

"I'm sure it's felt like ages since you've felt whole, Hawke," Uraj said. His own eyes had changed too, deepening to a hazel so dark they were almost black. He wrenched Symphony from where it still lodged in his armor and tossed it across the floor. It slid until it struck Hawke's foot. My friend made no move to pick it up.

The Forge shrugged and took his seat on the throne again, arms curling around their rests. Seeing him sitting there, resplendent in his battle raiment and hardened features regarding us, I could understand why people would bow their head to him as their king.

"I assume an explanation is in order," he said after some time.

"Damn right," Hawke snapped. He turned his eyes of quicksilver on his former colleague, boiling with anger.

"Long story short, I made a plan where Rouge would help me gain your power of rejuvenation. Things went horribly wrong," Uraj summed up quickly. Hawke narrowed his eyes.

"Uh, I want the long version, jackass," was his reply. Uraj leaned his forehead on steepled fingers.

"Yes, of course you would," Uraj mumbled. If I didn't know better, I would have said he looked embarrassed. He cleared his throat.

"Hawke, we've been trying to scrape together some semblance of life for humanity for over four centuries. That's a long time." Uraj raised an eyebrow, "Honestly, longer than either of us have any right to living. And yet how far have we really gotten? We've eked out this meager existence on our little pile of dirt we call Astra, yet the grinel still hold the only remaining continent on the planet; one almost thrice the size of our island. Their resources far outstrip ours, their numbers are greater, and their average citizen could be a match for ten of our greatest warriors."

"What's this have to do with my situation?" Hawke said impatiently. Uraj bared his teeth.

"Think about something other than yourself for once!" he snarled. "Why are we allowed to continue to live here? These aren't the days of old. The grinel have ships now. They could easily sail here and overwhelm us, wreaking havoc the likes of which we haven't seen since the Pilgrimage. What's to stop them?"

Uraj seemed to be waiting for an answer, but when none came, he sighed.

"*We're* here, Hawke. The grinel still fear us, they fear what we did to the grinel who were here before. They might be able to conquer us with their full force, but the damage they sustain would be catastrophic. They don't want to risk it."

"Okay, I can see where you're coming from," Hawke acquiesced. "So you wanted my healing was because you feared that if you died, we'd lose half our bargaining power."

"Basically," Uraj said. "I may be able to resurrect myself, but it takes far too long for me to regain my strength afterwards. Time that the grinel could use to undo all our work. If I could gain your healing, though, that would never be an issue again."

Hawke flopped onto the ground and crossed his legs. Leaning his cheek against a hand, he stared at the ground lost in thought. "So why take my Scholar power? Why not just take my healing and be done with it?"

"Hawke, whatever disagreements we have, I would never want you dead or irreparably injured," the Forge said. For a man with such a hardened face, I wouldn't have thought it possible to see tears streaking down his face. Yet there they were, tracing shining lines along the old soldier's face.

He didn't strike me as the type who could fake something like that.

"I didn't want to *steal* the power from you," he elaborated. "If I had just taken a shinestone with your healing, I'd have to keep it. No, I wanted to *copy* it."

Hawke nodded. "And the only way to do that was the power of the Scholar."

"Exactly." Uraj idly drummed his fingers on his knee, twirled a lock of his hair, and fidgeted incessantly as he talked. He was clearly uncomfortable with where the story was leading. He took a deep breath to steady himself and pressed on.

"The plan seemed simple. Rouge would give me your power of the Scholar; I give you some minor injury when you come back to take it. Then you heal, I copy it, and I give you back the Scholar's power."

"When did you even have time to plan this?" Hawke interjected.

Uraj looked at him as if he were joking for a second. "You don't remember? Those seven odd years ago when Rouge and you came to Damkarei for a short visit?" When Hawke shook his head, Uraj's brow furrowed. "I thought all your memories were together."

"They were. Some slave owner had them. He had me working for him too." Hawke's glare returned. "You still haven't explained how *that* happened."

"Well," Uraj dragged the word out, "there was a complication when Rouge tried to pull the power of the Scholar out of you. Turns out that your other powers were tied to it, so to speak. When she broke that one piece of your essence away, your entire soul fragmented.

"Rouge wasn't expecting that, and in her panic, she did her best to contain what pieces she could. Unfortunately, the core of your essence escaped. Without that, she couldn't put the fragments she had caught back in you. She came to me in hysterics, begging me to help. That was the second big mistake, though, because she left you alone in the rooms you two were sharing. By the time we came back to check on you, you were gone."

"She *left* me like that?" Hawke's voice was choked with disbelief.

"Rouge wasn't thinking logically at that point, Hawke. She assumed in your condition, you couldn't get yourself into any trouble. We're not sure whether your soulless body wandered away on its own or if you were abducted, but we found out soon after that you had fallen into the clutches of slave traders.

"Rouge left me the power of the Scholar and rushed off to find you. I would have come too, but you saw the state I was in just a short while ago. Even seven years ago, I was long past any shape for extended travel."

Uraj's knees were jittering now. "I didn't hear from her again for over three years. Finally, she returned one day, looking as if she had hardly rested since her departure. She had found you in the clutches of the slave owner you mentioned. She tried to fix you there, but your core was still missing. Try as she might, she couldn't put your essence back in you. She feared that if she tried to steal you away, you would be killed, whether by your captor or on the journey home.

"In a last desperate effort to try and fix the problem, she left you there and placed your memories in the care of the man, threatening dire consequences if either were harmed. You know how much people fear the wrath of the gypsies; it was that fear she bet on to keep him compliant. Nobody wishing you harm would think to look for you serving under some lowly plantation owner, or at least that's what she hoped.

"She couldn't trust him enough to keep all your power, though, lest he use it for himself. Instead, she bestowed the others to the protection of people who had been indebted to you through your endeavors abroad: 'a young former student, an ex-soldier once saved on the battlefield, and an old caretaker,' as well as Char, Luke, and Lady Lheona, she told me. The only chance she saw was if your core could find its way back to your body on its own, and once done, you would be able to recollect your essence bit by bit."

All throughout the rest of Uraj's tale, Hawke listened with rapt attention. The Forge paused, looking to his old friend for some sort of reaction. Silent as stone, Hawke stood from the ground and popped the kinks in his neck.

"You knew I would return," Hawke stated at last. I wasn't sure if he was asking Uraj or confirming a thought. Either way, the Old King leaned forward and nodded.

"Your body still lived. If the core of your essence – your soul – had moved on, you would have simply died. What saved you was my own power. The first power you had ever learned."

"But isn't your power control over fire?" I blurted. Uraj startled, apparently having forgotten I was still standing there.

"Hawke, you still haven't told me who the girl is," he said. I flinched, expecting him to be upset. His eyes danced over me, but they were filled with curiosity more than irritation. Hawke briefly explained the situation that had led to our adventures.

"A slave girl and budding savant of essence, no less," the Forge mused when at last Hawke finished. He regarded me gently. "Well, you're partially right, Micasa. My power does allow control over flame, as it did when I first discovered it. Has Hawke ever told you about how powers can expand over time with practice?"

I thought of how my own power had changed over the course of our journey, growing to the point where I could work locks without even touching them. Uraj was watching me still with those dark eyes, waiting for a response. It felt like he was reading my slightest movement, drinking in my most subtle quirks. He would know if I was lying. I nodded.

"Well," he said, "my own power goes beyond simply controlling fire. I can control energy itself.

To put it simpler," he waved his hand around trying to grasp for the words, "think of my essence as the fire of my life. Because of that, I can control it too. Does that make sense?"

It didn't, and my befuddlement must have read on my face, because Uraj sighed and rubbed his temple.

"Then let me ask this. On your journeys, did Hawke ever show you that he could control fire?"

I was about to deny it, but memories of our trip to Sapir filled my head. I remembered his demonstration with the lantern: my first introduction to the concept of "powers." My silence told Uraj everything he wanted to know. He leaned back and smirked.

"The power he gained from me so long ago is as much a part of him as it is a part of me," he concluded. "I knew that core would one day find a way back to its owner. It's why I've waited here, for this very day: the day he would return and the Old Kings would both be restored to their former glory."

He turned back to my friend, his former companion. "Hawke, I understand there is no way for me to simply apologize for what we schemed. This plan of mine almost cost us everything. Our lives, the lives of everyone on Astra, everything we have worked towards for hundreds of years." Uraj covered his face with a large, gauntleted hand.

"Yet now we have another chance to try and set things right in our world. We can work together, without worry of time or age, to try and build that better world for humans we originally worked for. I know I have no right to ask more of you, but I beg you–" he clasped his hands and looked up, "–for the good of everyone, take your place beside me again. Rule with me, make the Old Kings two once more."

Hawke had been frightfully quiet for a very long time. Uraj and I were both looking to him for some response. A nod, a grimace, a yawn, anything. He only held his place stubbornly. His eyes, on the other hand, told of the storm raging inside him. They were heated mercury, on the cusp of boiling over.

At last, he moved. He bent at the waist and picked up his precious Symphony.

"You think this is over?" he said. His fingers tightened around the hilt. "You think everything is solved?"

The air came alive. Sparks danced around us, and a wind picked up like a hurricane. Was this

Hawke's real strength? I wondered, as his energy crackled against my skin. There was malice in that energy, but it wasn't pointed at me. It was aimed straight ahead, at the figure watching with widening eyes.

This time Hawke didn't vanish as he had before. His feet pounded on the stone, his face twisting in rage, his sword levied towards the Forge. Uraj made no move to defend himself. Arms lowered, face passive, it almost looked as if he *wanted* Hawke to attack. He got his wish.

The blade pierced steel and flesh and muscle and stone alike, skewering straight through Uraj's armored body and embedding deep into the occupied granite throne. Uraj grunted, flinched, but didn't fight back. A stream of crimson trickled from the hole in his breastplate. It flowed past his legs and spilled over the edge of the throne, pooling at the foot.

"Tell me what you said," Hawke grunted through clenched teeth. "What you threatened, what you did to Rouge. Tell me how you forced her to do this to me." He gave his sword a sharp twist. Even I winced at the sound of blade and essence tearing Uraj's armor further. Uraj himself shuddered, but still kept his composure. Of course, I knew that at this point the platinum-haired king could not be killed, and surely Hawke remembered too. Did his anger blind him so much he had forgotten?

Uraj's gaze flickered between Hawke and me. Then the Forge licked his lips and leaned in towards Hawke, pushing himself until the blade was buried in him to the hilt. He leaned until his mouth was so close to Hawke's ear their faces were brushing. His lips moved, but so quietly did he whisper that I couldn't tell if he was saying a word at all.

He must have, for Hawke went pale as a new woolen sheet. The man who was once a king fell on his ass, staring up as befuddled as a child.

"No, that's ridiculous," he muttered. "That doesn't…how would that…"

"It matters not now," Uraj dismissed. With a stifled cry of pain, he ripped Symphony from his chest and tossed it aside. The back to his throne crumbled with the sword's removal, unable to handle one more chink in its weathered surface.

Uraj frowned at the chair. "Dammit all. I've had that for centuries." The bleeding from his wound had already stopped.

"Hawke," he looked back with sadness in his eyes, "what's past is past. I can't undo my mistakes and what they cost you. What I can give you is another chance to stand beside me and make the change in the world you've always wanted. Take your place as king once more. The people need you. The kingdom needs you." He offered a hand to his comrade. "*I* need you."

Chapter 22

The Scholar

Hawke didn't move from where he landed. He looked to the hand being proffered, then to me, then back to the hand, then at a random spot on the floor.

"I can't just leave Micasa behind and start ruling again," he said.

"You don't have to leave her behind," Uraj said irritably, "She can live here in Damkarei. Hell, she can live in the castle if you want. You can keep raising her like before, in addition to your duties!"

That gave Hawke pause. He looked back at me again for a long moment. "Is that something you want, Micasa? To stay here?"

Was that what I wanted? Our stay with the gypsies had given me a taste of what free life could be like without the stress of constant travel. A place I could call my own, being able to make friends and keep close to them. There was certainly temptation in that.

There was something even more important to me than any of those things, though.

"I'll do whatever you want to do, Hawke," I decided. It was an excuse not to make a decision, sure, but it really didn't make a difference to me either way. Hawke gave a small smile.

"See? There's no problem then," Uraj declared. His hand was still extended, and he gave it a little shake towards Hawke. My friend regarded what that offer meant, what taking that hand would signify. Then, he scooted back and pulled himself to his feet. Uraj's hand slowly dropped to his side.

"Do you really hate me so much that you would damn your people just to spite me?" the Forge asked with a frown. Hawke dusted off his kilt while shaking his head.

"It's that kind of reasoning that makes me certain our place isn't here," Hawke said.

Uraj fumed. "What, that I decide to stay and work for the good of everyone!? Are you really so self-centered!?" His fingers clenched and unclenched. He looked ready to strike out at my friend, but his fist stayed. Hawke only gave him a cool stare.

"You still think that sitting around and acting like a lord is what will change things around here," he shot back. "Sitting in a castle, making plans that go nowhere, while the people out there – *our* people, as you so love to remind me – are constantly suffering. And you call me self-centered."

Hawke strode past Uraj and collected his sword where it lay. Symphony was guided back into its sheath with a quiet *ping* that filled the quiet room.

"I've never been able to stomach trying to delegate how to fix problems to other people," spoke Hawke. "I've always believed there's I can do so much more good by using all these gifts I've been given, out there. Not letting them rot in here," He turned his silvery glare to his fellow king. "It's why I left in the first place. And it's why I'm leaving again."

He shifted his eyes towards me, raising an eyebrow and nodding towards the door. I understood his meaning and returned the nod. His long strides carried him past me quickly, and I hurried to keep pace.

"Wait."

We were nearly out of the audience chamber when Uraj spoke up. His face was like the stone making up his falling castle, all edges and pebbled.

Hawke looked ready to walk away in spite of the command, but in the end, he lingered.

"I was hoping to give you this as a token of good faith, but it looks like it'll be a parting gift instead," Uraj grumbled. "Watch closely."

As he spoke, his body burst into flames. His sudden combustion startled a cry out of me, but Uraj just chuckled darkly. He looked as comfortable being on fire as one might in a plush bathrobe. Even at a distance, I could feel the waves of heat washing off of him.

Slowly the orange and yellow tongues licking over him began to shift to a bright blue. The entire room became stifling, like we had stepped into a brick oven. No longer did the fires dance, instead tapering straight upwards and coalescing into a single massive flame. It gave Uraj the appearance of a candle wick, though no candle I had ever seen could match the brilliance of his light.

Then the single flame enveloping him brightened to pure white, filling the room with such brightness it made even the sunniest day look dim. I couldn't bear to look at him anymore, but just as I was covering my face the light smoldered and flickered, retreating. As quickly as it had come, the inferno that had engulfed Uraj vanished. The only sign anything untoward had happened were the deep scorch marks left in the tone at his feet, streaks of soot that flared outward like a star with Uraj in the center.

"Micasa, get away from me. *Now.*"

It was Hawke who had spoken. When I faced him to ask what he was talking about, I quickly swallowed my words and hopped away. The intensity with which he stared at Uraj sent goosebumps over my skin: his silver irises had grown to fill the entirety of his eyes, and his pupils contracted to near invisible pin pricks. Unblinking, unmoving, they were eyes that saw something far beyond anything I could comprehend.

Then Hawke's body erupted, just as Uraj's had. Sizzling orange gave way to blazing gold to searing blue to blistering white. He burned just as fiercely as his former comrade had, and extinguished just as quickly too. He stood ponderously in his own star of blackened stone, looking at Uraj.

"That was..." he trailed off, unable to grasp the words he was looking for. Uraj flashed a smirk at him.

"In the end, I'm always a blacksmith at heart," the Forge said, "and any good blacksmith knows that something strong but brittle is a chancy ally at best. Seeing how exposed you became when your soul was shattered, I spent the last few years figuring out how to temper essence itself. What you just saw and experienced were my results."

Hawke stared ponderously at his hands. The flames hadn't so much as singed his clothing, but still, he checked over his whole body like he had turned into someone else.

"Feels strange, doesn't it?" continued Uraj. "Don't worry, you'll get used to it quickly. Doesn't have a lot of practical use, honestly, but you should find that anyone trying to break off pieces of your soul again will have a much harder time."

Hawke eyed Uraj with suspicion. "What's the catch?"

"Catch? Why would there be?"

"After all that's happened, of course I'm uneasy with you 'giving' me something right as I'm leaving."

Uraj sighed. "I suppose that's my own fault. But no, there's no catch. You helped me, without your consent at that, to shore up my weaknesses. I was just returning the favor." He stepped forward and held out his hand one more time. Hawke hesitated, but finally gave his own sigh, clasping the hand and shaking.

"Even if we both go our own ways, we *are* still both fighting for the kingdom, right?" Uraj asked.

Hawke's eyes flicked to me for a second, then back to meet Uraj's. "Yeah. For the kingdom."

"Take care of yourself out there, then," Uraj bade, casting his own glance at me. "Make sure you take care of her too. And maybe drop by for a visit someday." They released their grip. Uraj turned away, adding, "Goodness knows we have plenty of days ahead of us."

* * *

The atmosphere was tense as we left, but not for the same reasons as when we had first come. Hawke looked like his mind was a thousand miles away, on a thousand other things. I thought he would be ecstatic: we had reached the end of our journey at last. Instead, I found him lost in thought, somber, and tight-lipped.

The courtyard was empty when we emerged from the heavy iron gates we had come in from. Night had fallen during the meeting, but a plethora of torches and braziers cast away the darkness that we might find our way back. Samuel was nowhere to be found.

Hawke pulled up the hood on his cloak and led the way back. Bright lanterns lit the streets of Damkarei's after hours. A few people roamed the town, chatting amiably or doing business with the vendors taking advantage of those still about. The mood was palpably lighter than it had been hours ago, when Uraj's agitation weighed on them quite literally.

No one paid mind to two strangers slipping into the inn. A few patrons milled about the common room, but they had just as little interest in our comings and goings. A brief nod was all the greeting Hawke offered the proprietor before we were tucked back into our room.

I was ready to say anything to break the silence, to take a peek into what was going on behind my friend's sober exterior. He broke it first with a grin.

"Micasa, you still interested in seeing the beach tomorrow?"

It wasn't what I was expecting him to talk about, but it was such a huge relief to see him smiling I busted into a fit of giggles and wholeheartedly agreed. We called for a supper from the kitchens and spent the rest of the night in companionable quiet, drifting off with full bellies and minds at ease.

For the first time, I found myself rousing before he did. Of all the things we had overcome in our adventures, none struck me as bizarre as tiptoeing around to keep from waking him as I prepared for the day ahead. When he did wake, he was strangely embarrassed about the whole thing, which only made me laugh.

We breakfasted in the privacy of our room on fruits and oatmeal while he asked me how I slept and told me about the dream he had. When we finished, he gathered up some money from the supplies and donned his cloak, leading the way back into town.

We stopped at a general store where Hawke bought a wicker basket and a blanket. Then we spent the rest of the morning perusing several of the grocery stalls littering the streets. We ended up picking up some dried jerky, bread, a jar of honey, a few peaches, and some bottles of milk. He tossed everything into the basket and handed it to me to carry.

"A day at the beach wouldn't be as good without a picnic lunch," he told me. Considering that most of the meals we took on the road were more or less picnics, it tickled me that he made such a fuss over this instance. His enthusiasm for the day was infectious, though, and I went along with it happily.

A cobbled path led away from the town to the smell of salt and the calls of birds. The sky was a clear blue save for a few billowing puffs lounging above, and a cool breeze kissed us every so often. A few of the townsfolk were headed our way too, but none of them paid any mind to the man cloaked against the chill and his daughter taking a lunch to the shore.

If the sea had been a wonder from afar, it was almost too good to be true when I beheld it at the edge of the beach. The sun rippled on sapphire waves crested with milky white foam. Gulls circled overhead, their cawing to one another the only voices to be heard.

I kicked my sandals off and wriggled my toes into the sand. The sun warmed grains caught between my toes and under my nails. It felt so deliciously gritty. I ran off, kicking my feet through the sand to send up tufts of gold before me.

Hawke followed me at his own pace. Every few steps, he'd shake a foot to dislodge the sand gathering in his own sandals. It only took a couple minutes before he took a page from my book and pulled off his own footwear, taking them in hand alongside mine that he had picked up. I spun around once in a while to see where he had gotten to, but he was never far behind, and never without a smile.

We set up our blanket well away from the scarce few other beach goers and pinned it down with our basket. Neither of us were hungry yet, so Hawke took me down to the water. I must have spent hours splashing in the shallows and looking at all the odd little things that washed in with the waves. Hawke found a tide pool full of mussels and a lone starfish that we watched for some time.

Later, we returned to our spot to find it under attack by some gulls who were looking for a picnic too. We chased them off quick enough, but most of our food had already been sampled at that point. We contented ourselves to a more meager meal than expected, though even with only a few bites to eat, the scenery alone made it all sweeter than anything I had eaten before.

The sun climbed and dipped. Other people came and played and relaxed and went. We spent the entirety of the day there, exploring up and down the coast at our leisure, and we talked about the things we came across. And not once did we talk about where we had to go next.

* * *

Hawke had found enough dry driftwood to light a fire when the last rays of the day fled to wherever they go at night. We sat and watched the heat shimmer off the flames, our shadows dancing about us.

"Micasa," Hawke broke in out of nowhere, "back when we first started our journey, you wanted to see me pull off your trick, right?" When I nodded, he reached into his pocket and pulled out one of the padlocks he had bought for me in another lifetime.

"Work this lock for me a few times," he requested, tossing the device to me. It was a simple one, plain iron and no decoration. I must have practiced with that one a thousand times before. With one hand I snapped it open and closed a few times with deft flicks of my fingers.

Hawke was watching, but his eyes had changed just as they had in Uraj's audience chamber. Tiny ink pupils peered out of silver orbs as he drank in my every movement. When my hand started to grow tired, he snatched the lock back from my hands.

"I see, so that's how it is…" he mumbled, rolling the lock in his hand over and over. Then with a snap of his wrist, the lock came undone, quick as I could.

I gasped. "You really can copy anything!"

He chuckled at my astonishment. "It's not just a copy." He produced from the folds of his cloak several more padlocks. With each one at turn, Hawke observed it closely before snapping it open and closed. When he had played with each one, he took all of them in hand and amazed me by popping all of them open at once without touching the latching mechanisms. In a span of seconds, he had mastered what had taken me months of practice.

"Awesome!" I said with my hands to my face.

Hawke wasn't done yet, though. "Now, let me try something new," he said. He curled his fingers of his right hand and placed them on his chest, above his heart. He closed his eyes and sat still for some time, unmoving. Then his hand twisted. I thought I might have heard a faint 'click', although to this day I cannot be certain.

"What was that?" I asked.

"I 'locked' away your power within myself," he said. When I stared at him dumbfounded in response, he picked up the padlocks he had set aside and tugged at them again. This time, they stayed firm, refusing to yield open. "It's still here, inside me, and what I've learned I can't forget or learn again. As it is, though, I can't use it anymore."

"But... *why?*" was the best I could manage to blurt out. Hawke broke eye contact and turned to the campfire.

"It's hard to explain, but I guess I just felt like I didn't want to take something so special about you for myself." He gave a shrug. "I want to see how far you can bring your power yourself."

"I don't care about that!" I said heatedly. Hawke's glasses glinted mischievously in the fire-light.

"Well, it's too late now. I can't undo what's been done without that power. *Your* power." He raised an eyebrow. "If you want something to be done about it, it'll have to be done by your hands."

I hadn't any idea where to start to accomplish what he was suggesting. It was just like Hawke, to turn anything he could into a lesson for me. "So what do I do then?"

"There's no need to rush it, Micasa," he assured me. "You'll figure it out along the way, I'm sure. And I'll help any way I can."

Along the way, he had said. "So where do we go now?" I asked.

Hawke looked into the night sky, to the waning moon slipping along and the stars it swam through. "Not sure. I have a lot of favors I need to repay, after everything we've been through. There's so much of Astra you haven't seen yet. I also recall you saying there were a lot of people you wanted to see again?"

"Yeah!" I said excitedly. He turned and looked back at me, silver eyes glittering with his own excitement.

"Well then, what adventure do you feel like taking on?" he asked with a giant smile on his face. It was a smile filled with the warmth of a campfire at night, the comfort of shelter in a storm, the assurance of a friend unwavering and unbroken.

Dear reader,

We hope you enjoyed reading *Broken Soul*. Please take a moment to leave a review, even if it's a short one. Your opinion is important to us.

Discover more books by Joshua Buller at https://www.nextchapter.pub/authors/joshua-buller

Want to know when one of our books is free or discounted? Join the newsletter at http://eepurl.com/bqqB3H

Best regards,
Joshua Buller and the Next Chapter Team

The story continues in:

Savants of Humanity

To read the first chapter for free, please head to:
https://www.nextchapter.pub/books/savants-of-
humanity

About the Author

Hey there! My name's Joshua, and I've been fascinated with storytelling practically since I was old enough to talk.

A bit about myself, I suppose. I'm in my early 30s, born and raised in Sacramento (that's the capital of California, in case you're confused). I'm the second of five children, and I. Love. Fantasy.

Growing up I was one of those kids who would blurt out the first thing that came to mind and got all the awkward stares. Even at the age of five, I could go on tangential rants for almost an hour that went nowhere.

In elementary school, I had my first brush with the dark side of fantasy: fan fiction. I spent several of my formative years writing stories based off of favorite tv shows and video games of mine.

This continued on through high school as a group of friends and I made a roleplaying forum where we tried to collaborate on writing a single narrative between almost a dozen people. It's about as easy as it sounds. Of course, it was moments like that that spurred me to eventually start trying my hand at writing original stories.

I've been working full time in the customer service industry since high school. It pays the bills, but doesn't give me a lot of time to write, so I usually have to really make it count when I can. When I'm not writing, I tend to be either reading or playing video games. Fantasy and sci-fi novels, Japanese manga, RPGs- if it has a fantastical element to it, I'm interested. Reading in particular has always been a huge passion of mine. There's nothing I enjoy more than a well told narrative and engaging characters.

On the other hand, I have a bit of a masochistic streak when it comes to movies and books as well. Oddly enough, I find immense satisfaction in reading a terrible book or watching a horrible movie. Well, part of that enjoyment probably comes from subjecting my friends to the same thing afterwards. Take it from me: if you show a friend Birdemic, and they're still friends with you after that, they're keepers.

Lightning Source UK Ltd.
Milton Keynes UK
UKHW011828010421
381406UK00001B/58